LUCY BLUE, WHERE ARE YOU?

Lucy Blue is not the sort of girl to pick up a stranger in a snow-bound airport and she's certainly not the sort to then leap into bed with him in a motorway motel . . . Yet this is a strange, once-in-a-lifetime day, and in any case nobody will know and they'll never meet again . . . But actions can catch up with you and secrets have a way of being told, and a spectacular gesture means that this time Lucy just can't walk away.

Books by Louise Harwood
Published by The House of Ulverscroft:

CALLING ON LILY

LOUISE HARWOOD

LUCY BLUE, WHERE ARE YOU?

Complete and Unabridged

ULVERSCROFT
Leicester

First published in Great Britain in 2005 by
Pan Books
an imprint of
Pan Macmillan Limited
London

First Large Print Edition
published 2006
by arrangement with
Pan Macmillan Limited
London

British Library CIP Data

Harwood, Louise
    Lucy Blue, where are you?.—Large print ed.—
Ulverscroft large print series: romance
1. Love stories
2. Large type books
I. Title
823.9'2 [F]

ISBN 1–84617–210–1

Published by
F. A. Thorpe (Publishing)
Anstey, Leicestershire

Set by Words & Graphics Ltd.
Anstey, Leicestershire
Printed and bound in Great Britain by
T. J. International Ltd., Padstow, Cornwall

This book is printed on acid-free paper

For my wonderful sister Jo

Acknowledgements

Special thanks to Imogen Taylor and the fantastic team at Pan, and to Jo Frank and Araminta Whitley for all their support and encouragement; to Russell Jones and Aileen Richards; to my family, especially Josie, for coming up with so many great ideas; and to wonderful Ant, Tom and Jack for looking after me so well and for making it happen.

1

Clutching a red duffel-coat in one hand and a telescope wrapped in silver paper in the other, nudging a heavy suitcase along with her knee, Gabriella struggled to keep walking, trying not to let the train's violent twists and turns throw her off her feet.

She didn't quite make it to the door to the next carriage. Just as she reached the last row of seats, and with Lipton St Lucy station only a few hundred yards away, the driver finally outmanoeuvred her, accelerating fast and then braking violently with a series of jolting lurches that lifted her first off one foot and then, a few long seconds later, off the other. Dropping the coat and the telescope on the floor, she landed in the last row of seats, deep in the lap of a surprised fifty-something business man. And as the train shuddered into the station, she felt his hand slide beneath her bottom.

'Stop that!' she snapped, but he pulled out a Mont Blanc fountain pen and pointed to the nib.

'I hope that didn't hurt?'

'Oh no!' She put her hands to her face, her

cheeks hot with embarrassment.

'I'm sorry.'

He smiled at her and settled comfortably back in his seat. 'So, where did you come from?'

'Italy,' she said, misunderstanding, scrabbling for the ground with her feet and trying to stand up. The train was stopping now.

He nodded. 'I thought you looked Italian, all that dark hair. I was in Rome myself, back in 1976.'

She'd been born in Rome in 1976 but she certainly wasn't about to tell him so.

She put her hand on the table in front of them and began to lever herself upright, and he stared at her in disappointed surprise. 'Oh, are you getting off?'

'Of course I am!'

And then he glanced around and caught the amused glances of his fellow passengers, saw what a fool he was making of himself, and so, with a good deal of tutting and sighing, he finally helped her back to her feet. Knowing the train must be about to pull away again, she reached for the suitcase and telescope, praying it hadn't been broken by the fall, ran to the door and jumped off the train just as the whistle blew.

Standing on the platform, she slipped on her coat, grateful for its warmth in the cold afternoon air, then picked up her luggage and walked towards the exit, her carriage accompanying her for a few strides before the train picked up speed and pulled away.

She'd been the only passenger to disembark, and Lipton St Lucy station was as dark and deserted as she'd expected. She looked around and wondered where Jude was, hoping he wouldn't be late.

Gabriella had been aiming for the four o'clock train, but she had arrived at Paddington to find that an earlier one was still on the platform, just about to depart. She'd run awkwardly through the barriers and clambered aboard, and it was only after she'd settled down in her seat that it occurred to her that perhaps it hadn't been such a good idea, catching a train that would bring her into Lipton St Lucy forty minutes earlier than expected, with no guarantee that she could summon any of the Middletons to pick her up. Too late to change her mind, she'd called the house twice before anyone had answered the phone and finally she'd got Jude, dragging him from a deep sleep on the sofa in front of the fire. He'd been left all alone in the house, he told her. The rest of his mad family were out in the freezing rain, climbing Dixie Hill and working off their Sunday lunch. Of course he'd come to the station to pick her up.

But he hadn't come *yet*.

Gabriella turned away from the tracks, making for the bridge that led over to the station car park, then stopped and felt in her coat pockets for money for a cup of tea, thinking she'd be better off in the waiting-room than out in the open. And then she heard him, running across the bridge, his long strides ringing out above her head.

Just a few seconds later he leapt down the last five steps and all but collided with her, dressed only in jeans and a shirt, with a smile to soften the hardest of hearts.

'So good to see you.' He slipped an arm around her shoulders. 'I'm sorry, Gabriella. Don't look like that. I'm not late. Your train was early, it's only five to.' He pulled her against him and kissed her, catching the side of her head with his lips. 'You know I'd never be late for you.'

'Don't start, Jude.'

'But it's true. I'd spend my whole life waiting.'

'Shut up.' She reached up and kissed him on the cheek.

'Anyway,' he told her, 'there was this bull. A mad, dangerous bull, rampaging down the lane just outside the station.'

'A bull?'

4

'You know, one of those daddy cows.'

She pushed him away from her.

'And it might have hurt someone,' he said, replacing his arm round her shoulders and steering her towards the car park. 'You can imagine, a little kid, an old lady. There was no way I could leave it there.'

'So what did you do?'

He looked down at her and his arm tightened around her shoulders. 'Caught it, *of course.*'

'And then?'

'Found it a stable. Gave it some hay.'

'Bull-shit, Jude,' she said carefully, but laughing all the same. 'You went back to sleep, didn't you?'

'Sleep!' He laughed, kissing her again. 'With you here waiting? You think I'd fall asleep again?'

★   ★   ★

Three-thirty on the afternoon of 28 December and already it was nearly dark. They reached the car and then they were away, Jude picking his way carefully along the narrow lanes, through the dark afternoon towards Lipton Hall and the Middletons, where Luke and Suzie and James would surely all be back from their walk and waiting for them now. Gabriella thought of the belated Christmas presents she was bringing for all of them: the backgammon board for James; the leather holdall for Jude, boring she knew, but she'd found herself struggling and failing to find the right present for him. She'd bought the telescope for Luke and a lovely set of carved wooden angels for Suzie that she'd found in a Christmas market in Rome. Five of them, hands clasped, heads bowed, tiny and beautiful. By rights she should have given them to her own mother, and if they didn't get her into Suzie's permanent good books nothing would. Guiltily, Gabriella thought how extravagant she'd been, how much more money and time she'd spent choosing things for the Middletons than she had for her own family. But they had been so much more difficult to choose for, and it seemed to matter so much more that she got these presents right. Next year, she silently promised her parents, next year I'll make it up to you. But for now she was in Oxfordshire, speeding through the country-side to give these presents away and to spend a few days with her lovely boyfriend and his gorgeous family, and she was suddenly filled with excitement that it was so.

She turned to Jude, about to ask if he thought the others would be back from their walk by the time they arrived, but the words never came, because, suddenly, out of the empty darkness there was now a car, arcing fast around the bend, swinging over on to their side of the road as it came towards them, crazy headlights dazzling.

We'll hit each other, Gabriella thought, but there was no time for fear. She heard Jude swear, felt him pull desperately on the wheel even though there was nowhere for them to go, and then she felt the breathtaking slam as the two cars collided. And then they were spinning, she and Jude, sharing a ride on a giant, malevolent waltzer that whirled them twice, then hurled them off the road. High in the air, she looked out and saw black clouds racing across the moon and glittering leaves swirling around the windscreen, caught in the wild beam of the headlights. And then they were hitting the ground again, forcing their way through a hedge before falling downwards, the ground now dropping steeply away beneath them.

And waiting for them at the bottom of the bank was a tree, slamming through the windscreen as they came. And then, of course, they were still and Gabriella felt the cold night air touch her forehead and heard herself whisper, just once, *oh please God no.*

2

A year later

'You're so soft,' whispered Gordon, drink-fumed breath tickling Lucy's ear. 'Your skin is soft as, soft as a . . . ' He dropped two kisses on to her bare shoulder while he thought about it, and then, when nothing came to mind, encircled her with his arms, so that Lucy found herself being rocked gently and smothered by the scratchy wool of his dinner jacket at the same time.

He was quite sweet but very drunk. He was completely unfanciable, but this was better than sitting by herself watching everyone else dance. That was what she'd told herself, anyway, when he'd first taken her hand and pulled her to her feet. Now she was fast changing her mind.

'As soft as a pigeon,' he sighed, and Lucy felt his fingers slowly working their way down the bare knuckles of her spine, stopping abruptly when he reached her bottom. Obviously Gordon was a gentleman at heart, or perhaps simply gay? She pushed him upright and instantly he toppled forward again.

'Gordon?'

Now he was leaning so heavily against her that she wondered if he'd dropped off.

He didn't answer. She slipped her arm around him and steered him away from the dance floor back towards the tables, kicking out a spare chair with her foot and pushing him down.

This was not why she'd come, Lucy thought, looking down at him as he stared, hypnotized by her cleavage. She'd not travelled five hundred miles, left behind Jane and all her other friends on New Year's Eve, only to meet a drunken arse like Gordon. He looked up at her with eyes so thickly glazed she could see her reflection.

'Lovely boobies.'

She looked longingly over to the door.

'Sorry,' he said immediately. 'Ver . . . ver . . . '

She patted him on the shoulder, left him there, and walked away, past the dance floor — disco had given way to yet another round of Scottish dancing and she was happier still to be leaving when she saw that — through the door and past reception, calling good-night to the woman behind the desk and then running up the stairs, pulling her key from her mother-of-pearl evening bag as she went.

It was five to midnight. Reaching the second floor she turned left, stopped at the

9

third door down and slipped her key into the lock, let the door of her bedroom slam shut behind her, bent and undid the straps of her sandals, kicked them off, wriggled and flexed her way out of her dress and tossed it over a chair, unhooked her bra and stepped out of her pants, then pulled back the bedclothes and climbed into bed. She took out her contact lenses, turned off the light, lay down, rolled on to her side, pulled her knees up close to her chin and closed her eyes. She hadn't even made it to New Year.

⋆ ⋆ ⋆

Next morning the Kirk Castle Hotel ballroom looked hungover and not at all pleased to be disturbed. The crimson velvet curtains looped across its windows gave the impression of heavy lidded eyes squinting irritably at the interruption, and on the opposite side of the room, in a huge stone fireplace, a burnt log poked up from the ashes like a dirty broken tooth.

When Lucy had left last night, the room had still been full of people, hoarse men and horsy women, drunkenly groping each other under the tables or twirling streamers into the antlers of the stags' heads mounted on the walls. But now it was silent in the dusty light, empty but for Lucy, standing there in the doorway, looking around to see if anyone had seen or heard her, wondering if anybody else was about.

It seemed that nobody was. She closed the door again and turned away, retracing her steps back across the hall to reception. At the desk she put down her overnight bag, laid her handbag on the scuffed wooden surface and fought the urge to lay her cheek down beside it and close her eyes. She'd fallen asleep at dawn, and now she was up again and it was much, much too early. Why had she booked a flight at ten a.m. when she could have slept half the day away?

Instead, she'd given herself to the very last second of seven-forty-five, leaving five minutes to sit up, stick in her contact lenses, as scratchy and uncomfortable as Velcro, rub deodorant under each arm, pull on yesterday's jeans, shirt and cardigan and get out of the door, and allowing a further ten minutes to check out. Then one and a half hours to drive back to Inverness airport. Check-in nine-thirty a.m., flight departing at ten-thirty.

But five minutes had passed since she'd left her room and still nobody had materialized to help her, and if she didn't get a move on she was going to miss her plane. What was worse, as she'd walked down the ornate wrought-iron staircase, suitcase in hand, she'd looked out of the window and had been shocked to see the snow, falling thickly through the still-dark trees. This was snow that was going to slow her journey to a crawl and might mean she'd never make it to the airport at all.

Above her a wall clock ticked, and she bit her lip as the knot of worry tangled some more. She peered around the room again, as if by looking more carefully she'd magic someone to appear. This was where the party had begun last night, where she'd sipped her first drink and looked curiously around the room. But now the smell of old cigarette smoke and sweat seemed to be the only link with the evening before. In the candlelight the room had seemed romantic, but by daylight it was shabby and dirty, painted in a yellowing cream, shiny orange curtains hanging limply at each of the long rectangular windows. Orange, Lucy thought. Who could possibly have flipped through the sample book and chosen orange?

To the left of the fireplace there was a painting of a flock of sheep standing in just the kind of blizzard she presumed was now raging outside, and below that was an armchair covered in green tartan and to the right of it a dinner gong made from brass and suspended on a wooden frame, with a padded wooden beater on a length of wire. She walked over to it. From the layer of dust, Lucy guessed this was a gong long since retired from active service, but it was too tempting to ignore. She brushed the beater gently against the brass, producing a muffled hum that wasn't going to summon anybody, and then, before she could change her mind, she struck it hard, whereupon sound crashed out across the silent room, growing louder and louder with each second, the echoes and reverberations falling in on each other, building into a tidal wave of noise. The whole room was sounding the alarm: here, waiting at reception, was the least patient, most obnoxious hotel guest imaginable.

Mortified, Lucy dropped the beater and placed a hand on the angrily vibrating brass to stifle the sound, then sat down in the armchair, overcome with the effort. She rested her head against the wall behind, and closed her eyes and waited. Slowly peace returned to the room.

The minutes continued to tick past and still Lucy continued to wait, and very soon she found herself yawning, unable to stop her eyes slowly sealing shut, seduced by her soft wool coat and the heavy warmth of the room, no longer worried about skidding off the road or missing her flight. Instead her mind was slipping back to the start of the party the night before, and she was catching again the sweet smell of hyacinths in the cold night air, pushing her way through a crush of people, all of them knocking back drinks, laughing and noisy, and she felt again the pang of trepidation mixed with excitement that had come from walking in alone. Apart from the host, an old school-friend, she had known nobody and nobody had known her. She remembered staring across the room at the wonderful kaleidoscope of taffeta and tartan swaying gently in the candlelight. At that stage, the evening had felt full of promise.

She had found her table, heavy cutlery laid out against white table linen, the stiff place setting announcing that on her left would be someone called Neil Armstrong, and she'd had to smother her smile because he was there already, pulling out her chair, with a buzz cut and a sweet, earnest smile.

She'd eaten hot-smoked salmon and drunk glass after glass of pale gold wine, ice cold and delicious. Sitting opposite her had been Neil's wife, Philly, and on Philly's lap their six-month-old son, Josh, who had made sure of both parents' full attention all evening. And on her right had been poor Gavin Singleton, fleshy and rather flashy too, more than happy to hold Lucy's attention and anything else he could get his hands on. But Gavin had choked on his salmon, his face turning fiery red, only recovering when the chunk of pink fish that had been blocking his windpipe had leapt out of his mouth in a perfect arc and into her glass of wine. Laughing, she'd said she'd never seen salmon leap so far, but after that he had barely been able to speak to her again. Not in itself a great loss, but from then on Lucy had had nobody to talk to on either side. And as the tables were so big, the people on the other side were out of range. It was then that she'd first thought wistfully of London and all her friends, dancing away New Year's Eve without her.

She opened her eyes and wiggled her bruised toes. She'd worn strappy silver sandals, not ideal footwear for Hogmanay with a crowd of twirling Scottish dancers, but they'd gone with her pale pink sequined dress. Not that the dress had been very suitable either. When Teddy had seen it in her suitcase he'd held it up and asked, dubiously, how it had got there. Teddy preferred his women well covered up.

She pushed herself upright in her chair. Why had she done it? Spent three hundred pounds on a beautiful dress and two hundred more to fly away from everyone she knew to wear it? Yes, she'd escaped Teddy, but with just a little effort she could have escaped him in London too. What had she hoped to find here? *Who* had she hoped to find here? Because from the moment she'd slipped the dress over her head, right to the moment when she'd pulled it off again, she knew she'd been waiting for someone.

And whoever it was she'd been waiting for, they hadn't turned up. Being in Inverness on her own, rather than in London with her friends, had proved not to be such a liberating devil-may-care experience after all. Fun at the beginning, to put proper make-up on again and to walk into the room in her new high heels and know she was free to behave as badly as she wanted, but that had lasted only as long as it had taken to see that there was nobody to behave badly with.

And now, sitting on her own on such a hard uncomfortable chair, looking around at the shabby walls, the peeling gilt picture-frames and the thick layer of dust on the table beside her, thinking of the snow cascading down outside, she felt let down and a little bit silly. She could almost hear Teddy's laugh. *Look how well you're getting on. Admit it, Lucy, it's not so much fun without me, is it?*

She leaned back against the wall and at that moment the door from the hall opened and at last someone appeared, a thick-set, frowning woman, striding across the room as the door slammed behind her, in lace-ups, a tweed skirt and thick, ribbed tights, iron-grey hair springing with each step. Lucy got to her feet and walked over to join her, but without acknowledging her at all the woman crammed herself between the reception desk and a swivel chair and then, only when she was ready, did she finally turn her attention to her guest.

'So sorry to keep you waiting . . . ' The sarcasm was heavy in her voice and she was breathing heavily, her large body rising and falling to the rhythm. She settled herself down in the chair and began to check over some paper-work.

'And I'm sorry to have used the gong,' Lucy replied to the bent head, 'but I'm catching a plane. I have to check out.'

'No need to apologize,' the woman sniffed, 'but I'll be surprised if you haven't broken it, all the same.' She looked up suddenly and caught Lucy's amused grin, hastily smothered. 'I was in the kitchen,' she said defiantly, 'making everyone breakfast, breakfast in bed being rather popular on a Sunday morning.'

Oh, how mean of them, Lucy almost

snapped back. How selfish they all are to want breakfast in bed on a Sunday *in your hotel*. But she bit back the retort because this was Mrs E. Sutherland, according to the plastic name badge on her lapel, whose thick brown foundation and floury face powder failed to disguise the grey skin and eyes sunken with fatigue. Mrs Sutherland, who had been there yesterday afternoon to check her in, had still been there behind the desk when she'd come down to dinner, and who had *still* been there when Lucy had walked up the stairs at five to midnight.

'Have you been to bed at all?' Lucy asked instead.

'For an hour or two.'

'How do you cope? When do you ever get a break?'

'When my son gets up. Thank you for asking.' She gave Lucy an unexpected smile. 'I'll kick his lazy backside out of bed after I've seen you off.'

She bent her head back to her computer and Lucy watched her work, fascinated by the way her soft fleshy neck folded and extended like a concertina as Mrs Sutherland alternately bent to scowl at her notes, then peer forwards at the computer screen.

'I'll have you know that you don't look so marvellous yourself.'

She said it suddenly, without looking up or pausing in her typing, jolting Lucy abruptly back to reality, and Lucy felt herself blush as she realized how she had been staring. Not that she was in the least surprised to hear she didn't look so good. She probably didn't smell so good either, seeing that she hadn't brushed her teeth or washed since the evening before.

'You're in a great hurry to leave?'

'I wanted to catch the first plane back to London.'

Mrs Sutherland looked up sharply. 'Have you had a miserable time?'

Lucy smiled. 'Not great.'

'I'm not surprised to hear it.'

She took Lucy's key and turned to hang it on the row of hooks behind her.

'My room was very comfortable,' Lucy said hastily, 'but the party was . . .'

'Appalling!' Mrs Sutherland shuddered. 'And there was I thinking I'd seen it all.'

'Sorry,' Lucy said again.

'I understand your need to get away, but even so you should have something to eat or you'll be falling asleep on the road.'

Lucy swallowed uneasily as Mrs Sutherland started to rattle off all the different things she could and would prepare, the fried eggs, fried bread, potatoes, bacon, hash browns and pork sausages, pausing only to elaborate on the juiciness of the black pudding. She couldn't be sure whether she was doing it deliberately, turning Lucy's stomach into a butter churn, or whether she genuinely thought she was being kind.

She turned away, glanced out of the window, and Mrs Sutherland's voice faded away as she looked at the winter wonderland that lay before her. Suddenly the darkness had lifted and the world outside had been transformed. The cars, the roads, the little stone bridge just beyond the garden wall, were all covered in deep snow and still it was tipping out of the sky. Somewhere out there she knew there were hedges and a low wall that divided the garden from the car park, where she'd left her hire car, and further on there was a drive and a road that would take her towards the airport. But Lucy no longer recognized any of it, wasn't even sure where the garden ended and the car park began, couldn't have even said if she should turn left or right out of the hotel gates, couldn't even see the hotel gates.

'Who would have thought it?' Mrs Sutherland teased. 'Snow, in the Highlands, in January.' And she laughed at the dismay on Lucy's face. 'Don't you worry. It's a straight road to Scarth Ross. And once you get down there you'll meet the snowploughs.' She paused. 'Let's hope not head on.'

'Let's hope not.'

From inside the office Lucy heard a printer run through its routine and begin to print. When it had finished, Mrs Sutherland stretched her arm through the doorway and came back with Lucy's bill in her hand.

★   ★   ★

Outside, the fresh air made her feel a little better. The problem was that each of the vague white bumps looked identical and she wondered how she would ever find her car. In the end she pulled up the hood of her coat and determinedly marched from row to row, firing her alarm key at every bump until eventually she heard the satisfying sound of locks clunking open in response. Knocking off the snow, she rediscovered her little red car.

Driving painfully slowly, she slithered out of the drive, remembering that Mrs Sutherland had told her to turn right on to a tiny lane where the snow was already so deep it reached half-way up the hedges. For the first ten miles she drove very slowly, rigid with concentration, her shoulders hunched up level with her ears, leaning forwards, her eyes

21

wide and unblinking, her hands gripping the wheel so tightly that her knuckles went white, convinced it was only a matter of time before she skidded off the road.

But mile after mile passed by and the crash didn't come, and slowly she realized that the brakes still braked and the steering-wheel steered, that the snow, while still falling, was no longer blizzard-like and that she could see perfectly well and then she started to relax and picked up speed.

An hour later and she still hadn't seen another car or any signs of life at all. She'd passed a few isolated houses and a handful of tiny villages, but they were all so tightly closed down against the weather that she doubted anyone could be living in them, and she wondered if she was right to believe that for as far as she could see and beyond, in every direction, she was the only person there.

She opened the glove compartment as she drove, fished out a bottle of water, unscrewed the top with her teeth and took a long drink, then dropped the bottle on to the map on the seat beside her and turned on the radio, guiding the car with one hand as she moved between the stations, letting her head fall back against the headrest, grinning to herself as the music filled the car. Now that her doom was no longer certain, she was even having fun.

She drove on, mile after mile, picking up more speed, gliding silently and smoothly through the endless white expanse of snow-covered highlands. And gradually, as the snow lulled her, hypnotized her even, she began to feel that here at last, on this journey home, she was free again and loving it: here, all alone, a stranger in a strange place, skiing along in this car, cut off from the world outside. This was what she'd been hoping to feel when she'd left London, this exhilaration, this enjoyment in her own company, the relief of being answerable to no one, least of all Teddy. But it had taken all this time, and now she was on her way home again and she wished very much that her journey wasn't going to end so soon. She dared to take her eyes off the road to look at the clock and saw that she'd be reaching Inverness in about half an hour, and even as she registered this the road widened into a dual carriageway and a huge green road sign, almost completely obscured by snow, flashed past with only the letters INV visible at the top. Seeing it, she took her foot off the accelerator and reached again for the water, willing everything she was feeling now to soak into her and last beyond this day.

And then, just as she had one hand on the wheel and the bottle of water back to her lips, out of the whiteness came a stag, leaping out of nowhere as quiet as a ghost, clearing her speeding bonnet with a foot to spare and disappearing again even before she had closed her eyes tight, stamped down on the brake and wrenched around the wheel. The car spun in perfect three-hundred-and-sixty degree circles, twice, three times, and left her pointing in precisely the same direction as before. She opened her eyes again to find herself travelling smoothly on down the road.

Oh my God, she breathed, as the shock caught up with her. She snapped off her music and slowed down to only a few miles an hour, feeling her heart slamming against her chest, her palms suddenly slippery with sweat. How could the stag not have hit her? How had she managed to stay on the road? Even the bottle of water had landed upright on the map, not a drop spilled.

Then, as she recovered and her pulse settled and she picked up speed again, it seemed as if the stag had shown her something important: that today, on this journey home, nothing bad could happen to her. That she could do whatever she wanted, that for now she was invincible. It was snowing harder than ever, but now she knew that however deep and impenetrable it became, however fast or slowly she drove, whether she kept her eyes open or closed, steered or didn't steer, it didn't matter. The car would somehow keep on driving, would follow the road, and she would be safe.

Signs of life returned as she approached the outskirts of Inverness. A snowplough suddenly looming in front of her, headlights full on as it noisily cleared the road, other cars idling at the traffic lights, all of them carrying heavy white duvets on their roofs and bonnets. Ahead of her she saw a bareheaded man in a suit and black leather shoes stepping daintily along the pavement, Sunday newspapers clutched to his chest.

Squinting through the snow for the road signs, Lucy reached the airport and found the Deals on Wheels car park where she was to leave the car. She found a space alongside a dark red Range Rover — surely far too smart to be owned by Deals on Wheels — and parked neatly, turned off the engine, unclipped her seat belt and stretched back in her seat. Just beyond her danced two excited little girls in matching pink ski-suits and bobble hats. Their parents, lugging heavy suitcases, staggered along behind them.

But she was not leaving for a holiday, she was returning home. She watched the holiday-bound family slipping one by one through the doors into the airport and thought how any moment now she would be walking through those doors too. And she thought about why she'd come here in the first place. How much she'd wanted it to mark the end of Teddy and the start of something new. She sat there for a few moments more, watching people walking all around her but not seeing them at all, aware only of how she was feeling: brave, happy, her own person again. How this was New Year's Day, a day for changes. How she was going to catch her plane and go home. And once she got there, how she was going to sort out her life. And how she would begin with Teddy.

3

The airport was busy, people constantly arriving, stamping their feet, shaking their heads free of snow. Lucy followed the signs for the Deals on Wheels desk and, having been prepared for a long queue, was relieved to see that there were only five people in front of her. She'd soon be handing over her keys and making her way to the check-in, she thought. In under an hour she'd be in the air. Impatience to be off overwhelmed her, making her clutch her bag in her hand and keep her eyes fixed on the woman at the front of the queue.

Ten minutes later, there were still five people between her and the desk. Lucy shifted restlessly from foot to foot and again cast her eye towards the front of the queue, where the woman in a shiny pink plastic raincoat was still arguing with the Deals on Wheels rep, hands waving furiously in the air, exactly as she had been doing since Lucy had joined the queue. Lucy swung her overnight bag off her shoulder and on to the ground and sat on it, telling herself again that she had plenty of time and the woman couldn't go on for ever. The nervous-looking couple behind her glanced at her uneasily, then craned their necks again to watch what was happening. Lucy shuffled around on her bag and saw that the woman was now leaning so far over the rep's desk that her feet, in high stilettos, had lifted clean off the ground and her pink coat had ridden high up her thighs, revealing more of the backs of her chunky legs than Lucy could stomach so early in the morning.

Next thing she knew, there was a rush of air as someone came striding past her. She glanced up and saw a man, dark-haired, a long black coat flowing behind him as he headed towards the front of the queue. Lucy stood up, interested, and wished that she'd caught a glimpse of his face. He touched the back of the pink raincoat and the woman dropped back to her feet and turned around to him in surprise. And then Lucy watched him move in on the Deals on Wheels rep, how threateningly he towered over the desk. She watched him lean in closer, the pink-coated woman nodding excitedly. And then, finally, the rep rose up from behind his desk, a small defiant-looking man in a navy Deals on Wheels blazer, and, as Lucy watched, he reluctantly placed something on the desk that the pink lady instantly snatched away, smiling jubilantly, first sideways at her rescuer, then turning to include the queue of people waiting behind her.

'I'm so sorry, everybody,' she giggled nervously, blinking sticky Barbara Cartland eyelashes at them all, still managing completely to block Lucy's view of the man. 'So sorry to keep you all waiting. But this man owed me fifty pounds and I didn't see why he should get away with it.' She nodded flirtatiously to her Knight in a Black Coat. 'Thanks to you, I'm glad to report he hasn't.'

Out of the way, Lucy thought impatiently, *let me see his face* — because of course he was going to be gorgeous. And, of course, once he finally turned around, he was going to notice Lucy standing in the queue (by now, her teeth would have miraculously self-cleaned and she would be looking great, better than she'd ever looked in her life before). And he'd come over, say something, make her laugh, and she'd say exactly the right thing back and then they'd check in together, sit beside each other on the plane, talk all the way back to London . . .

The pink-coated lady stepped aside but still the man didn't turn around.

No. Abruptly Lucy changed her mind. She should prepare to be disappointed. The expensive coat and the broad shoulders were sure to be misleading. When he turned around she'd see he had pitted skin and criss-cross teeth, less the kind of man to fantasize about sitting next to on the plane, more the kind of man to cross the airport to avoid.

And then, just as she was about to sit down on her bag again, he did turn around, slowly, taking his time, as if he knew that every eye was upon him. He walked back and took his place at the back of the queue and as he passed he caught her eye and flashed her a brief brilliant smile.

Lucy opened her handbag, peering deep and intently inside it, fighting the urge to laugh, because he'd been so shockingly good-looking and so obviously had known it too, with his carefully knotted scarf, just a touch of stubble and that dazzling super-white smile. He looked as if he'd just finished filming a commercial for Ralph Lauren, and all down the queue people were still turning their heads after him, as if it had been Prince William who had just strolled past.

Lucy turned her back on them and sat down again on her bag. With the pink plastic lady despatched it wouldn't be long till her turn. She opened her bag again, brought out the Deals on Wheels paperwork and slipped it into her coat pocket. She could see her flight ticket tucked neatly between her purse and the turquoise leather photo frame with the pictures of Teddy inside. Immediately she felt herself shrinking inside her skin and yet, even though it was the very last thing she wanted to do, she found herself reaching for the frame, lifting it out of her bag, opening it like a book, so that she could see the photos of Teddy, two of them, one on each side. Neither of them ones she had picked, certainly not ones she had ever liked. They'd been chosen by him, the photo frame his birthday present to her. On the left he was wearing a sports jacket and tie, and was standing alone, looking confident and determined, and on the right he was with Lucy, who'd been caught at a particularly bad angle, the wind that was making her tightly screw up her eyes lending Teddy a spirited, dashing air of vitality that he certainly didn't have in real life. Now, in both the photos, he seemed to stare back at her accusingly, a double dose of disapproval. She wanted to take them over to the nearest bin, throw them in among the cigarette butts and fast-food wrappers and half empty cans of drink, but she didn't want to lose her place in the queue.

She looked at them again. *You're history*, she whispered at them both, and the two Teddys seemed almost to start in surprise at her words. You're gone. You and your fuzzy hair and your big white teeth and your loud voice and your bad temper, and your Golf GTI and your snooty ridiculous parents and your control-freakery and your extra-strong mints. Gone, gone gone. She glanced up quickly. The man in the black coat was standing with his back to her, directly in her eyeline. And yes, Teddy, she thought defiantly, snapping shut the frame and dropping it back into her bag, he did smile at me. And yes, he is gorgeous, isn't he?

The queue was moving quickly now. Only two more people and it would be her turn. Lucy picked up her bag and moved a few more paces forwards. And at the same moment, the airport's PA system suddenly boomed into life, making her stop again in surprise, announcing that due to adverse weather conditions, all flights were grounded with immediate effect. The airport was closing until further notice and more details would follow shortly, but in the meantime could the airport authorities please advise anyone leaving the airport to do so in a manner in accordance with the treacherous conditions.

Groans rippled down the Deals on Wheels queue. How could this possibly be so, Lucy thought disbelievingly? Snow in the Highlands? In January? Was the airport not used to this? They'd got snowploughs and gritters, she'd seen them clearing the roads around the airport. In fact, she could see some more of them now, their headlights cutting through the blizzard that was hurling itself against the airport windows. And seeing what was now going on outside, Lucy reluctantly had to admit to herself that she was grateful not to be out on the runway in a plane, attempting to take off.

But what to do instead? How were they all going to get home? It could be days before the snow stopped, weeks even. How was she to get back to London? She looked around the airport, at the rows of seats already full of people. She couldn't stay here, sitting it out with hundreds of others. She had work tomorrow and she needed to get back to her flat. She wanted to be home, beginning the new year, behind her desk the next morning. She wanted to be gone.

And then she looked down at the keys in her hand and pictured the red car waiting in the car park, remembered how it had felt to drive it, how she'd even wished for more time to drive. Now, here was the chance. Unlike most of her fellow travellers, she had a way out.

It seemed that everybody else in the airport simultaneously had the same idea. As the man ahead of her finally finished his negotiations with the Deals on Wheels rep and Lucy was nudged forward for her turn, she could see a dozen or so people, striding — but not quite shameless enough to break into a run — to reach the end of the queue first. Surely Deals on Wheels wouldn't have enough cars for them all?

She turned back to the rep, who immediately reached forwards and tried to snatch the car keys out of her hand before she'd even said a word.

'Don't do that!' She lifted the keys out of reach. He'd obviously been smarting ever since losing the battle with the pink raincoat woman and was dying for someone to push around. But it wasn't going to be her. She'd met him too many times before to be bullied by him now, dealt with him in the boiling heat of Nice airport and the sleety cold of Belfast, disbelievingly filled out his endless forms and argued over the hundreds of extra pounds in spurious supplements, the accidental-death-of-a-wild-animal insurance, the extra-large-suitcase premium, the using-all-four-seats-of-the-car premium. She'd been over them all.

'I would like to extend my rental for another day,' she told him firmly.

The rep shook his head.

'I'd like to extend my rental,' Lucy said

again, 'and take the car back to London. I'll return it to one of your London branches tomorrow.'

'Not a chance, madam.'

'What do you mean?'

'Let me rephrase that. Your car has already been reassigned.' He held out his hand. 'Keys, please.'

Lucy reached into her pocket and brought out her Deals on Wheels documents. In her mind the little red car had taken on the lovable qualities of Chitty Chitty Bang Bang. She was not about to give it up.

'You can't reassign it. Look at the agreement — the car is mine until ten p.m.'

She handed the papers over. Behind her the queue had been listening to what was going on and now started muttering noisily, supportive of her, she hoped, even though they were being held up yet again. But the truth was, she really didn't care whether they were on her side or not. She was keeping the car.

'Yesterday's Deals on Wheels rep insisted that I paid for the whole of today, even though he knew I would be delivering the car back first thing this morning,' she told him. 'You've taken my money, so you can't reassign my car to someone else. Not before ten p.m. 'Stare at me as much as you like,'

Lucy went on, seeing a savage look on his face, 'but I'm keeping the car.' Any more trouble and she would simply walk away, out of the airport, drive off and sort it out from London. 'I'll deliver it back by ten p.m. tonight.'

He studied the agreement and laid it down upon the desk in front of him. 'Very well,' he sighed after a long pause. 'Deliver it back by ten p.m. Any Deals on Wheels garage . . . '

Now Lucy wasn't sure whether or not to believe him.

'That is, any Deals on Wheels garage *in Scotland*. Because, madam, I would advise you not to drive over the border without insurance.'

'I've got insurance.'

'No, you haven't. You are insured to drive the vehicle *in Scotland*.' Now he was enjoying the chance to spell it out to her. 'Look at your agreement. If you want to take the vehicle over the border you need to pay the *international* insurance supplement. That'll be a further four hundred and twenty-two pounds and fifty pence, minimum forty-eight hours cover, payable in advance.' He looked her in the eye, gleefully taking in the doubt. 'Now, do you want to give me those keys?'

Behind her the whole queue came noisily to life, no longer a long thin snake of individuals but a cooperative and indignant huddle. As Lucy stood there, at a loss as to what to do, a smiley woman in a pompom hat stepped forwards and stood beside her.

'Hold on,' she said first to the rep, sounding polite and jolly, but with a don't-mess-with-me edge. 'I'll be with you in a second.' Then she gave Lucy a great grin. 'I've been hatching the most wonderful plan,' she said, nodding back to a group of triumphant-looking Deals on Wheels customers. 'We're going to give each other lifts. We can't believe there are many axe-murderers here among us, and it makes it all so much cheaper. And more fun too, don't you think? Is Manchester any good for you? There's a three who could do with one more. Then you won't even need his stupid little car.'

'I did want to get back to London tonight . . . ' Was it such a good idea? Did she want to share? Lucy knew she had to decide fast but she couldn't seem to think it through clearly.

'Well, we've got three lots of four going to London already. And we've got a four sharing to Luton and a people-carrier going to Gatwick, but they're both full too, and I've agreed with the couple behind you,' the lady pointed to the nervous couple who'd been standing directly behind Lucy, 'to share a lift to Ashford. We've got room for one more for Ashford.'

'Did you say Ashford?' It was an old man, appearing from the very back of the queue, hobbling up to the pompom-hatted lady on a silver-tipped cane and giving Lucy a few seconds to think. 'Ashford would be marvellous.'

'Actually, I was just offering the space to this young lady . . . ' The woman looked enquiringly back to Lucy.

'But you must have it,' Lucy told him.

'Are you sure?'

Lucy nodded. 'It's a great idea, but I want to go to London. Surely there must be more of us . . . '

'I could do you Kings Lynn,' a good-looking man in a pin-stripe suit came up and told her, giving a reassuring, trust-me-I'm-a-doctor sort of smile. 'Promise I won't bite.'

'I'll share with you,' replied a morose-looking woman. She had plaits and a nose like a bent finger and was sitting on her rucksack. 'But I can't drive.'

They'd moved so fast it seemed that Lucy had been left behind.

'Anyone else for London?' she called out loudly, taking the plunge. 'Share the insurance and I've got the car.'

'I do not approve of this. I do not approve

38

of this *at all*.' The rep's face was mottled purple. 'Deals on Wheels does not sanction this action.'

'Hey, you nearly made it rhyme!' the woman in the pompom hat congratulated him. 'And we can do what we jolly well like. We're not breaking your silly rules.'

The man looked at her incredulously, picked up his telephone and urgently tapped in a number. 'You are being extremely foolhardy.'

'Oh, give up,' she told him. 'Just stop it.'

'I was going to London,' someone said to Lucy.

And of all the people standing in the queue, of course it had to be him, quietly arriving at her shoulder.

'London,' she called out again to the rest of the queue, not acknowledging him, hoping someone out there would come to her aid. 'Anyone want to go to London?'

'Yes, I do,' the man said agreeably.

She turned to him. 'I'm sorry, but I don't want to share with you.'

Had she actually said it out loud?

The rep turned to Lucy and put his hand over the receiver of the telephone. 'Have to say, madam,' he said with a gleeful smile, 'I think that's wise.'

Lucy looked away. She knew it would

sound ridiculous to anyone she tried to explain it to, but it was the truth. She really didn't want to share with him. Ten, twelve hours alone in a car with him would be impossible. He was too pristine and perfect, with his shiny shoes and his cashmere coat. He made her feel hungover and out of her depth. If she had to share with anyone she wanted it to be some safe, comforting middle-aged couple who would listen to Classic FM and let her sleep on the back seat while they took on all the driving.

She glanced at him, wondering how he'd taken it, and was irritated to catch the amusement in his eyes, because of course he thought she was joking. He might even admit she was being quite funny, as long as she didn't keep it up any longer.

'Come on,' he said impatiently when she said nothing more. 'I'm just what you're looking for.'

Now he'd really blown it.

He waited for a moment more but when she continued to ignore him he shrugged and turned away.

'Anyone like to share a lift to London?' he called, standing shoulder to shoulder with Lucy, who then asked exactly the same thing, a little louder. Neither of them got any response.

'Gatwick? Birmingham?' Lucy tried, colour rising in her cheeks, feeling completely ridiculous. 'I've got the car.' There was still no response. 'Glasgow?' she said more half-heartedly.

'Looks as if it's just you and me.'

'I said I don't want to share a lift with — '

'Oh, go on with you!' The lady in the pompom hat interrupted Lucy in exasperation. 'You ninny, what are you shouting about if you don't want to share a lift with someone? Don't spoil everything! We're sorting it all out great, apart from you two. What's the matter with you?'

'It's none of your business,' Lucy told her, feeling stupid, because of course the woman was right. She was abruptly manoeuvred out of earshot of the man.

'I agree, it's none of my business,' the pompom hat lady whispered at her. 'But even so, I'll remind you that it is five hundred miles to London. On your own that's twelve, thirteen hours driving *at least*, non-stop and in this filthy weather. Just how are you planning to do it?'

Lucy shrugged. 'Slowly.'

'But I thought you wanted to be back in London today?'

'I do.'

'Then trust me.' Rather too enthusiastically

41

the woman patted Lucy's cheek. 'Silly girl,' she said. 'I know he looks smoother than a jar of face cream but you'll be safe with him. I've stood next to him in the queue for the past twenty minutes and I can tell he's a gentleman.'

'I doubt he'd be interested in being anything else,' piped up the woman with the nose and the plaits, giving Lucy a critical once-over.

Lucy was quite hurt. She didn't look that bad. And what was this? Were all these people completely mad? Hadn't any of them heard that you didn't get into cars with strangers, especially strangers you had doubts about, whatever they looked like? And the truth was, she thought, looking glumly down at her feet, that it was precisely because he looked so smooth that he made her feel so rough. Because he was so assured and capable that she felt so stubbornly determined not to have him around.

'You know, I do understand.' He was looking over the pompom hat directly at Lucy, staring at her with what were now rather soulful brown eyes, and there was a new sincerity in his voice. 'I'd say the same thing if I was you.'

'Would you? Then why did you ask me?'

'I guess I was trying my luck. Because I do

42

very much want to get back to London tonight. But it's perfectly OK. You don't know me. You shouldn't feel any pressure to share a car with me.'

Lucy nodded. Now, of course, he was getting somewhere. She dithered, wondering whether to relent or listen to the panicky voice that still gabbled on in her head about how it was too early in the morning to cope with someone like him, how she needed time to herself, time to think. She looked at him uncertainly.

'So I'm sorry I asked.' He turned back to the rep, who was still waiting for his call to be answered. 'I need a car for London. I'll take anything.'

'No, *sir*, you won't.' It gave the rep great pleasure to say so. 'We have no vehicles available. Very few of our customers made it back to the airport this morning. Perhaps you might like to come back in a couple of hours and try again?'

'Perhaps I'll do that.' He turned to go, then looked back at Lucy and gave her a nod of farewell. 'Drive carefully.'

Lucy reached into her handbag, found her purse and turned swiftly to the rep, presenting him with her Visa card. 'I'll pay for the international insurance,' she told him. 'Four hundred quid, whatever it was.' Perhaps her travel insurance would kick in. She doubted it. 'And put this man on the insurance, too.'

The rep put down his telephone. He looked so disappointed Lucy thought he might be about to cry.

'And name him as a driver. He'll definitely be sharing the driving with me.'

'Thank you,' the man said, coming back to her, looking genuinely surprised and relieved.

'No problem. What's your name? You need to tell the rep.'

He held out his hand and she shook it, noticing his shiny pink nails.

'It's Jude. Jude Middleton,' he told the rep.

'I'm Lucy Blue.'

He turned back to her. 'What a wonderful name. But people must say that to you all the time?'

'Hey Jude, you're right. They do.'

He laughed, and as she found herself smiling back at him again she imagined telling her friend Jane about him the next day; how indignant Jane'd be. *What do you mean you nearly didn't give him a lift?* And then, *How come this kind of thing always happens to you? How come I never get to share a lift with a gorgeous man?*

But that wasn't why I did it, Lucy would insist, truly I did it because he made me feel sorry for him, absolutely nothing to do with that smile. She'd changed her mind and had offered him the lift because the pompom lady was right, it was ridiculous to think she could drive the whole way back to London on her own, and she would almost certainly be safer with him than without him. And what was more, now she'd be saving at least two hundred quid on the insurance. And then there was the bonus of being able to annoy the Deals on Wheels rep again.

★   ★   ★

'Do you mind if I make a quick call before we leave?' he asked, just as they reached the car. 'I had someone picking me up at Gatwick. I'd like to let them know I won't be there.'

He pulled out his mobile and walked away from her and Lucy stood for a moment, letting the snowflakes fall on her upturned hands, then tilted her face to the sky and caught a few more on her tongue. The wind had dropped away but the snow was still falling solidly, and she wondered whether she and Jude and everyone else in the Deals on Wheels queue were mad to think about driving through it. She guessed they would find out soon enough. She turned back to her car and unlocked it, swept an armful of snow off the windscreen and wiped her wing mirrors, opened the boot and threw in her overnight bag before slamming it shut again and dislodging a great heap of snow from the roof on to her feet as she did so. She walked around to the driver's side, shaking the snow away, then took off her coat, climbed in and started the engine, turned on the heating, took the map off the passenger seat, dropped it on to the seat behind her and prepared to wait.

She watched Jude through the windscreen. Now that they were out of the airport terminal and the journey was about to begin, she was regretting it all over again. She wished she'd at least put on some make-up to combat the effects of the night before. She wondered if this made her a very superficial person and decided that it probably did, but she had fair skin, and eyelashes that came to life with a little mascara and disappeared without it. Of course what she looked like hadn't mattered when she'd got out of bed. And it hadn't mattered when she'd entered the airport because she'd thought she would scuttle through, meeting nobody. But it was mattering now, now that she'd set eyes on Jude Middleton.

She ran her hands through her hair and checked herself in the mirror, then surreptitiously breathed on the back of her hand and sniffed. How long would they be on the road? She'd guessed ten hours, but the pompom lady had said thirteen. She was going to be sharing a lift with this man until approximately eleven that night, no distractions, nothing for them to do but get to know each other, and the least she should do, and for Jude's sake not hers, was gargle with a bit of toothpaste.

She looked out of the window again, watched him sliding his fingers through his silky hair as he talked on his phone, smoothing and straightening it perfectly into place as he walked slowly away from the car, across the car park, disappearing into the snow, clearly completely absorbed. She wondered who he was talking to . . . his girlfriend perhaps? *Baby, you won't believe it, my flight's been cancelled. Yes, I know, me too, me too . . . But I'm driving down! I've persuaded someone to share a lift . . . yes, darling, a girl . . . God, don't worry about that, you're quite safe. Breath like a dead badger . . .*

She opened the car door, crouching down and slipping to the back of the car, opened the boot and unzipped her overnight bag, finding her toothbrush and toothpaste, then rezipped the bag, shut the boot gently and slipped back to her seat again. Toothpaste on brush, swig of water, furious brushing, a surreptitious gargle and spit into the snow. She opened her handbag, and quickly stuffed in the toothpaste and brush and zipped it shut again just as Jude opened the door. He paused, seeming to sniff the air appreciatively.

'OK if I drive first?' she asked him as he took off his scarf, a pair of soft leather gloves, then carefully unbuttoned his beautiful black coat, folded it and dropped it on to the back seat. She wanted to be in control at least until she'd had a chance to get the measure of him. 'We could swap over when we stop for petrol.'

'Whatever you want,' he said, bending his head and climbing in beside her.

'I guess we should just head south?' she asked, starting the engine and thinking how big he seemed in the little car.

'We need to follow the signs for Fort William, and then to Perth.' He leaned round and reached for the back seat, practically kissing her as he did so, and took the map from under his coat. He cupped his hands and blew on them, then opened it and started to turn the pages. 'We'll cross the Slochd summit and then go over the Drumochter Pass. We want the A9 and after that we'll drop down on to the M74 and join the motorways. I guess the snow won't be so bad down there.'

'You sound as if you know the route.'

'Some of it.'

Jude didn't elaborate, so Lucy started the car and tentatively followed her nose out of the airport and looked for the signs to Fort William.

'Got some petrol?'

She nodded. She could hear a deliberate formality in his tone now, which she supposed wasn't surprising after the awkwardness in the airport, and the megawatt smile was nowhere to be seen. He'd probably concluded that she was mouthy and charmless and best left alone. She wondered whether she should say something, try to explain, and then she stopped herself. No regrets and no apologies. She didn't have to make him like her. It was her car. She'd chosen to share it with him. And anyway, she hadn't really been rude to him, she'd just been honest, looking after herself, cautious about travelling with a stranger, a lone man. And she'd brushed her teeth for him, after all.

The car suddenly skidded in the snow, sending them sliding sideways towards the ditch, and belatedly she woke up to the fact that she was driving again. In the short time since she'd first arrived at the airport the snow had clearly deepened and become more treacherous. Even within the ring roads of Inverness, with the gritters and snowploughs working hard, the road was still covered in deep fresh snow. Turning corners would need care and attention and a certain degree of luck.

'It's OK,' she reassured Jude the third time his head shot up from the map in alarm. 'I had the same trouble all the way here, although perhaps it wasn't quite so bad. But as long as there's nothing coming the other way, I find it's best to let the car right itself.'

He nodded and swallowed but said nothing, watching with her as she waited for a space in the traffic before slowly pulling out on to a roundabout.

'I nearly hit a stag on the way here . . . ' She flicked on the indicator and turned off to the left as she talked. 'Well, I say *nearly hit* but actually it leapt over the bonnet of the car.' She paused and glanced across to him, unnerved by the cold, flat look on his face. 'It was beautiful . . . ' she tailed off.

'I'd put the headlights on,' he said, looking down at the map again, 'and speed up the windscreen wipers.'

'I was just about to.'

She carefully moved up into third gear, then fourth, and when he said nothing more she told herself it was perfect if he didn't want to talk to her, that silence was what she wanted too. But who was she kidding? Now that she and Jude were in the car together, Lucy desperately wanted to talk to him, to lay the ghost of awkwardness hanging over them since the airport. Already this journey was so different from when she'd been on her own. Then she had thrived on the silence, but now the two of them, sitting side by side but not talking, didn't feel good at all but awkward and spiky. Once or twice she opened her mouth to speak, to ask him what it was he'd been doing in Inverness, where he was going once he got back to London, even who it was he'd been calling on his phone, but each time the look on his face made her close it again and say nothing.

She drove on, thinking how unexpected this was. In her imagination he'd been charming and flirtatious, intimidating even, dominating the conversation and tying her sleepy brain into knots with his witty chat. Instead, as she peered through the windscreen, carefully giving him the mother of all lifts, having kindly saved him from hours and hours at Inverness airport, he looked as if he was falling asleep. And Lucy imagined the shock on his face if she suddenly pulled the car over and stopped, told him that it simply wasn't good enough, that his behaviour wasn't up to scratch, that she felt he'd misled her and if he wasn't prepared to contribute to the mood of the journey he could get out.

'Are you OK?' he asked suddenly.

'Yes. Why?'

'You sighed.'

'Did I?' She knew she hadn't made a sound.

'Or was it a sneeze?' She looked at him, eyebrows raised, and he nodded towards the windscreen. 'You should watch the road.'

'I am watching the road.'

'You're OK then?'

'I'm fine!'

'And you know we want the A9 at the next roundabout?'

'Yes, I do.'

'Not too tired to drive me safely home?'

'I want to drive myself safely home, remember.'

'Sure you do. But any time you want to change over, you should let me know.'

She nodded and stared irritably through the windscreen, keeping her eyes away from him. And when at last she did sneak a look, it was to see that he'd stretched out his legs and turned away from her.

'I don't think you should go to sleep.'

His looked back at her. 'Were you talking to me?'

'Of course I was talking to you. Who else is sitting in this car?'

'I'm sorry.'

'I was thinking it would be nice if you talked to me,' she said.

He pushed himself up in his seat. 'And I was thinking it was better to leave you alone. Because you're clearly not a morning person, are you?' He waited. 'Or is it me?'

How dare he say that? What a bloody cheek! Yet she couldn't stop herself beginning to smile as she stared straight ahead at the road.

'It's you,' she retorted. 'Falling asleep instead of keeping me company.'

'I wasn't asleep, I was just resting my eyes.'

'That's rubbish. And aren't you interested in finding something out about your chauffeur?'

He pretended to think about it, then shook his head. 'I don't think so, no.'

'I'll drop you off at a bus stop then, shall I?' It was almost impossible not to keep looking at him, but the road was twisting and turning and great gusts of snow were being ripped about by the wind. 'Let me concentrate on driving.'

'You're doing fine, as long as you remember to keep looking ahead and not at me all the time.'

'That's easy enough.'

'And of course I want to talk to you. I got the impression you didn't want to talk to me, that's all. Not yet, anyway. But I think it's wonderful, you and me, sharing a lift, not knowing each other at all. It's such a one-off, don't you think? We could get back to London and find that the drive down from Inverness, experiencing the entire M6 motorway along the way — was a wonderful, life-changing experience.'

She wasn't sure if he was being serious. 'Strangers share journeys all the time,' she said crisply. 'It's just that ours is going to be longer than most.'

'I think that's what I meant.'

She heaved a sigh. 'I'm sorry.'

'That's OK.'

'I had too little sleep last night.'

He nodded. 'So did you have a good time?'

'Awful.' She saw him start to smile, then think that perhaps he shouldn't. 'That's right, you're not allowed to laugh because, as far as I can remember, the evening wasn't in the slightest bit funny.'

'Mine was. I had great fun.'

'Good for you. The best bit of my stay was leaving this morning.'

'The best bit of mine was dancing to the Sugarbabes with my eleven-year-old-cousins.'

She laughed in surprise. 'How did you manage that?'

'My mother got her sister to invite me

54

because she was worried I'd be on my own for New Year's Eve. So I came from Aberdeen last night, only to find the parents were off to a party and I'd been brought down as the babysitter.'

'How mean of them.'

'No. The girls were lovely. We made banana and rum milkshakes.'

'You fed them rum!'

'Just a teaspoon.'

Lucy risked a quick glance. 'And otherwise you'd have done nothing? Didn't you have hundreds of swanky parties to choose from?'

'Now why would you think that?'

'Because you look the sort.'

'Said with true disdain.'

She shook her head. 'Not at all.'

'So what is my sort? What do you think I do in Aberdeen?'

'I've no idea.'

'Have a go.'

'Are we going to have to spend the whole journey talking about you?'

'No. We could spend it talking about you.'

She shook her head. 'I don't think so.'

'No? Then I suppose we could talk about aquaculture in the Inner Hebrides, or the long-term implications of the Criminal Justice Bill? What would you like to talk about?'

'I'd guess you sell aftershave,' she said, just to shut him up.

Jude spluttered satisfyingly. 'You can't say that.'

'Yes I can. You asked me what I think you do and I'm telling you.'

'You mean I'm a model? I'm flattered.'

'Did I say that?'

'No,' he admitted. 'Actually I work on the rigs.'

This was obviously meant to silence her, but for a long moment Lucy couldn't imagine what he meant, wondering vaguely if The Rigs could be some trendy Scottish magazine.

'Doing what?'

'I fly the guys out and I bring them back again.'

'Fly them out?' she repeated, knowing she was sounding really slow. He even looked disappointed, as if he'd had high hopes for her and what a shame to find she'd only got half a brain after all. But right now, even her half brain wouldn't do its business and work. In fact her whole head felt as if it hadn't been screwed on properly.

'I fly helicopters on and off the oil-rigs,' he said slowly. 'I work off the coast of Aberdeen. North Sea oil, Lucy, maybe you've heard of it?'

But this fashion statement in his long

cashmere coat, with his spiky eyelashes and his glossy hair, could *not* work on oil-rigs. He was tea-tree oil, not North Sea oil; cashmere coats, not oilskins. Oil-rigs had men in boiler-suits with grimy faces shouting to be heard above the hundred-mile-an-hour winds. Oil-rigs had tiny cabins, with no room to balance a bar of soap let alone the several washbags worth of expensive products that Jude would no doubt need beside him.

'You don't!' she laughed.

'Yes, I do. Why do you think it's so strange?'

'You're too clean.'

'I live in Aberdeen. I don't live on the rigs.'

She nodded, taking it in. 'So, do you get to see any of the drilling?' she asked, trying to sound serious. 'Or is it all done by computer now? No need to get your hands dirty, just a question of moving things around on a screen?'

He shrugged. 'I fly the helicopters on and off the rigs. The men out there work two- or three-week shifts. They need bringing back to shore and the new shift needs flying out. I've been doing it for about eight months.' He leaned close towards her so that she could feel his breath warm on her face. 'And yes, sometimes I watch the drilling.'

Do that again, she thought. Involuntarily

she touched her hand to her cheek.

'It must be so wet and so cold?'

'I tend not to land in the sea.'

'You know what I mean. It must be a hard life.' She'd wanted to say a windswept, miserable, lonely life. 'Surely there are other places to fly helicopters, warmer places?'

'I've done that too. I used to fly helicopters for the Navy. I left last year.'

That was more like it. A suntan, aviator shades, gleaming white teeth. She could picture him in the Navy.

'Why did you leave?'

'Fancied the change.'

And the suddenly clipped way that he said it told her not to ask why.

*   *   *

They reached the Drumochter Pass relieved to find that it hadn't yet been closed, then threaded their way painstakingly slowly between the mountains which, even on this day, with the sky low and visibility so poor, were stark against the snow and very bleak. Lucy could only glance up, awestruck, as Jude did, catching the briefest of glimpses of the huge wet boulders, the steep granite slopes, before the snow enveloped them again.

As soon as they'd crossed the pass the road widened again, but still visibility was so bad that Lucy had to concentrate completely on the road and neither of them spoke at all. All she could think, as she gritted her teeth and drove carefully on, was how very relieved she was to have Jude beside her. How scary and daunting this journey would have been if she'd been making it alone.

'Were you in Aberdeen over Christmas?' she asked him eventually, when she was able slowly to pick up speed again. 'I guess the rigs don't close down for the holidays?'

'Yes, I was, and no, they don't.'

'It must have been hard.'

'There was tinsel and a turkey,' he said flippantly. 'What more did I need?'

'Family? Friends?' She didn't want to let it go. 'Didn't you miss them?'

'Of course, but that's why I'm here with you now, heading home. And I expect there'll still be a Christmas tree and some leftover turkey.'

'So are you the prodigal son?'

'No, I think his mother *cooked* him a fatted calf,' he grinned at her. 'Mine will have been *burned*.' But even though he was joking there was an edge to his words. 'And then it will have had a bottle of wine poured over it, always my mother's solution to a crisis.'

So's that where the problems lie, Lucy wondered. And the way she'd stepped in to set up his New Year's Eve perhaps meant his mother was rather interfering too. Not surprising that Jude was wary of seeing her again.

'And my father will have planned a fun job for me, drainage pipes needing laying at the bottom of some freezing field, something like that.'

Perhaps his father liked keeping far out of the way too?

'I'm meeting my brother in London and then we're meant to be driving on to Oxford tonight. Three and a half days of family bonding.' He turned to her and grinned. 'You know what? It's my idea of hell.'

She was surprised that he'd admit such a thing, but she kept her voice light. 'You shouldn't have made such an effort to persuade me to give you a lift.'

He was still looking at her. 'I decided you were worth it.'

It was so unexpected that as she kept her eyes on the road she could feel herself start to blush, and hoped desperately that he wouldn't notice. Ignore it. Don't react at all, she told herself. Twelve more hours in the car with him could only be survived if she didn't react at all.

'So is it ages since they've seen you?'

'A few months, not so long.'

There was a long pause.

'Where does he live, your brother?'

'In Notting Hill, off Moreton Road.'

'How funny. I'm going to a party there next weekend.'

'Come and knock on my door?'

'We'll have had enough of each other by then.'

'You know that's not true.'

And immediately she felt it again, anticipation and excitement, and again she tried to stamp it out. But the tune had begun now inside her head and it wasn't going to stop. 'I could drive you back there tonight, if you like.'

'That would be very nice of you.'

She nodded, saying nothing.

'So where do you live?' he asked.

'Barons Court.'

'Deals on Wheels has an office in Hammersmith.'

'How do you know that?'

'I asked at the desk when I was filling out the forms.'

'Jude!'

'What's the problem? I knew one of us had to take the car back. I was being efficient. And, any other time, of course I'd be offering.

But I haven't been home for such a long time. And we're going to be so late . . . And now they know I'm still coming, they'll be waiting up.'

Nothing about her plans, she noticed. It didn't occur to him that someone might have been waiting up for her too. But she had offered to drop him back.

'This trip home is such a big deal.'

'It's OK,' she said quietly. 'I don't mind taking you to your brother's.'

'Thank you, Lucy. Luke and I . . . ' he paused again, clasping his hands together tightly on his lap. 'Oh, sod it. If I'd got stuck in Inverness, I know they'd have thought I was making some excuse . . . '

'Why don't you want to go home?'

He turned to her. 'Why does it bother you if I don't?'

'Because it's sad.'

'Don't say it like that. Everything's fine. I love them, they love me.'

But even as she heard herself apologizing, she was thinking it had been a natural enough question to ask. He'd made so little attempt to disguise his feelings, it was almost as if he'd wanted to provoke her into asking.

'I'm sorry,' Jude said. 'I mean, they're used to me being late, that's all, not turning up for things, forgetting birthdays, being unreliable.'

He was smoothing everything over again, the charm back in his voice, the smile back on his face. 'And they'll be waiting up, telling each other how hopeless I am and what a shame poor Luke — my brother — has had to spend the whole day waiting for me. You know, family stuff.'

'But you couldn't help the snow.'

'I couldn't help the snow. Will you tell them that for me?'

'I'll tell your brother if I meet him.'

'I expect he'll be out on the steps the moment we reach his front door.' He looked at his watch, then back at her. 'An hour and a half down. What do you think, twelve more to go?' Restlessly he drummed his hands on his knees. 'Guilt,' he said shortly. 'That's what it is — the closer I get to them, the more guilty I feel.'

He veered between openness and evasiveness so constantly that Lucy was at a loss as to how to react.

'Tell me about your party,' he demanded, immediately moving on. 'Was it really so bad?'

'Terrible.'

'Why?'

'Honestly? Because I think I'd imagined myself waltzing into the room in my sexy pink dress, wowing everybody with my glamour and my air of mystery. And it didn't exactly work out like that.'

Seeing surprise on his face, Lucy cringed. What was she doing, telling him that? Honesty was so rarely the best policy and now she imagined him thinking, *How funny, you seriously thought you could wow an entire room?*

'Mad Blind Idiots of Inverness, was that who the party was for?'

She grinned at him gratefully.

'I'd have been wowed.'

'Oh, shut up. Just because I said I'd drive you home.'

'No, of course I'd have noticed you. And your sexy pink dress.'

'Someone called Julia Clegg, an old school-friend, invited me. But I hadn't seen her for years.'

'And then you remembered why.'

She laughed. 'Exactly.'

'So why did you go?'

'Because she invited me at just the right moment. I needed some time on my own.' She glanced at him. 'You know that feeling, don't you? When it's time to get away for a bit . . . ' *Of course he knew what she meant. It was why he was in Aberdeen, wasn't it?*

But Jude wasn't about to admit it. He simply sat there, silently, letting the momentum of the conversation die away. And Lucy drove on, thinking how every time she sensed he was about to take her cue and talk more openly, he moved out of reach again. And so she didn't say any more, although she'd like to have told him about Teddy. She'd have explained how she'd finally binned him just before Christmas to cheers from her family and friends, and to tears of relief from her friend Jane, who'd immediately announced that at times she'd wondered if she'd lost Lucy for good. She'd have told Jude how Teddy had refused to believe her when she'd said it was over. How he had persisted in calling her every day over Christmas, much to her family's dismay: clearly Lucy hadn't been quite convincing enough. Didn't she realize there was no point trying to be his friend? And how she knew she was going to have to be that bit more convincing once she got back to London, this time telling him so firmly that he'd have no choice but to believe it. She'd have told Jude how difficult it was because she and Teddy worked in the same company and how they had to continue to get on for the sake of their work, how he was bound to be there at her desk first thing the next morning. If Jude had wanted to listen, she could have spent the next hour telling him all about Teddy.

She remembered him as she'd seen him

last, just before she'd left to join her family for Christmas. He'd watched as she'd packed, occasionally commenting on the things he liked, or didn't like, dismissing her pink party dress, then flicking at a lovely black shift dress and asking where she'd be wearing *that*? And she'd told him: drinks party, Christmas Eve, friends of her parents, keeping her head down, thinking to herself over and over again that this was it. And she'd waited until she was standing in the communal hall of the mansion block where she lived, with her coat on and her handbag in hand, her suitcase packed at her feet and the taxi waiting for her outside, and then, out of the blue, she'd told him that she wasn't coming to Norfolk for New Year with his parents after all, she was going to Inverness, to a party on her own. And then she told him how she didn't want to see him when she got back to London again either. And once he'd got the gist of what she was saying, he'd talked loudly through every next word she'd said as if he hadn't taken in a thing. He'd held the door open for her and had steered her out on to the street, packed her into the taxi, refusing to listen, saying that he would call her that evening and that he'd see her when she got back on Boxing Day. And that he hoped she liked his Christmas present. And she'd stopped, in a way so elated that she'd said anything at all and so grateful to be getting away from him that she'd hardly cared he hadn't listened. But then, just as the taxi was preparing to drive off, her courage had returned, and she'd called out of the window that she wasn't coming back to London on Boxing Day, she was staying away until after New Year. She would go to Scotland for New Year's Eve, straight from her parents' house. And she'd seen from the way he stopped and stared back at her in surprise that finally she'd got through to him.

Now she looked across at Jude again and saw in frustration that he'd closed his eyes once more. Open them, she wanted to insist. I need you to tell me what to do with him when I walk into my office tomorrow morning. But closing his eyes was clearly Jude's way of cutting short a conversation he didn't like. Why he mightn't like it she didn't know, because surely she was demanding nothing of him? Was it that he was wary of getting personal? Or was it simply that he was afraid she was about to bore him, to pour out her heart for hours and hours?

With one hand on the steering-wheel she stretched to reach the back seat and her handbag, and beside her Jude opened his eyes.

'What do you want?'

'My phone. Can you find it in my bag and turn it off for me?'

He asked for no explanation. She watched him unlock the phone for her and switch it off, and she felt first relief wash through her — that Teddy was no longer able to burst in on them in the car — and then anger with herself that he could still make her feel anything at all. Then Jude put the phone back in her bag and dropped it behind her seat and moved forward to switch on the radio and music suddenly filled her head, drowning out all thoughts of Teddy.

He moved them from station to station, gauging her opinion of what was playing as he went — Radiohead moving into Simon and Garfunkel's *America*. Kings of Convenience into the Alabama 3, the Black Eyed Peas and the Red Hot Chilli Peppers. And the music lifted her spirits again, helped her remember and rediscover the person she'd been on that journey to the airport. And they sat there silently together, gradually building up the soundtrack of their own road-movie, as another hour slipped by.

And when they turned the radio off again, it was as if the music had loosened Jude's hold on himself because finally he started to talk, still not much about himself but happy to tell her more about the oilfields and his life on board the rigs, how they towered hundreds of feet above the sea and how they could creak in storms like huge ships. And she would sometimes not even be able to hear what he was saying but she'd smile anyway and nod, enjoying the sound of the calm rise and fall of his voice against the mesmerizing hum of the car on the snowy road. And now she was relaxed because she knew that Jude was relaxed too, and sometimes she was leaning in to listen to him and sometimes she was hearing no words at all but was simply liking him being there beside her. And then occasionally he'd break into her thoughts and ask her something, and she'd turn to him briefly as she drove and would be suddenly acutely aware of him there, so close. Or she'd think he was about to speak and she'd glance across but he'd say nothing at all, would just be looking at her, waiting for her to look at him, and then she'd feel a fingertip of excitement slide softly down her spine, and she'd grip the wheel and fix her eyes straight ahead at the road and not at him.

4

'Don't you wish we'd found some Hip Hotel and holed up for a few days?'

She darted a look at him, and he stretched in his seat and raised his eyebrows back at her.

'I meant don't you wish you were taking advantage of the snow? It's a good excuse not to go back to work, isn't it?'

She kept her eyes on the road, forcing herself not to react.

'I don't mean like that. Although I'm sure like that would be good.'

'I'm responsible. I'm very hard-working. Don't talk to me about skiving off.'

'What do you do?'

'Headhunting,' she said crisply. 'First I trained as a vet but then I became a headhunter instead.'

'Why did you do that? Why did you change?'

'Because I realized I didn't like animals enough.'

He laughed in surprise.

'But when I say I don't like them — ' she was smiling too, still going over what he'd said about the Hip Hotel — 'I mean I don't like *little* animals, pregnant gerbils and guinea-pigs with ingrowing toenails, that kind of thing. I like horses, cattle . . . but you don't get that many of them in London. So last year I changed direction and became a headhunter instead.'

'And who do you hunt? Are you good at it? Do you like it?'

'I hunt anyone — producers, directors, graphic designers, marketing directors. I could be hunting on behalf of someone who's ready to change jobs, or for a company with a space to fill. But I sometimes wonder if I'm making a mistake.' She nodded towards the window, out towards the distant highlands where the snow was clearing and they could now see light across the farthest hills, and for a moment she held her breath, it was so beautiful. 'No more Barons Court station at seven in the morning. Find somewhere like this to live instead.' She stopped abruptly, thinking of heels and fifteen-denier tights, of getting up at six when it was still pitch dark, of arriving at her office, of how the adrenalin cranked up her heart rate whenever she pushed her way through those heavy glass doors. 'But after a holiday the first morning's always a horrible experience, isn't it? By lunchtime I won't even remember I've been away. You must feel it too?' She glanced across to Jude but he had turned away, looking out of the window, and she wasn't even sure he was still listening and again she was left feeling excluded from what was going on in his head.

Then the road narrowed and darkened again and they entered a deep, dark forest of pine trees, adding a spooky edge to the muffled sound of wheels on snow, paths twisting between the trees where the snow had not yet reached, and then they were out on the other side, back in the daylight, grey light, once more, and it was clear that the snow really had eased off. At times it had been rushing at them, so aggressively gusting and beating on the windscreen with rage that it had been almost impossible to see the road, but now it was tumbling softly, the downy flakes taking their time to fall, and from the vague ache in the back of her eyes that heralded the lifting of the clouds, Lucy guessed that soon the snow would stop completely.

She thought about Julia, whose New Year's Eve party it had been and who lived here all year round, in an old hunting-lodge a few miles from the Kirk Castle Hotel. Julia Clegg, who could gut a stag where it had fallen, kneeling in the heather with her hunting knife, a velvet scrunchie holding back her fine blonde hair, but who had passed out last night after only a few glasses of wine. Four seasons in one day, Julia had said, while she could still talk, that's what she loved about where she lived. Lucy had arrived in darkness and hadn't understood but now she could look out of her windscreen and appreciate exactly what Julia meant.

Far in the distance, across the huge flat expanse of moorland and up towards the mountains, the clouds had broken and shafts of pale sunlight had started to fall upon the peaks, making the snow around them glow with an alabaster light. She could even see a sliver of cobalt-blue sky.

And then Jude said quietly, 'Such a perfect day,' and Lucy turned to him in surprise and he reached for her hand and squeezed it gently. 'I'm glad I'm sharing it with you.'

But a strange, inexplicable sadness reached into her at his words and she found herself stretching for his hand again, but letting it go almost before she'd touched him.

'I'm glad I'm sharing it with you.'

He said nothing more, and for a long time they drove on in silence, but by touching her hand he'd reached something inside her too, so that whereas before she'd sat beside him so comfortably, so light-hearted, now she found herself disrupted, intensely aware of him there next to her.

They passed a garage that looked shut up for the winter, and Lucy checked the petrol gauge and saw that they had just under a third of a tank left. She flicked on the car's computer, to find that they had now travelled a hundred and eighty-seven miles at an average speed of fifty-six miles per hour and that the temperature outside was minus four. She drove on, thinking of sleety rain and an oily black North Sea, roaring and crashing against the huge oil-rigs, and wondered how Jude could have ended up there, what it was that had taken him from the Navy, whether he'd been asked to leave or had chosen to go. She wondered about his life, whether he had a girlfriend, and if he did, how serious it could be with him away so much. She wondered where he lived in Aberdeen, whether he was planning on staying for another year, whether he might be thinking like her, that New Year's Day was a day for changes. And then he coughed, shifted in his seat and turned towards her, and she looked and saw that he'd fallen asleep, his mouth a little open, his head wedged between the headrest and the seatbelt, and when he didn't stir she looked again, in snatched glances as she drove.

She wanted to touch him. Asleep he was so defenceless and sweet and alone and tired, his closed eyes sunk deep into their sockets, his full lips chapped and rough and the skin beneath his stubbly cheeks a pale biscuit brown, as if he'd seen a lot of sun but a long, long time ago, with a faint smattering of freckles there below his eyes. Awake, he was perhaps too vain, and it annoyed her that he barely listened when she talked about herself and did the disappearing act on her once too often, that he was flippant and evasive and that she could hardly say she knew him any better now than when he'd first got into the car. But asleep, her hand so badly wanted to stroke his face that she had almost reached his cheek before she realized what she was doing.

He was wearing baggy dark jeans but all she could see were the long muscular legs beneath them, and a heavy zip-up jumper she wanted to unzip. She took in the breadth of his shoulders and the narrowness of his waist. No doubt his mother would tell him he was far too thin, would bring him a huge breakfast in bed and inedible suppers of leftover, over-cooked turkey and Christmas pudding. She looked at his sleeping face, at the soft black hair cut close to his scalp, and wondered what she looked like, what kind of mother would have such a beautiful son as Jude. And then, what kind of girl might have a boyfriend like him.

They were approaching another roundabout now, with signs to the motorway ahead of them, and she changed down a gear and slowed ready for the turn, and Jude stirred with the movement and stretched out his arms. She wondered if they'd ever see each other again after she dropped him off at his brother's house, whether they'd swap phone numbers, at least pretending that they'd stay in touch. And she knew even then that she wouldn't want to. That Jude was part of this strange one-off day and it wouldn't be the same to see him again.

Then he swallowed and shifted again in his seat, turning to face her and at the same time his hand fell into her lap, palm up, where it stayed resting lightly on her thighs. And by the time she realized what she was doing she'd crossed both lanes of the roundabout and veered back in again, just missing the kerb, before finally righting the car and driving on. *You silly bugger*, she whispered at him. *See what you made me do?* But Jude didn't stir, his head stayed just where it was, and all Lucy could think was that Teddy had never, ever had that effect on her.

She looked at his long fingers still there in her lap and imagined them coming to life, wondered what they'd do, where they'd go next, and her stomach flipped over at the thought. She lifted his hand off her legs and dropped it back on his own. He was just a good looking man hitching a lift, taking advantage of the fact that they were alone together to have some fun, see how many knots he could tie her into, he wasn't going to think about her once he got home. And so she couldn't let him get to her. She couldn't, mustn't behave in the wholly predictable way he expected her to.

But why not? a little voice asked inside her head. After all, they'd been in the car alone together for nearly four hours *and now he was lying asleep beside her* and he wasn't so much good-looking as walk-into-a-lamppost gorgeous. Of course her mind was bound to wander and she was bound to wonder. Since when was that so wrong? She looked across at him for a third time, and he seemed to smile up at her in his sleep.

But then as she drove over the brow of a hill she saw another petrol station ahead, this one lit up against the snowy road. And she knew that it would be the last before the motorway, that she would have to stop to fill up the car and that that would wake Jude again, and that the daydream was coming to end before it had even really begun.

★　★　★

He opened his eyes as she turned into the empty garage, driving across the spotless pristine snow and pulling up beside a pump.

'Welcome back,' she said, feeling his eyes upon her.

He stretched and yawned lazily. 'I was dreaming about you. We were on a beach, sitting in the surf . . . You had no . . .'

'If only,' she said, turning off the engine, and Jude sat up in his seat.

'I'm sorry,' he said, rubbing his eyes and making a big deal of looking all around him. 'How could I have fallen asleep, how could I have left you all on your own? Were you all right?'

'You only had about half an hour.'

He reached on to the back seat for his coat and pulled out his wallet.

'Stay here and keep warm,' he said. 'I'll do this.'

Which was the right thing to say.

She watched him through the window as he stood beside her door and filled up the petrol tank, his back turned to the wind. They were the only people there apart from an old man sitting huddled behind the counter in the brightly lit shop; she could almost believe he was there specially for them, as if they truly were the only two people travelling that day.

She watched Jude jog over to the shop to pay for the petrol and then, as if he knew she was watching, he suddenly turned and grinned at her. She waved back at him and felt her heart stop. *Don't,* she told herself, bringing her hand down on to her lap, clasping hold of it with the other. Fancy him but don't fall for him. That way danger lies.

She opened her car door and got out hurriedly, gasping at the icy cold but enjoying the movement after sitting still for so long. She walked round to the other side, slipped into the passenger seat, still warm from his body, and sat waiting for him. When he returned he waved a floppy hot-dog in a bread roll at her through the window, and she wrinkled up her nose at him. He opened his door, leaned across and went to hand it to her.

'What's the matter?' he asked when she shook her head.

'I can't eat that.'

'Are you sure? Aren't you hungry?'

'I've never seen anything so bright.' Her

stomach was clenched tight as a fist. She didn't think she could ever eat anything again.

'Or a Twix?' He pulled it out of his pocket.

She shook her head, remembering the time Teddy had removed a Twix from her fingers just as she was about to take a bite. *You're getting fat*, he'd told her cheerfully.

'I'll have your hot-dog,' Jude decided. 'Give it back to me once we're on the motorway. I need both my hands.'

I could use both your hands, she thought, and she took it from him, held it, smelled it, and felt what little breakfast she'd had rising again in the back of her throat.

Jude started the car and pulled out on to the road, testing the windscreen wipers, flicking the indicators, adjusting the seat as he went. They climbed a hill, dropped down the other side, and immediately ahead of them saw a huge green destination board with signs to the M74 and the M6, with Gretna Green as the first destination at the top of the list.

'Lucy, look, we could get married!' Jude said, laughing, turning to her. 'Please say yes.'

'I'll need a very big diamond.'

He glanced at her again. 'Are you always so demanding?' He was challenging her, asking her in such a way that it was perfectly clear diamonds were not on his mind.

'Sometimes, if I have to be.' She could feel the heat in her cheeks, her heart starting to race and she looked away, out of the window, because it was as if something had happened to him while he'd been asleep, as if he'd had a dream that had shown him how she'd been thinking and was now matching her, challenging her to take it further.

'Here,' she said, sounding so calm she almost convinced herself. 'Have this disgusting thing before it goes cold.'

The hot-dog sausage had fallen half out of the bread, and ketchup and vivid yellow mustard were dripping on to her fingers. He saw the distaste on her face and laughed. 'Go on. Eat some.'

'Take it off me,' she insisted, holding it out to him, and he took the hot-dog in her hand and lifted it carefully to his mouth and then let her go.

'Any more?' she asked when he'd finished the mouthful, holding it out to him again, but he shook his head, opened his window to an icy blast of cold air, took it out of her hand and flung it away.

When the window was shut and the car warm again she put her arms above her head and stretched in her seat, and thought about how the next few hours might map out. It had been deliberate, the way he'd taken her hand just then, no mistaking the way he'd looked at her, how it had felt when they'd touched each other, and yet, despite what he'd said, she suspected that that was as far as he would want to go. The reticence in him, the way he turned away from her as often as he came close, made her suspect that there was more going on than she knew, and that the rest of the journey would now turn into a marathon flirt that would end when they got back to London, when they'd walk away from each other without a backward glance. All too easy to spend the rest of the journey alert to every move that he made, watching him talk, watching him laugh and blink and swallow, watching his hands grip the steering-wheel, imagining how they would feel if they were touching her, brushing the hair from her face, stroking her cheek, imagining but never finding out. And she thought how she'd trade never seeing him again for him to stop the car and kiss her here and now.

'Are you asleep?' Jude asked.

She almost told him.

'I'm daydreaming.'

'Are they nice daydreams?'

She nodded.

He rested his hand lightly on her shoulder and there had been no reason to do that, no reason at all but that he'd wanted to, and that he'd known she wanted him to.

'You had your eyes closed.'

'I was a million miles away from being asleep.'

'You should try. You look tired.'

'That's sweet of you to say so.'

'You know what I mean. Go to sleep,' he insisted. 'I promise I'll drive you safely home.'

'But I should keep you company.'

'I've slept, remember? And there's time for us when you wake up.'

Time for us? Anticipation leaped inside her again and she felt sparklingly, electrifyingly awake.

She lay there with her eyes tightly closed, her body rigid. What was he doing? Why did he want her asleep? She imagined Jude looking at her, checking her out, taking his time like she had with him, studying her hair, the curve of her hip, the shape of her lips . . . She licked them, then stopped abruptly, feeling colour stealing up her cheeks again, and had to fight the urge to open her eyes.

And lost. She opened her eyes, to find Jude wasn't looking at her at all but was staring straight ahead, concentrating on the road and tapping the steering-wheel to some imaginary beat.

She turned slowly away, disappointed, still alert to every flicker of movement he made, every sound, and then she took herself in hand, listened to the scolding voice telling her to stop getting everything out of proportion, to stop acting like a lovesick teenager.

She stared out across the flat expanse of snow-covered fields stretching away on either side of the motorway. There was a train in the distance and she watched as it dipped in and out of view, keeping pace with them, and felt herself floating away on the sea of sleep, half-conscious, half-drifting. Through half-open lids she took in a cluster of houses, chimney-smoke hanging in the air.

Having been the only car on the road, they were now one in a multitude of others, most of them no doubt full of people travelling home from the Christmas break, in every sense changing gear, mentally limbering up for the Monday morning onslaught. As far as Lucy was concerned, Monday morning seemed still to be light years away.

Mostly Jude drove much more cautiously than she had done, staying well below the speed limit and hugging the inside lane even though the motorway was gritted and the snow, still falling in fits and starts, was causing them no problems, but occasionally he would put his foot down and overtake another car and then she would take a good look as they passed, checking out the luggage and what the passengers looked like. A family, their estate car piled high with duvets and dogs, then a clapped-out Golf with four men squashed inside, heads bent at right angles against the roof, and then a glamorous-looking man and immaculately groomed woman in a Mercedes sports convertible, both of them looking fixedly ahead, neither of them speaking. Definitely a couple, Lucy decided, peering at them nosily. They matched each other so perfectly. And then the woman caught her eye and looked curiously back at her and Jude, and sleepily Lucy wondered what conclusions she might be reaching about them, convinced she wouldn't come close to the truth.

'Where are we?' she asked, opening her eyes again and stretching slowly as she woke.

'About half-way down the M6. You've been asleep for the last two hours.'

'No!' she said in disbelief. 'I couldn't have been.' She looked at the clock and saw that it was nearly six o'clock, registering belatedly that it was dark outside and that the dashboard lights were on.

'I had no idea,' she said, stretching again. 'I could do with a break and a cup of tea.'

'We'll stop soon.'

She sat there watching him drive, unable to

stop herself grinning into the darkness — it was so damn nice to wake up and find him there.

'I have to say,' she let out a giant yawn, 'that I feel miles better for having slept.'

She reached into the glove compartment of the car for the bottle of water and drank some then passed it to him, watching him tip back his head, his lips round the top where hers had just been. He handed her back the bottle.

'I missed you, while you were sleeping.'

She wondered if she was wrong to be reading an entire romantic novel into that one line. Jude waited but said nothing else, only left the silence hanging there in an utterly disconcerting kind of way, and when she looked across to him again he didn't react at all.

'Do you know why people got married in Gretna Green?' she asked, suddenly very keen to break the silence.

'It's bothering you, isn't it? That you could have had me and you turned me down.'

'In your dreams, Jude.'

'I don't know. Why did they choose Gretna Green?'

'Because it's so close to the border. The laws changed in England, you see.'

'That's very interesting, Lucy.'

'It was some time in the mid-eighteenth

century. Suddenly you had to be twenty-one to be married without your parents' consent. But gallop over the border and you could be married in Scotland at sixteen.'

'How reckless and irresponsible of them.'

'Don't say that. It must have been exciting, eloping with your true love, parents in hot pursuit.' She looked at him. 'Trust me, the girls would have found it exciting.'

'Are you asking me to turn around?'

'I am not.'

'Sure?'

'Someone who used to work in my office got married there last year. She had a piper and a chimney-sweep, very traditional apparently. And she was married in a blacksmith's shop, just like in the olden days, because the blacksmith's shop was where they always aimed for. And the man who married her was called an anvil priest. And afterwards, I suppose they probably went on honeymoon somewhere in Scotland.'

She knew she was starting to burble, recounting details of a wedding she hadn't even been to and had had no great interest in at the time. But her mouth was suddenly running away with her, her heart starting to race again, because although the thought of kissing him still seemed illicit and dangerous, now she knew it was going to happen.

'Loch Ness, perhaps? Or I suppose they could have flown anywhere from Inverness? Or maybe they crossed back over the border.' She paused briefly. 'Did you know ninety-seven couples got married in Gretna Green last Valentine's Day?'

'I'd rather shoot myself.'

'You're so unromantic.'

'No,' Jude said.

She looked across to him. 'No what?'

'I am romantic.'

She turned away from him, not sure what to do, what to say.

'Tell me some more,' he said.

'You're not interested.'

'I am. I like hearing about Gretna Green. I like the sound of your voice.'

'But you've talked the whole way down. Gretna Green's all I've got to talk about.'

'Lucy?' He reached for her hand.

'Yes?' she whispered.

'I wondered if you know any good games?'

'Games?' she repeated. 'I don't understand, like *Botticelli* or *Twenty Questions*?'

'Yes,' he said, 'or *I Spy*?'

'You are joking?'

'Yes.'

'Why?'

'Because I was about to say something else,

but then I thought I shouldn't.'

She stilled. 'What was it? Please tell me.'

'I want to kiss you.'

'I thought you did,' she managed to whisper back.

'And I've been sitting beside you watching you sleep, eat, talk, laugh, wondering if it would be the last thing you wanted to hear. Chuck me out of the car if you have to, I can't not tell you any longer. Is it such an awful thought?'

'No!' she cried. 'The best thought I've heard for ages.' She laughed, then reached out for his face with a shaky hand. 'I badly want to kiss you too.'

'I was thinking it most when you were asleep,' he said. 'And the way you stretched just then, as you woke up. If I wasn't driving this crappy little car . . . '

'Perhaps we could stop . . . ' she ventured.

He caught her hand against his cheek. 'Lucy, darling. Why didn't I tell you five miles ago? That's what I want to know. Because we've just passed a turn-off and there probably won't be another one for a hundred miles.' He banged the steering-wheel in frustration and she leaned forward, laughing because he sounded so cross, brushing his cheek with her lips, breathing in the scent of him.

'Don't.' He stiffened. 'I have to keep you safe.'

She drew back again and sat beside him, quietly, feeling so alive, aware of the blood in her veins, the weight of her limbs, a strange languorous heaviness in her body that made her want to lie down, and at the same time doubting it was really happening, because everything that day had felt so dreamlike and strange . . . She looked over at Jude. He was there, beside her. He had just said something that felt momentous, and now he was about to turn off the motorway. And then what was going to happen? She imagined them together in the car, steaming up the windows, it getting farcical as they were jabbed by the gearstick, or accidentally sat on the horn.

'What's the matter?' he asked. 'You're having second thoughts?'

'No.' She reached to stroke back his hair, loving it that she could, and with the knowledge that she could came a recklessness, and a determination not to doubt, not to hesitate, but to go wherever the moment took her.

5

Fifteen minutes later and they had still not come to a motorway junction. And because it was dark, and Jude was having to concentrate on the road, they had slipped into an easy silence, their hands, gripping tightly, binding them close.

'Did you expect this to happen?' Lucy asked suddenly.

'You know I hoped it would. Did you?'

'I thought about it.' She looked at him in the darkness. 'But I didn't believe it.'

'I knew you were thinking about me.'

'Oh, yes?'

'When you nearly drove us off the road when I touched your hand.'

'I thought you were asleep!'

'Of course I wasn't.'

'You're such a schemer.'

'But I had to *know*. You were being way too cool and it was driving me nuts.'

'All that yawning and stretching when you woke up. Remind me never to trust you again. And why were you so keen to get me to sleep? Why didn't you say anything?'

'I guess I felt I could take my time.'

As he spoke he braked to join a long queue of traffic, three HGVs in front of them, spread out across all three lanes of the motorway. Lucy looked ahead to see three long trails of red tail-lights, stretching away as far as she could see. This felt so disappointingly wrong, still to be talking, talking, talking, when all she wanted to do was stop the car and grab hold of him before the heat of the moment cooled and all the excitement and spontaneity passed them by.

'We're going to stop as soon as we can,' Jude said. And then he looked at her again. 'Bloody fucking traffic.' And he picked up her hand and kissed it tenderly.

Finally the traffic started to move again, crawling at first but eventually picking up speed, and then at last a sign for services flashed past them. And all at once the steady tick-tick-ticking of the indicator seemed to be counting down the seconds to when they would stop.

Jude drove them between crudely landscaped traffic islands, past a children's playground and into the lorry park, stopped the car, pulled on the handbrake and turned to her.

'No,' she cried, looking out of the window in panic. 'Jude, we can't stop *here*. I don't want a bunch of lorry drivers watching us though the windows.'

He looked around. 'No one can see us.'

But he started the engine again and pulled away, taking them down the slip road towards the brightly lit service station.

'Go left,' she told him, and immediately he swerved left, towards a completely empty car park. He stopped the car.

'Choose a space.'

'Shut up,' she muttered.

He rolled the car forward into the first space in front of them, then turned off the engine and undid his seatbelt, Lucy did the same, then turned to look at him. Keeping his eyes fixed on hers, he reached beneath his seat and then, with a terrible scraping sound, shot it backwards, away from the steering-wheel.

'Oh, you're so cool,' Lucy said, laughing, and barely a second later she was sitting on his lap, her arms around his neck.

'I'm glad you think so.'

He pulled her closer, holding her, both of them understanding that what was happening was still precarious and still so unexpected and all the more exciting because of it. And then he was kissing her gently and insistently, opening her lips with his tongue, holding her face in his big hands, and then suddenly kissing her much harder, all the waiting, the drawn-out longing, finally able to find its expression so that they were lost in their kiss — lost to the car park, to who they were and where they were going and what they were doing. Just kissing and kissing, unable to stop. She closed her eyes to the hot smell of him, ran her fingers through his soft black hair, felt his hands, hard and strong, as they held her close, and his mouth, warm and addictive, sending her shivery with lust. And hearing him sigh, feeling him shiver, seeing how he stared at her, tipping up his face to her kiss, she felt powerful and desirable and reckless, so that the last thing she wanted to do was stop.

She had slid half-way down the passenger seat, twisted at the waist, and somehow had her head resting against the door handle with one leg bent over the gear-stick and under him.

'Is that a groan of pleasure or of pain?' he asked.

She winced and pushed him away. 'I can't bear to stop you but I'm in pain.'

He swivelled to kiss her again. His upper body was bent towards her, with his legs still facing forwards beneath the steering-wheel. 'I am too.'

She felt her way underneath him. 'That's because you're lying on the handbrake,' she said against his mouth.

He whispered back. 'What are you going to do about it?'

'Take you inside, I think, as we're parked outside a Milestone Motel Travel Lodge.'

She hadn't planned on saying it, and she could see how much she'd surprised him.

'Are you sure?'

And she could see doubt there just for a brief moment, a bedroom and a double bed being a whole lot more serious than a romp on the back seat of the car. And then she saw the surprise turn to excitement, as if he couldn't quite believe his luck, knew that he wouldn't have dared to suggest it himself. This is it, she thought. Do or die.

He glanced out of the window across the dark car park, the lights of the Milestone Motel Travel Lodge winking at them brightly, and then he turned back to her.

'That was not what I expected you to say.'

'You mean you're thinking *what a slapper*?'

'No. You're incredible.' He pulled her towards him again, burying his face in her hair. 'I would like to walk, sprint, leap into that Milestone Motel with you more than anything in the world.'

'But?' She waited for what it might be, dread spreading through her. A girlfriend? An illness? An embarrassing disability?

'I'm thinking that soon we'll be back in London.' He gently touched his nose to hers. 'I feel I should remind you that tomorrow you'll be starting your day, going to work. I don't want you wondering what the hell you were doing.'

She looked steadily back at him. 'Will you?'

'No.'

'Then neither will I. Tomorrow has nothing to do with it.'

'But I can't say I'll — '

'And I won't be wondering,' she cut in, 'if I'll see you again. Because I know that I won't.' She said it impulsively but she meant it definitely. 'Not that I don't think you're amazing because I do, you know I do. But it could never be like this again, never as good. Don't you agree? This is New Year's Day and I want to grab hold of it with you. And let whatever we want to happen, happen. And then let it go again. Because I think if I walk in there, wondering about tomorrow, it will be spoiled.' She kissed him softly. 'We don't know anything about each other, Jude. We're not part of each other's lives, and that's good. We don't owe each other anything.' She leaned over to him, and he put his arms around her and held her close. 'I want to keep it like that.'

For a long moment he held her, saying

nothing, and then he stirred, his breath hot against her neck.

'Has someone been talking to you about me?'

'Why?' she smiled.

'I can't believe you said that.'

'That's because you were thinking it too.'

★　★　★

They stood close together for a few moments in the dark of the car park, the snow falling lightly around them, neither of them wearing a coat, Jude looking more handsome than ever, snow settling on his dark hair as he looked down at her. And then he turned back to the car, leaning into the back seat and feeling in the front pockets of his overnight bag, and Lucy glimpsed the silver foil of a condom packet. This was a reality check, bringing her up short, and she stood rather warily watching him rezipping his bag and tucking the condom into his pocket. Then he slammed his door shut and turned back to her.

Lucy led them through frosted glass swing doors, across a purple carpet to where two girls in purple jackets and skirts waited behind a partitioned reception area.

'We'd like a room,' she said.

One of the women gave them a bright smile, the other didn't look up from her magazine.

'Of course. How long would you be staying for?'

'Just the one night,' Jude said.

The woman nodded. 'The room rate is forty-five pounds plus VAT.'

She took Jude's credit card and handed him back a registration form to sign. 'Thank you, sir, and if you'll be wanting supper, Milestone Motel restaurants serve a fine selection of both hot and cold foods, available twenty-four hours a day. Take the next left after the signs for petrol.'

'Thank you.'

Behind her Jude slipped his arms around Lucy's waist and she leaned back against him. 'You wanted a cup of tea, Lucy, didn't you?' he murmured against her hair.

'I don't think I do, not any more.'

'And will you require an early morning wake-up call?'

Jude's arms tightened around her. 'Definitely not.'

'And will you need to fetch any luggage from your car?'

They both shook their heads.

'Right then,' she said brightly. 'I'll show you up to your room. If you'd like to follow me.'

She took them in a tiny lift to the second floor, standing with her back pressed into a corner, eyes carefully averted, and marched them down a narrow, windowless corridor, walking so fast she was almost running and Lucy was twice nearly overcome with giggles.

Out of breath, they stopped at the last room, number 25, and the woman pushed a keycard into the lock, opened the door and walked into the room.

'Check-out is at eleven. There's tea and coffee on the table. There's an en suite — '

'It's great,' Lucy interrupted her, standing with Jude in the doorway and looking through to a square room with a purple nylon carpet in the centre of which was a double bed covered in a striped purple and green counterpane. 'We'll find it all out for ourselves.'

They went on into the room, making way for the woman, who turned back at the door. 'Dial zero for reception if you need anything and we'll do our best to help you.' She was obviously nearing the end of her spiel.

'I think we'll be fine, thank you,' said Jude, walking over and sitting down on the bed.

Lucy closed the door after the woman, locked it, then leaned back against it. 'What's your name again?'

'Come here.'

She stood in the doorway and didn't move.

'What's the matter?'

'I need the loo.'

'At last,' he laughed. 'I was worried about you.'

When she came out of the bathroom she stopped against the doorway again and Jude, misinterpreting the doubt on her face, reached across the bed to a small bedside lamp and turned off the light, leaving the room lit only by the soft glow of the car park outside.

'Are you OK?'

'I'm great.'

She sat down hard beside him, wincing at the jolt to the base of her spine. 'Don't you think that this has to be the hardest, most uncomfortable bed you've ever sat on?'

'Lain on,' Jude said, rolling away from her and on to his back, and Lucy moved over to join him, stretching herself out beside him, both of them now lying on their backs, staring up at the ceiling. She slid her hand into his and breathed deeply, letting her brain calm down and concentrate on the fact that Jude was lying there beside her. She moved her hand away from his and stroked his collarbones, then pushed herself close against him, nestling against his neck, breathing him in. She could feel his heart beating against her chest, one long leg sliding over hers.

'You've got glitter on your cheek,' he told her, touching it with the edge of a finger.

'Party last night.'

'I wish I'd been there. I'd like to have seen the pink dress.' He reached forwards and kissed her. 'I could have helped you with the buttons.'

'No chance.'

'Why, was it a zip?'

She looked up into his eyes. 'You have to realize, Jude, that I only feel like this on very, very special days.'

'Which days are those?'

'It has to have snowed for at least ten hours.' She kissed him slowly on his warm soft mouth, lust rising up so fast it was difficult to keep speaking. 'It has to be dark. I have to have eaten nothing since breakfast . . . '

'And then, only then, someone might get to undo your buttons?'

'Yup,' she said weakly, because his fingers were now on the button of her jeans, undoing them, tugging down the zip.

'Then I am the luckiest man, to be here with you at just the right time, in just the right place.'

'Only you,' Lucy whispered. 'This could only have happened with you.'

He didn't answer, just tugged up her shirt until it was clear of her jeans and he could spread his hands across her bare back. Then he groaned, reaching for her mouth, covering her face with slow, soft, open kisses. She stared up at the ceiling, seeing a sparkling glittering sun dancing on a blue sea, felt heat slide up through her legs, unable to move other than to twist the counterpane in her fingers and curl her toes inside her socks.

And then they were kicking off shoes, pulling at each other's clothes, and what had begun cautiously and hesitantly became more daring and purposeful, her hands undoing the zip on his jeans, a finger tracing the edge of her pants, a fumble of buttons and belts and zips as they pulled free of all their clothes and then the bliss as hot, naked skin touched skin and her whole body started to beat and she thought, *I want him, I want him, I want him*.

'Lucy . . . ' he stopped suddenly, leaning back and somehow looking at her with such incredulity and tenderness in his eyes that she stilled. 'You are wonderful, amazing. I can't imagine this is true, can't believe you're here.'

* * *

The curtains were still open but the light from the car park outside was not bright

102

enough for Lucy to see his face clearly. She knew that he was lying on his stomach facing her and that his eyes were open. As she lay there naked next to him, staring at the shadow of his face, feeling his breath gentle on her cheeks but not touching at all, she felt her body slowly coming back to her again, her heart steadying, and a languorous sleepiness stealing over her. She stroked his cheek with her fingertip, searching out his eyes in the darkness, but at her touch he rolled on to his back and sat up, then reached across to the bedside lamp and turned it on, so that she had to cover her eyes with her hand.

'Time to get up,' he said, looking down at her.

She lay still in the pillows, half-expecting him to fall back beside her, but then he jumped out of bed, pulling half the covers with him, and walked across the room to close the curtains. Lucy pulled the remaining covers back over herself again and watched as he prowled round the room, picking up his socks from the floor and sitting down on the end of the bed to pull them on before setting off again with nothing else on, bending down beside her to search under the bed.

'What time is it?'

He looked at his watch. 'Ten past seven.'

And they'd walked in, what, an hour

before? Less perhaps. She watched as he continued to look for his clothes, for the first time looking at him properly, taking in the breadth of his shoulders, his sturdy thighs and well-muscled calves. There was a heaviness about him that she hadn't noticed before. It was ironic, thought Lucy, watching him turn away, that he should seem less familiar now than he had done before. Even his voice and his face seemed different now.

'Don't go all off-hand with me now. Please, Jude.'

He stared back at her, and in the movement of his body and the way he held himself at such a deliberate distance she could see none of the tenderness that had radiated from him before. He came back to her, bent his head and kissed her briefly on the cheek. 'I just think we should get up.'

Was this the horribly predictable ending she hadn't seen coming at all? She watched him moving around the room, waiting for him to say something else, anything at all.

'I've lost my trousers.'

'And your pants?'

'Pants I can do without. Trousers and I think people might notice.' Once again he returned to the bed and kissed her, and at his touch she relaxed. She was being way too sensitive, she told herself. It wasn't her he was suddenly desperate to get away from, it was the horrible purple hotel room. She looked around, taking in her surroundings properly for the first time. In the bright electric light the purple seemed to emit a toxic glow. But even so, she didn't want to leave quite so fast. She wanted time to take in the fact that they were here, take in what had just happened. After the long journey in the car, she felt like a bath.

She asked him to run her one and immediately he disappeared into the bathroom. Seconds later she heard the crash of water as the taps were turned on, then the door closed and she was left alone.

She was in a motorway service station off the M6, wrapped in a purple sheet, in this strange room with this strange man dressed only in his socks who was running her a bath, and yet however he behaved now, she was feeling more real, more comfortable in her own skin than she had done for years. Because just for once she'd broken free and done what other people did, let instinct and passion and devil-may-care recklessness sweep her up and carry her away. And if there in the background was the timid under-confident Lucy who was still trying to get her attention, who couldn't help but notice how effortlessly Jude was detaching from her, who couldn't help but think it strange and rather sad that they wouldn't ever see each other again, she could ignore her without a second's hesitation.

She got out of bed and walked around the room, picking up her jeans from the carpet, untangling her knickers from the sheet at the bottom of the bed, finding her long wool cardigan and pulling it back on, hiding her nakedness in preparation for the moment when Jude came back into the room. It wasn't that she wanted him to declare undying love, she thought, laying her bra and knickers and jeans neatly on the bed for when she'd had her bath. And she certainly didn't want him to plead with her to see him again. All that would sadden her would be if, now, they'd lost the easy relationship they'd had before they'd walked into this room. And she wondered if that was inevitable, whether she was stupid to think it might be otherwise.

She jumped back into bed, turned on the television and, as she guessed, it immediately drew Jude out of the bathroom.

He had damp hair and a towel around his neck and another in his hands. He walked around to the other side of the bed and sat down. 'I've run you a bath, I've even found you bubble bath. Guess what colour it is?'

She smiled at him, lifted the covers and

stepped out of bed, wrapping the cardigan round her, and went into the bathroom deliberately leaving the door open, not so that he could look at her but so that he wouldn't think she was shutting him out. She tested the water, dropped the cardigan on the floor and climbed in, sliding down so that the bubbles came up to her chin.

'I cannot believe my purple bath,' she called out to Jude, and immediately she heard him get off the bed. Then he was there, standing in the doorway, dressed and ready to go.

'Your purple what?'

She turned to look at him. 'Bath.'

He grinned back at her, and now it was the same old smile but this time with a shared understanding and new knowledge of each other, an intimacy in the look that hadn't been there before. 'OK in there?'

'Yes, thank you.'

And then he was gone again.

Lucy looked down at her two white knees pointing up through the foam, listened to the bubbles popping against the sides of the bath. Then she found herself slowly flexing her toes, rolling her ankles round and round, slowly and methodically, and, even as she thought how silly it was, she knew she was doing it to try to find out if she was the same person she'd always been, checking that everything about her was exactly the same. All day she'd felt like a different person, an actor playing out a day in the life of Lucy Blue, free of any sense of caution, ballsy and determined to do what she wanted to do. And now, she thought, opening the rectangular packet of soap and sliding it around in her hands, she was not going to change back into the old Lucy again, the Lucy who could be manipulated by Teddy, crushed by some of her friends, daunted by evil bosses at work, easily silenced by everyone else. She liked this Lucy who'd not run away, not thought too much about what was best, but had followed her instincts. She liked who it had made her be.

She turned on the hot tap with her foot, flinching at the scalding burst of heat, then washed quickly and with a whoosh of water stood up and climbed out of the bath. Reaching for a towel she found that Jude, thoughtful guy that he was, had taken both of them, leaving her with a tiny square of hand towel. His problem, then, if she walked back into the room and reminded him of exactly what he wasn't ever getting again. She dried herself as best she could and came back into the bedroom.

Jude was sitting on the bed waiting for her,

hands folded in front of him.

'Was it much too quick?' he said as soon as she came through the door. 'I'm sorry. I could tell you wanted to take your time and I rushed you, didn't I?'

'I didn't mind at all. I was flattered.'

It was only then, when he opened his mouth and then shut it slowly, looking completely taken aback, that Lucy realized that of course he'd been talking about her bath. She ran across the bedroom and threw her arms around him, bursting into giggles.

'Oh no, ask me again!'

He sat there stiffly. 'I can't believe you said that.'

'Please, please ask me again.'

'I'm crushed. I am a ruined man.' He looked mournfully across at her.

And the new Lucy didn't care. 'Shut up and go and get my bag for me from the car, please,' she told him, dropping a kiss on to his head. 'I really need some clean clothes.'

He nodded silently and turned around, and he reached for the car key from the bedside table and let himself quietly out of the room.

While he was gone, she lay back on the bed and channel-hopped idly. But once she'd dried off completely and Jude still hadn't come back, foreboding slowly rose up inside her.

Stupid man, she thought, getting up off the bed and walking around the room. Surely he hadn't been so offended by what she'd said that he'd left her here? But what if he had — taken the car and abandoned her in this horrible place? How would she get home? She imagined the humiliation of asking the woman at reception for a taxi to the nearest railway station, rifling through her purse for enough cash, then hours of sitting on a snowy platform waiting for a train. And what about the Deals on Wheels car? She'd be responsible if it disappeared. She'd probably be interviewed by the police. *So what exactly were you doing in the Milestone Motel with Mr Middleton?* Perhaps she was only one of many other girls. *You do realize that Mr Middleton has done this before? Don't think you're the first to be tricked like this.*

Jude might nick both the bathtowels but surely he wouldn't do that to her? She leapt out of bed and peered down through the curtains into the car park below, and saw with relief that he was there, standing next to the car, talking on his mobile. As she looked down, holding the curtain to cover her naked body, he looked up, caught her eye, waved to her and grinned. She raised her hand back to him and turned away, not wanting him to think she was spying on him. She sat down on the edge of the bed and wrapped her cardigan around her.

After the fear of thinking he'd left her, why did the sight of him smiling up at her fill her with such sadness? Was it simply because he was on the telephone to someone she definitely didn't know and was certainly never going to meet? Because, whatever she told herself, it made her aware of the whole huge life he had that she knew nothing about at all. And perhaps she wasn't that woman after all, who could walk away from him now without a backward glance?

Soon she heard him walking back down the corridor and then the door opened and he appeared in the doorway with her bag. She didn't move from the bed. Her cardigan was pulled around her, reaching half-way down her pale thighs, her hair spread out on the bed, her feet bare. Jude stood for a long moment, looking at her.

'Hello, gorgeous.'

'I thought you'd driven off.'

'You silly softie.' He came and sat beside her on the bed, dropping her bag on the floor beside him. 'Why would I do that?'

'I don't know. Thanks for bringing my bag.'

He dropped his hand and gently stroked her hair back from her forehead as if saying goodbye. But he didn't go, just sat beside her

111

on the bed, playing with a thick strand of her hair.

'It's the colour of barley.'

'Wet straw, someone told me.'

'Trust me, I'm a farmer. It's the colour of barley.'

'You're not a farmer, you fly helicopters.' And as she said it she wondered if everything he'd told her was true. Then, if anything he'd told her was true.

'Farmer's son, then.'

'Where was your farm?'

'It's still there, as far as I know. In Oxfordshire, near Woodstock, a little village called Lipton St Lucy.'

'It's my name.'

He nodded. 'So you see I won't be able to get away from you after all.'

'Lipton St Lucy. Do you like it there? Is it a nice place?'

'It's a beautiful place. There are soft, undulating, kind of curvy hills. Deep valleys, secret paths, places you can get lost in.'

'Stop it,' she said, laughing. 'And you're going there tonight?'

'Yes. I was just calling Luke when you looked out of the window. I wanted to let him know where we are.'

'Not *exactly* where we are, I presume?'

'No,' he agreed.

And although he was still sitting beside her on the bed, teasing her and stroking her hair, she knew he was a long way away from her at that moment. Still it was the same, the restlessness whenever she tried to get him to talk about his life, his unwillingness to reveal anything about himself, the way he persistently dodged getting personal, and she knew, even after everything that had happened between them, that she wasn't going to get any more out of him now.

'Jude.' She wished her voice wouldn't wobble when she said his name.

'Yes?'

She could see the sudden wariness in his eyes.

'You're not sitting there worrying I'm going to tell you I love you or something?'

He laughed, still playing with her hair. 'No, because we both know that's not what this is about, don't we?'

She nodded.

'Although, I want you to know that if I was looking for — '

'Don't say it,' she interrupted him crossly. 'Let's not hear the crappy cliché, please. In any case *I'm* not interested either.'

He let out a long sigh. 'Fair enough.'

She sat up on the bed. 'But that doesn't mean you can't kiss me again, doesn't mean

113

you can go the rest of the journey not talking to me.' Four more hours in the car with him, Lucy was thinking. Keep it light. 'And you've got to meet my eye, too. After you got out of bed, you wouldn't even do that.'

'Not true!'

'It is true. And you leapt out of bed like the building was on fire.'

'All guys do that. Didn't you know? Girls rest, guys leap out of bed. We have to be alert, keep an eye out for danger.'

'Or girls like to have a bath.'

'They do,' Jude agreed, standing up abruptly. 'And now we should both be going.'

* * *

Lucy was driving again, and Jude sat quietly beside her as she backed the car out of its space and drove out of the car park. As they rejoined the motorway he returned to the radio, both of them understanding that music would release them from any pressure to talk.

By the time they had left the M6 and joined the M40, the snow had turned to sleet that spattered hard against the windscreen and sprayed out in great arcs of dirty slush, making passing lorries a test of nerves and will, and from feeling as if she was on fire at the thought of him beside her, now she was aware of an impatience to have him out of the car. It had gone on too long, this awkward postscript to what had happened in the Milestone Motel. Far better if they'd been able to go their separate ways at the front door.

The constant concentration made her gritty eyes ache, and the long hours sitting in the car were taking a heavy toll on her back, so that as they finally swished through Shepherd's Bush towards Notting Hill all she could think about was how soon he'd be getting out of the car, how soon she could finally be separated from him.

Finally, just after one o'clock, they pulled up outside Jude's brother's home in Moreton Street, an impressive four-storey midnight-blue house just off Elgin Crescent.

She turned off the engine, tired to the bone, listening to the sudden silence, the stillness after so much noise and constant movement, and she turned to Jude, who ran a practised hand through his hair.

'It's harder than I thought. Are you sure you don't want me to call? Not even just once?'

She shook her head, surprise making her stumble. 'You know it wouldn't work.'

'You don't want to come and say hello before your party next week? Luke and I will be coming back from Oxford that evening. I could make sure I'd be in.'

'It wouldn't work.'

He sighed deeply and reached for her, pulling her close. 'I know. But I won't forget you, Lucy. I really won't.'

She pushed him away again and looked towards the house, feeling irritation because it was so obvious he was trying to say all the right things in these last moments together when, truth be told, he had already moved on and away from her. It was clear in the way he was looking out through the window at the rain, in the hasty unfastening of his seatbelt even as he spoke. And in the way he hardly waited for her reply but snatched his coat from the back seat, dropping his wallet into the pocket as he did so.

She folded her hands on her lap and he caught her stare.

'One day we'll be old and decrepit and we'll be able to remember this year and that long, long drive down from Inverness. And every time you see a Milestone Motel, you'll have Milestone Motel thoughts about me.'

'Every time I drive to Lipton St Lucy I'll think of you. I'll tell my grandchildren about us.'

'Don't. They'll think you're a dirty old man.'

He leaned towards her and kissed her, once, twice, on the lips. 'You know that after you've gone it will be too late?'

'For what?'

'For either of us to change our minds. If we've got this wrong how would I ever find you again?'

'We're not wrong. Anyhow we'll probably get introduced to each other at some party in a few weeks' time.'

'I don't think so,' he said quietly. 'I'll be back in Aberdeen by then.'

'Yes, of course, hundreds of miles away. No chance of meeting then.' She paused again, then added awkwardly, 'Goodbye, Jude Middleton.'

'Goodbye, Lucy Blue.'

He opened the door, got out and slammed it shut. Then he walked round to the boot to get his bag and slammed that shut too. And seconds later a light came on in the hall of the house and the front door opened.

Even if she hadn't been expecting him, she would have known this was Jude's brother, Luke. Not simply because they were the same height and had the same dark hair — the similarity was there in the way Luke walked, coming down the flight of steps, then striding towards Jude with keys in his hand, wearing socks and jeans and a white T-shirt, his arms

117

wrapped around himself for warmth.

'I'd given up on you,' she heard him say. She watched him hesitate, then move forwards, swinging an arm around Jude's shoulders, and she saw how Jude immediately stepped away.

'You knew where I was. I told you what was going on.'

'I know, I know.'

Jude would be glad if she drove away quickly now, Lucy thought. And she wanted to. Her time with him was over, but even as she was thinking it, Luke had turned curiously and Jude was coming back to the car.

'Lucy,' he called, 'come and meet Luke.'

And so she had to undo her seatbelt and get out of the car, walk into Luke's interested gaze, dipping her head against the rain, then take his hand and shake it.

'Luke, meet Lucy.'

'Would you like to come in?' Luke asked her politely.

Lucy shook her head. 'I have to get the car back to the hire company. And, you know, after thirteen hours, I'd like to get home.'

'Jude, you're not leaving Lucy to take back the car on her own?'

Jude nodded at him sheepishly. 'I thought we wanted to get to Oxford tonight.'

'You lazy bastard. That's our problem.'

'I'll be fine,' Lucy insisted. 'Get inside. It's horrible out here.'

'But how will you get home?' Luke asked her, concerned.

She hadn't thought about it. Deals on Wheels probably wouldn't even be open this late. 'It's just up the road in Hammersmith. I'll get them to call me a cab. Seriously, I'll be fine.'

'I'll follow you in my car,' Luke told her. 'You go and wait in the house,' he instructed Jude, then he turned back to Lucy. 'I'll drive you home.'

'No,' Lucy insisted, knowing that was absolutely the last thing she wanted.

'There's no point arguing with her,' Jude told Luke. 'Is there, Lucy?'

She shook her head. She didn't want a lift with his fierce-looking brother, but she would have been happy if either of them had offered to find her a taxi, right there and then, if either of them had offered to take over responsibility for the car. But they were going to Oxford so of course they weren't about to do that.

She went to open the door of the car and then, suddenly, Jude was back in front of her, blocking Luke's view, putting his arms around her and swooping down to kiss her hard on her half-open mouth.

'I'm sorry I didn't think about the car and getting you home,' Jude whispered. 'And don't drive away from me now, regretting what happened, thinking I'm a selfish bastard like Luke says I am, someone who doesn't care about you at all. Because I do, I think you're wonderful. Remember me fondly, please.'

She was surprised to hear such sincerity in his voice and to see such an urgent look in his eyes.

'I will do. And you do the same for me, OK?'

She pushed him away from her and opened the car door, not wanting him to see the tears in her eyes. And then she climbed in and drove away.

6

By the time the cab pulled up outside Lucy's mansion block in Barons Court it was twenty past two. She stepped on to the pavement and felt her whole body buzzing with the exhaustion of having travelled for so long, a thousand headlights flickering and dancing in her head.

She unlocked the door, kicked her way through the usual rainforest's worth of junk mail and slowly climbed the two flights of stairs to her flat, dragging her bag behind her. The taxi had been much too warm and by the time she reached her own front door she could feel her knees buckling with exhaustion. She opened her door and staggered theatrically inside, overwhelmingly relieved to be back. Letting the door click shut behind her, she switched on the hall light, edged off her shoes, dropped her coat over the back of a chair and looked gratefully round, breathing in the wonderful stillness and peace after the movement and noise of all those hours on the road.

She'd rented the flat six months ago and was surprised to find how much she liked living alone. Not that she'd been alone very often, with Teddy staying over at least two or three nights every week. But there'd be no more of that now. And with that knowledge there in her mind, she looked around and the whole flat felt different, hers in a way it had never been before.

She pulled off her socks and the coolness of the painted wooden floorboards felt blissful against the soles of her feet. She wandered into the bathroom, filled the basin with warm water and splashed her face, then caught her own eye in the mirror and couldn't stop smiling at herself because now, here at home, everything seemed to have settled back into a new sense of proportion. She'd had a great one-night stand. She'd celebrated her New Year with Jude, unexpected, unbelievable Jude. Jude who she was surprised to discover was already receding in her mind, becoming less and less real, leaving only a new confidence and sense of purpose in his place.

She left the bathroom and took the two strides necessary to reach the kitchen, through an archway at the other end of the hall. In the dim light she poured herself a tall glass of orange juice, visions of her soft bed with its cool white sheets drawing her towards her bedroom. She went back to the hall to pick up her bag and then, at long last, pushed open the bedroom door and walked in.

Teddy was in her bed.

He was lying asleep on his back, his arms stretched out wide as if ready to grab her the moment she came close enough, the light from the hall falling straight on to his face.

Teddy was in her bed. If she hadn't been so desperate not to make a sound she'd have cried. Instead she turned swiftly round, reached for the hall light and switched it off, returning the room to inky darkness, then closed the door quietly behind her and tiptoed quickly away, back down the hall to the sitting-room. She shut the door behind her and dropped on to the sofa, immediately aware of the horrible familiar churn in her stomach, the fluttery panicky need to pacify him even in sleep.

Bloody buggering hell, she thought, dropping her head onto her arms. He was not coming back. She'd allowed their mess of a relationship to begin and then to continue. And she thought she'd finished. She'd tried to get out — but clearly not hard enough — how could it possibly be that Teddy *still* thought he was in with a chance? And, worse, how could she not have remembered to ask him for his keys to the flat?

She rubbed at her face with her hands. She wanted to be asleep in her lovely bed, which she'd been waiting to fall into for so long. How *could* he do this to her after all that had happened? And yet, if she'd thought about it before, she might have guessed that he would do this. It was perfectly timed and exactly the sort of stubborn, defiant thing Teddy would come up with.

She stood up again, wandering around the room, racking her brain for some brilliant way of emptying him out of the bed and out of her flat too, preferably without him knowing what was happening. Because at that moment there was nothing in the world she wanted less than a conversation with him. But short of knocking him out with her Le Creuset frying-pan and dragging him feet-first down the stairs, there was no clever Plan A.

And so she came around to Plan B, which was to open the sitting-room door for a second time and creep back to retrieve her bag. She took it over to the sofa, unzipped it and started to pull everything out on to the floor, finding her toothbrush, her contact lens case, her pyjamas. She'd make up the sofa-bed and sleep on that. And in the morning, in all of five hours' time, she'd wake and . . . Lucy shuddered at the thought of her and Teddy getting ready for work together, standing shoulder to shoulder in the tiny bathroom, brushing their teeth, because he'd know, he'd look at her, and without her saying a word he'd know exactly what she'd been up to. But it was so different now, she tried to tell herself. She was none of his business any more, and at some time before they left for work she was going to have to remind him of that and in a way he'd never heard before.

How could they ever have got close, she thought despairingly as she unbuttoned her cardigan and pulled off her jeans. How could she ever have thought it was funny and sweet that he was called Teddy and looked so like one too, with his golden fuzz of body hair and that little disapproving smile permanently stitched to his face?

The office softball team had everything to answer for. If she hadn't been pressganged into playing she'd never have met him. He worked with her at Barley & Bross, but it was a huge company — she'd been there a year and had never even set eyes on him — then someone came up with idea of forming a softball team, to join one of the company leagues that played in the London parks every Tuesday night.

He'd joined the team and she'd fancied him simply because he'd been so good, making the most impossible catches without really trying at all, cracking the ball the length of the park and beyond, scoring them a home run every time he strolled up to the plate. Slowly he'd become part of those long summer evenings, lying beside her watching the shadows lengthen across the grass and the sun dip behind the tower blocks of Kennington or the neat redbrick rows of houses in Wandsworth and Fulham. And then, sitting with her and the rest of the team outside the pub after dark, he'd surprised her one evening by taking hold of her hand under the table. And that was how it had begun. She wasn't to know then what she was letting herself in for, just how far from an uncomplicated summer romance theirs would turn out to be. She would have laughed in disbelief to hear that Teddy would soon be buying her clothes for a weekend with his parents, would not only feel free to take a Twix from between her fingers but would wipe off her lipstick at the same time with his thumb. The depressing part of it was that she'd let him get away with it for so long. The force of his will, his occasionally furious loss of temper when he didn't get his own way, coupled with her hopeless inability to confront him success-fully, meant that they'd still been together right up until Christmas, right until that moment outside her flat when she'd told him she didn't want to see him after she got back — and had managed to forget to ask him for his keys.

And now he was here again, and his timing really couldn't have been worse.

★   ★   ★

In the cupboard in the hall was a spare duvet, kept for when she had *invited* friends to stay. The sofa would fold out into a bed but she couldn't be bothered to do it tonight. Despite Teddy's presence, she knew that the second she curled up on the sofa, under the duvet, she would be asleep. So she tiptoed back into the hall a second time and dragged the duvet out of the cupboard and back to the sitting-room. She needed the loo but she couldn't take the risk that Teddy would hear her, so she ignored that and instead spread the duvet out on the sofa and set her alarm for work the next morning.

She laid out her T-shirt and pyjama bottoms on top of the duvet, then took out her contact lenses, pulled off her knickers and bra and stretched to pull the T-shirt over her head. And then her heart leapt in alarm because, through her blurry eyes, she could just about make out that Teddy was no longer asleep in her bed but was standing in the doorway watching her.

This time she couldn't help but cry out. Not a full-blooded yell that would have roused her kind and well-meaning neighbours, but a strangled yelp, of fright and anger that he should see her naked, and despair that whatever she did it seemed she couldn't get away from him. She leapt onto the sofa, pulled the duvet high around her shoulders, then fumbled for her glasses and put them on. As if he'd been waiting only for her to see him properly, Teddy took two quick steps towards her and dropped to his knees, skidding across the polished floorboards like an amorous ice-skater to kneel beside her makeshift bed.

'Please, Lucy, I know I shouldn't have let myself in but I've been missing you so much and I've been waiting for you to call.' He was giving her what he clearly thought was a winning smile, trying to turn the awful invasiveness of what he had done into some kind of grand romantic gesture.

She gave him a hard stare back. 'I want you to get dressed and get out of my flat. And give me my keys back while you're at it.'

The winning smile flickered and died. He hadn't ever heard her talk like this, so cold and calm, so certain.

'But I was so worried,' he retaliated, recovering fast.

'You didn't need to sleep in my bed.'

She paused, knowing she should be following up her advantage, leaping off the sofa to manhandle him out of the door before he got any more words in. But she was lying on the sofa with no knickers on and that put her at a huge disadvantage.

'I wanted to be sure you were safe, that was all.' And then, awkwardly, he leaned forwards and kissed her cheek. 'Hello darling, happy New Year.'

If he'd been hoping for a sudden melting of her heart he didn't get it.

'Go home, Teddy.' She gritted her teeth and pulled the duvet higher up her shoulders.

'I can't go! It's nearly three o'clock in the morning.' He rubbed at his face. 'Come to bed?'

'You're joking.'

'Lucy, please,' he pleaded. 'What's the matter with you tonight? I wanted to talk to you, to tell you how terrible I felt when you left in that cab, what you said . . . ' He shook his head, looking at her sorrowfully. 'I know you didn't mean half of it. You were stressed out and I wasn't making it any easier.' He shook his head again. 'But you were off before I could explain. And there was so much I wanted to say.'

'Teddy, listen to me.'

He looked at her warily. 'I don't think I want to.'

She stopped, aware that this time she had to get it right. And perhaps he'd already sensed what was coming, had seen in her eyes how much she'd changed in so short a time.

'Don't, Lucy. I know exactly what you want to say,' he ploughed on, no longer dominant, no longer certain, wobbly-voiced, pleading. 'I think I was as angry with you as you were with me. And I'm sorry about that, really sorry. You were probably right to give us a break, it certainly gave me time to realize how much I missed you . . . But I was hoping that now you've had a chance to think things through . . . you might have had time to miss me, too, just a little? Even if you didn't call.'

She shook her head. 'I didn't miss you.' She surprised herself by how absolutely definite she sounded. She stretched out an arm and pulled her jeans off the chair, dragging them under the duvet, taking her time to find the leg-holes with her feet and feeling such relief when she did because now she would be able to pull up the zip and do up the buckle of the belt, then get up and walk straight over to the door.

'I wish you'd called. We should have talked.'

She stayed where she was. 'I didn't want to speak to you.'

'What's happened to you, Lucy? Why are you being so tough?' His voice was still very quiet, none of the fast-boiling anger she sometimes saw. 'Last time I saw you I was still allowed to talk to you, to come to your flat. Last time I saw you I was still allowed to care about you and worry. My gorgeous honey, my beautiful girl, of course I'm going to care. I don't understand what's changed.'

'Yes you do.'

'Oh, what was it you said? Some dreadful cliché. *You don't allow me space to be myself*, was that the one?'

Had she really said that? He was right, it was a dreadful cliché.

He pushed himself to his feet but made no move forward. 'It wasn't like you, Lucy, not to call. Whatever was said, however angry you were.'

Why wouldn't he let the telephone call go? It was almost as if he had a sixth sense telling him that this was his best chance of getting to her. And yet he couldn't possibly know that by asking her this one question he was sending her straight back to the little car on the darkened road. Of course she hadn't

131

called, and she'd switched off her phone so that he couldn't call her, because at that moment nothing had mattered but Jude.

'I didn't call because . . . ' she dared herself to say it, *because I was with someone else, and I was just about to shag him in the Milestone Motel service station, just off the M6, somewhere near Walsall, I think.* That would sock it to him between the eyes, end this ridiculous pretence that he was in her flat because he had been worried, when they both knew that it was only because she had finally slipped from his grasp and he hated it. But she couldn't bring herself to do it, partly because despite everything she didn't want to hurt him, partly from fear of what she'd provoke him into doing in response. 'My battery went flat.'

Her phone was on the table in front of him and she watched as he reached forward, picked it up and switched it on. And of course she knew from his bitter smile, and the way his face hardened when he looked back at her, that the phone had betrayed her with its full five fingers of power.

'It must have recharged. Anyway, I missed my flight. I've just driven down all the way from Inverness.'

He nodded, saying nothing, then walked over to the armchair in the corner of the room and sat down facing her. 'Tell me more.'

'Don't act like you've caught me out.'

'Then don't act guilty. Tell me about the party.' His voice was rising and getting louder. 'Did you have a good time?'

'I'm not in the mood for a chat, Teddy.'

'In your flimsy fuck-me dress, did you meet someone there? Is that why you didn't call?'

She shook her head. 'My business, Teddy, what I choose to wear. And I didn't call because I didn't want to speak to you.'

'I don't think that's true. I think you met some Scottish bastard.' He waited, then looked at her incredulously. 'You did, didn't you? I can see it in your eyes. Even better, I can see it on your little chin. Someone hadn't shaved, had they, Lucy?'

'I didn't meet anyone at the party, not that it's anything to do with you.'

'I don't believe you.'

'You should. The party was rubbish. There was no one to talk to at all.' Don't tell him anything, she told herself. Shut up. He has no right to know anything at all and if he knows any more it'll only make him explode with anger. But so much had happened to her that day that her brain was simply too full, and all the thoughts she wanted to keep safe were starting to spill back out of her mouth.

'I didn't even last until midnight. And then I was up again early this morning, and I have just spent the last fourteen hours driving five hundred miles home. I'm sorry I can't speak to you tonight but understand that I am tired. And yes, I forgot to cleanse, tone and moisturize before I walked through my own front door but, silly me, I didn't think there'd be anyone here.'

He hardly listened. 'Tell me there's not another guy,' he demanded. 'Tell me of course you couldn't have forgotten me so fast. Not when we had so much together . . . Lucy?' He stood up, crossed the room in two strides and took hold of her hand. 'Please.'

And she knew then that there was only one way to make him listen.

'I can't tell you that,' she said steadily. 'Because you're right. I did meet someone. Not at the party but in the airport coming home. We drove back to London together.'

'You drove back to London with him?'

She nodded.

'And?'

She stared impassively back at him and saw the anger unfold slowly in his stunned white face. He stared at her, silently, for long, horrible seconds.

'So where is he? Why isn't he here? I'm

surprised you haven't brought him upstairs — you weren't to know I'd be here after all.'

'I won't be seeing him again.'

'Oh.' Momentarily Teddy was thrown. 'So nothing happened? It was no big deal?'

'Actually yes, it was a very big deal, to me,' she said, holding his stare. 'So you see, you really should go home now.'

She opened the door for him.

He stood there swaying slightly, giving little barely perceptible shakes of his head.

'You know what?' he said eventually, very quietly. 'You're going to regret telling me that.' And then he walked out of the room and back to her bedroom and closed the door behind him.

She waited for him in the sitting-room, shivering and sad, and when he reappeared, dressed, he walked past her, not looking at her once, opened the front door and shut it quietly behind him. She heard his footsteps clattering down the stairs.

She took her bag and her dress, walked with them back to the bedroom and saw he'd left his keys on the bedside table. She walked over to the cupboard and hung up the dress, trying to make sense of what had happened, to evaluate how high up the Richter scale Teddy might have reached, what the implications might be for her next day in the office.

But she was simply too tired to do it. She numbly laid out her clothes ready for the morning on her bedroom chair, a pair of soft grey wool trousers, a high-necked black jumper and shiny black boots, forcing herself to think about anything but him. Then she looked at her watch and saw that it was now twenty past three. She climbed into the bed, still warm from Teddy's body, and sleep rose up and enveloped her.

7

Lucy arrived at work at eight-fifteen, showing what she felt was an impressive commitment to her job. In the past she'd arrived at work feeling so much worse than she did today. There'd been a very irresponsible day after Jane's birthday when she'd passed out in the lift, and in comparison to that morning she felt almost good. She was aware of a certain light-headedness, due as much to lack of food as to lack of sleep, which meant she still couldn't seem to pull her thoughts together, and a sick dread when she thought about seeing Teddy again, and she had a bruise on the base of her spine from landing too hard on the bed with Jude, therefore reminding her of the Milestone Motel every time she sat down, but otherwise she felt fine.

It was a beautiful day too. The tinted glass of the Barley & Bross building reflected the perfect turquoise blue sky and cotton-wool clouds, and the air was crisp but warm enough to remind Lucy of springtime and floaty cotton skirts and sunglasses. She imagined sitting outside a café with Jane at lunchtime, and hoped desperately that she would be able to escape her office and meet her.

She pushed open the doors, waved at Zoe, their office receptionist cum agony aunt — warm-hearted, unfailingly nosy and, Lucy suspected, more than half in love with Teddy too — and walked over to the lifts.

'Teddy's in,' Zoe called after her, just as the lift arrived and the doors glided open. 'I saw him about half an hour ago.'

And from the look on her face she'd heard something.

'He looked terrible.'

She had heard something.

Torn between jumping into the lift and returning to Zoe's desk to hear what she might have to say, Lucy hesitated and Zoe saw her chance and pounced.

'He's feeling really bad.'

Was he? Did she care? Lucy turned to look back at Zoe and Zoe's eyes pleaded with her to come back and talk.

Since Lucy and Teddy had started going out together, Zoe had enthusiastically monitored the state of their relationship from her vantage point just in front of the main door, logging their arrivals and departures, taking special notice of the times when either of them arrived or left alone, completely unabashed when it came to passing comment on either of them. *Such a sleepy-head, isn't he?* she'd usually offer to Lucy when she arrived in the morning before Teddy. And *Bounced out of bed this morning, did he?* when it was Teddy who had got in first. It certainly wasn't by chance that Zoe's remarks always seemed focused on Teddy in bed. The few mornings when they had arrived together had produced little more than a subdued *good morning.*

'I asked him what was wrong.'

The lift doors closed again and Lucy turned back and walked over to reception, staring into Zoe's huge, elaborately made-up eyes.

'I couldn't help it, he looked half-crazy.'

'What did he say?'

She shouldn't be asking. She should be walking into the lift. She should be opening the door to her office, sliding into her chair, preparing to behave like the responsible, conscientious headhunter extraordinaire she was supposed to be.

'Far more than he should have done.' Zoe shook her head disapprovingly.

You loved hearing every single word of it.

'But there was absolutely no stopping him,' Zoe went on eagerly. 'It all came pouring out.'

And it's not as if you'd tell anybody, apart from the hundred and twenty-seven members

139

of staff who walk past this desk every day.

'You see, I'm a good listener, everyone tells me so, although, quite frankly, sometimes it can be a bit of a curse.'

'What did Teddy say?'

Zoe looked sharply right and left. 'Lucy, I'm sorry but he told me stuff I'm sure you'd rather I didn't know.'

'Oh God, tell me.'

'It doesn't seem right, so early in the morning.' Zoe swallowed awkwardly. 'He told me, well, why you two split up. How impossible it would be for him now — '

'Oh, yes?'

'Now that he knows. OK,' she went on, taking a deep breath, 'he said how you two had been happy together, in many, many ways, but that you'd never hit it off,' she dropped her voice, '*in the bedroom*. And until yesterday he never knew why!'

'And now he does?'

'Look, I know it's none of my business, I know you'd never have dreamed of telling me something so personal, but Teddy did, OK?'

Lucy shrugged helplessly. 'I don't blame you at all.'

'And don't blame yourself either.'

'Zoe, what did he say *exactly*?'

Zoe stopped, looking at her uncertainly.

'I'd really like to know.'

'Teddy said . . . Teddy explained . . . '

'Yes?' Lucy leaned closer in towards her. 'Tell me.'

'That you like to have sex with strangers,' Zoe whispered. 'Strangers, low-life, high life, you don't know and you don't care.'

Lucy leapt back from the desk in shock.

'Pick them up off the street, day-time, night-time, the less you know about them the better,' she went on with relish. 'And Teddy explained . . . that yesterday, he found out about it.' She looked at Lucy warily, then judged it was safe to go on. 'Well, you told him, didn't you? And he couldn't take it.' She looked at Lucy sympathetically now. 'He says he feels terrible because he knows he should forgive you — that you can't help it, that it's not your fault. He said perhaps he will forgive you eventually.'

'He said that?'

'Lucy, to tell you the truth I wouldn't try too hard to get him back. You and Teddy? Let's face it, you were never quite right for each other, were you?'

Wordlessly Lucy shook her head.

'And you know what? I take my hat off to you.' She grinned. 'I suppose it's not something I'd like to do myself, but if you've found out what makes you happy . . . ' She leaned forward, looking at Lucy, and her face

141

dropped in concern. She took her hand. 'Take care, love, won't you? Lucy?' She looked at her closely. 'Lucy, if you're not happy, there's lots of things you can try.' She nodded enthusiastically. 'Lots of things. There was a seaweed I was reading about only last week, from Zanzibar I think it was. It was in a magazine. It's meant to make you just *explode* inside.' She paused again. 'Perhaps that way you might find you can have a meaningful relationship with someone — someone else? I thought I'd try some myself,' she added encouragingly as she took in Lucy's uncomprehending face. 'No? You don't think it would help?' she hesitated, uncertain now. 'Then maybe it's just a question of talking it through with someone? Somebody you really, really trust? I mean, there's all sorts of things to try. You shouldn't feel there's nothing you can do about it. Lucy?'

'Oh, no. I don't feel that.' Abruptly Lucy started to laugh, making Zoe start with alarm. 'I can't believe he told you that. He really told you?' She shook her head. 'But I know *exactly* what I'm going to do about it. I'm going to go up to his office and kill him.'

She walked quickly towards the lift, then turned back and saw the doubt, the dreadful uncertainty there on Zoe's face.

'I'm joking, Zoe.'

'Of course you are,' Zoe said emphatically. 'And you know Teddy was too?'

Lucy looked quickly round the reception area to ensure it was empty and then said loudly, '*Zoe, I do not have sex with strangers.* You know he's always been a terrible fantasist. He's pissed off because we split up last night, that's all. The truth is this is just his cheap, rather sad way of getting even.' She jabbed at the lift button with her finger. 'The seaweed sounds fun, though,' she added, as the lift doors opened and Zoe gave her a tentative, rather crushed smile back. 'Did you get an address?'

So this was what Teddy meant by revenge, Lucy thought as she was flown at lightning speed up to his floor, and yet how unlike him to show such imagination.

She found him crouching down beside the bottom drawer of his filing cabinet, half-hidden by his desk, and from the wary look on his face she guessed that he knew exactly why she was there.

'I was joking.' He stood up, protecting his face with a file, and then bent over his desk, not looking at her. 'Let's call it quits, shall we?'

'If you go down and explain that to Zoe.'

'What? Why would I do that?' He stood up

143

and moved round her, then suddenly set off across the open-plan office floor, walking so fast she almost had to run after him.

'Because I don't want the whole of Barley & Bross thinking it's true,' she hissed back, striding as fast as he was, aware that he was making for the double doors at the far end of the floor that took them out on to the staircases. If he thought he could lose her, either by running up or down them, he was mistaken. She was far fitter than him.

It was as if he had the same thought at the same moment, because he stopped suddenly and turned around again and she was immediately painfully aware of where they were, standing in the middle of the eighth floor. She took in the watchful faces all around her, people stopping what they were doing, lifting their fingers off their keyboards, aware they mustn't miss this, whatever it was about.

'It is true. You're a thrill-seeker, Lucy. A cheap, sleazy thrill-seeker,' Teddy said, coming up close. 'Admit it. That's why you don't even want to see him again.' He looked round the room, aware of everyone listening, seeing how much he could do to damage Lucy's reputation — new, young to the job, not nearly so established as him — but then he stopped. 'Go back to work. Leave me alone.' He turned dismissively away.

'How dare you do that to me?'

He swung back to her in surprise. 'Oh, I dare. It's you who should be careful.' He nodded around the room.

'Teddy.' She leaned in close to him. 'Don't threaten me.'

And there must have been something of her fury in her face because he looked, suddenly, rather taken aback, as if he simply hadn't expected her to come at him again — little docile Lucy, who never usually answered back — let alone here, amidst his colleagues. And now that she had, he didn't quite know what to do next.

He shook her away, sidestepping her, and started to walk back across the room. She followed him silently until they returned to his desk.

'Go away,' he said, once again not looking at her, pretending to be searching for a piece of paper on his desk.

She waited but he didn't stop, so she put her hands on his desk and leaned close to him once more.

'Once and I'm prepared to let you off. But if you say this again you are slandering me and I will stop you.'

She waited for a few seconds more but he didn't move, so she pushed herself upright

145

again and walked away, looking straight ahead, until she'd reached the double doors, swung them apart and arrived safely on the other side. Then she stopped, breathing deeply, aware that she'd been terrified the whole time but triumphant too, because she'd never ever behaved like that before, never dared to take him on.

Once outside her own offices, she put him out of her head, bracing herself for all the bustle and energy waiting for her on the other side of the swing doors, giving herself time to let calm, professional Lucy settle upon her. As the doors opened the smile was already breaking across her face, and she walked across the large open-plan area towards her desk, calling out hellos and Happy New Years, waving at her boss, Jon, who was sitting cross-legged on his desk, talking on the phone — and was she paranoid to think his beaming smile back at her was just that little bit too knowing?

She had a sudden fear that Teddy hadn't just talked to Zoe but had already targeted other significant members of Barley & Bross too. She looked across to her desk, wondering whether anonymous gifts of blindfolds and crotchless knickers would already be piling up, but when she stared more closely at Jon he gave her a surprised, what's-up-with-you, kind of look, so that she had to grin reassuringly and shake her head.

What's up with me, she wanted to shout across to everyone within earshot, is that *Teddy Arnold is a wanker* and you're not to listen to a word he says.

She went to her desk, sat down, switched on her table lamp and her computer and waited for it to boot up. Everything would be better once she'd spoken to Jane, tipped everything that had happened over the last couple of days out of her head and into Jane's lap.

By midday she'd drunk three cups of coffee, deleted several hundred spam emails, worked through fifty-six genuine ones, opened her post, gossiped and caught up with Jon, and started to pick up the threads of the two major projects that were still hanging over from the previous year.

First, Golden Mile Books. She'd been approached just before the Christmas break by the highly successful, highly aggressive Mr Galen, Director of Publishing, Sales and Marketing for Golden Mile Books, Edinburgh, who had finally decided to learn the art of delegation and hire a sales director. Lucy knew him by reputation, and during their first phone call it had become crystal clear how hard it was going to be persuading

147

anyone to work for him, how unlikely it was that he would ever give someone enough space and responsibility to make the job work. She suspected that he knew it too. Even so, she'd spent the last week before Christmas making notes, working her contacts, sifting through CVs, and now that she was back she would shortly be putting together a list of potential candidates, then beginning the delicate business of the first approaches.

The second project had begun in the autumn and should have been over by Christmas. It had involved the placing of a new head of graphic design for Stillman Sound, a fast-growing multimedia company in Chelsea led by the fantastically cool Stuart Stillman. They had approached Lucy back in October and almost immediately she'd found them someone called Greta Dolland. Greta had loved them, they'd loved Greta, Lucy herself loved Greta. They'd gone through the motions of wrangling over her starting salary, her package and her start date, and then, just as Lucy had thought she'd managed to put the whole deal to bed, Greta's current boss had thrown a wobbly and insisted on holding her to the letter of her contract, having verbally agreed to waive her three-month notice period so she could begin with Spillman Sound at the start of the New Year.

She sat at her desk, scrolling back through her December phone notes to remind herself exactly where they'd got to before the Christmas break. But ten minutes later Lucy realized that, although she was peering in what looked like complete concentration at her computer screen, she could just as well have been playing Spider Solitaire for the amount of information she was taking in. She got up impatiently and walked around her desk to the meeting-room, the only place where she could get some privacy. She closed the door and sat on the sofa, neatly hidden from view, tucking her feet up, mobile in hand. She had to speak to Jane. She'd tried to be motivated, she'd tried really hard, she'd even managed to do some good work, but now she just had to call Jane.

She curled around her mobile, imagining the signal from her phone in Hanover Square zipping through the atmosphere to Jane's in Broadwick Street in Soho, and then, just as the line crackled ominously and she heard Jane's tinny voice say 'Hello,' she remembered with a sinking heart that of course Jane wasn't in Broadwick Street. She was in the Lake District on holiday with her boyfriend and his parents, and wouldn't be back in London until the following week.

'It's me,' Lucy said, 'and I've just

remembered where you are. And I can't bear it. I thought you were going to be able to have lunch with me today.'

'Oh, Lucy,' she just about heard Jane cry, ' . . . sorry. Really . . . was.'

'I don't know how I could have forgotten.'

'Cold as a witch's tit . . . ' came back Jane. 'Too choppy, sick inside . . . but . . . games of Risk . . . my head in.'

Despite her disappointment Lucy laughed, then held the phone away from her ear, checking that it wasn't her mobile struggling, and tried again.

'Jane, you can't hear a word I'm saying, can you?'

' . . . signal . . . '

'But you're having a good time there, playing Risk with old Robin?'

Grisly and monosyllabic at the best of times, Robin Barraclough was Jane's boyfriend's father and in the early years she had despaired of ever holding his attention for longer than twenty seconds. But then had come the fateful day, the turning-point in their relationship, when Dillon had suggested Jane ask his father to teach her how to play Risk, because that was the game that made Robin come alive. *Do you secretly desire to conquer the world?* asked the back of the box. In Robin's case, yes, definitely, as soon as possible, and he executed his bold military manoeuvres with a precision and competitiveness that usually wiped his opponents off the board in record time. But not Jane. Jane, who was as competitive as he was, had proved a worthy adversary, and Robin's dad had decided he rather liked her company after all. He had no shame in bringing out the box every night when she came to stay.

'Sometimes six . . . ' Jane crackled, but even so Lucy could hear the outrage in her voice. 'Believe it! . . . mother . . . Cashmere . . . Fucking way I am . . . she said that?'

'No! Yes! Whatever!'

'How was Inverness?' Jane asked, suddenly crystal clear.

'Life-changing. Amazing.'

'God . . . Done!'

'You'll be proud of me.' But she knew it was hopeless, that Jane was perhaps hearing perhaps one word in six. 'And Teddy is being awful. And I need you to tell me what to do — again.' She waited. 'Did you hear any of that?'

'And . . . flights . . . sure . . . today.'

'No, I didn't think you did.'

' . . . wait to see you.'

'Listen to me, Jane.' Lucy raised her voice as loud as she dared. 'I need to see you this lunchtime in Mr Wa's, please.' Jane didn't answer. 'And I think if you explained to Dillon and got a train in the next hour or so you might still make it. Did you hear that?'

'Some . . . ' she heard Jane laugh, and then the phone cut out again. 'Can't . . . No point, is there . . . when I get home.'

Fuck it, Lucy hissed at her phone, holding it in front of her and glaring at it angrily. Couldn't the signal appreciate just how important this call was?

'Teddy . . . cunt.'

'I know.' Lucy closed her eyes.

'Another . . . days . . . Come home.'

'Jane, I met someone on the way home.' She tried again. 'I wish I could tell you about him.'

' . . . say that . . . nice?'

Lucy paused. 'Very nice. But this is driving me crazy. I'm going to have to wait to tell you about it, aren't I?'

Silence.

'I don't know if you can hear me any more. And I know that you don't have a phone in your lakeside prison, so I can't even expect you to call me back.'

There was another pause, then Jane said, ' . . . talk about Dillon.'

'No, please don't tell him.'

' . . . Not that . . . him and me.'

And then the signal died completely.

Lucy slipped the phone back into her pocket and then rubbed tiredly at her face. What had Jane meant about Dillon, about talking to her? Nothing could be wrong with the two of them, could it? Surely nothing beyond the usual moans and groans that Jane liked to fall back on every now and again? They were the most romantic couple Lucy knew, and seeing them together was all the proof she ever needed that there was such a thing as true love.

She stood up. She was imagining things. She was physically tired from all the driving the day before, emotionally drained from all that had happened, and she was therefore leaping to all the wrong conclusions. She pictured Jane, way too gorgeous for the freezing, dismal little living-room she'd be trapped in, cocooned in several layers of jumpers and huddled over the Risk board, convincing herself, as usual, that she was in the wrong house, with the wrong boyfriend.

'I'm going to the Lake District with Dillon and his parents for Christmas,' she'd announced glumly to Lucy as they'd fought their way up Oxford Street, battling it out with all the other Christmas shoppers. 'And we're going on a Christmas Day cruise.' With every day that passed she'd only looked forward to it less.

But the problem was that whatever she did with Dillon, whether it was a fantastic weekend at Le Manoir aux Quat' Saisons or the not-so-inspiring trip around freezing Lake Windermere, Jane carried the same question around with her wherever she went. *What am I to do about Dillon?* And it was a question she had never answered, no matter how many times she'd tried.

In Lucy's opinion it was very clear. Jane should stop asking and accept that there was nothing to do about Dillon. That Dillon was the love of her life and the fact that she'd met him at seventeen rather than later on, and had therefore never gone out with anybody else, was just one of those things. Yes, it meant that she'd had to alternate Christmases with his family and her own, trading her warm, exuberant parents for the difficult and strait-laced Robin and Dorothy. Yes, this would continue for countless years ahead. And yes, there were all those other men she was never going to get her hands on. But what was she getting instead? The brightest, most endearing, funniest, sweetest man she could ever hope to find, who loved her to distraction, who positively revelled in the fact that he'd found her so soon and could therefore misspend his youth with her as well as his responsible middle age. How much better, he believed, to do all the crazy, exciting things young people were supposed to do *with* her rather than before her. And when he talked about it like that, of course Jane was lit up too. It was when Dillon wasn't around that she became less certain, when she was out with Lucy (not that Lucy ever did anything other than tell her how lucky she was), when she heard about other people's see-sawing love affairs, which she'd never have, when she watched her friends light up with the dizzy excitement of new love. Even when her friends were weeping into pillows or losing weight with the misery of being dumped, she sometimes felt overwhelmed with jealousy simply because they were feeling so much, while her own cosy, familiar love for Dillon simply didn't compare. It was then that Lucy would give Jane a kick, remind her how she'd feel if she lost him, tell her to stop being self-indulgent, and Jane would shut up for a while.

They'd been friends all their lives. Lucy and Jane's mothers had lived in the same village in Dorset and had had their baby girls within a few months of each other, and until the age of eleven Lucy and Jane had played together nearly every day. But then, with many doubts and regrets, Jane's family had moved to London and Jane had been sent to a high-flying, exclusive girls' day school, turning her skinny and beautiful and neurotic almost overnight.

While Lucy continued to fumble around at the Chilton and District Pony Club disco and play variations on tennis on the bumpy grass court at the bottom of her friend Miranda's garden, Jane was having private lessons at the Harbour Club and was already catching her first glimpses of seventeen-year-old Dillon as he was being put through his paces by his father, rather more athletic then, not yet reduced to playing out his competitiveness on a board game.

Jane and Dillon had started to talk. Then they'd started playing doubles together, first on opposing sides but all too quickly as partners. Both sets of parents were delighted by their children's new passion for the game, neither of them realizing there was an ulterior motive. And then one day they'd found themselves in each other's arms, kissing behind the curtains that separated the courts from the walkways, and Robin had caught them *the very first time*. Jane had graphically described her agonizing embarrassment. How she'd been standing with her back to Robin, how he would have seen her knickers, thanks to Dillon and his big hands rucking up the back of her tennis dress. And she knew that

Robin still remembered it, now, nearly ten years on, every time they met. She could see it in the rather speculative look he always gave her whenever she reached forward to kiss him hello.

And so the long girly letters that they wrote to each other, funny letters that they'd both kept and reread when they were feeling drunk and sentimental, charted their teenage years and revealed that by the time she was eighteen Jane had only ever kissed two men, the second of whom was Dillon, the first a man she'd met at a Saints and Sinners party. It still galled her that the only other man she'd ever kissed had been dressed as a nun.

When Lucy had started university, Jane had got a job at LWT and a flat in Waterloo, sharing with a school-friend, and still she and Dillon had hung on together, at times only by the thinnest of threads, at other times so in love that Lucy wouldn't have been surprised to hear that the two of them had got engaged.

Two years on, Jane had jacked in her job and she and Dillon had done what he had always wanted them to do, taking a year off to travel around the world together. They had worked whenever they ran out of money and the rest of the time they'd lazed, doing exactly what they liked, crossing countries on a whim, climbing mountains and snorkelling on coral reefs, lazing around on a hundred beaches, canoeing down the Zambezi and climbing Mount Kilimanjaro. And then, finally, they'd come home, and at almost the same time Lucy had arrived in London and she and Jane had found themselves working only a couple of miles apart from each other, Jane at a production company in Soho, Lucy in Hanover Square.

Six months earlier, Dillon had suggested that Jane move in with him, into his flat, because it was bigger, even though it was in Balham rather than her rather more upmarket Gloucester Road. I don't want to live in blinking Balham, Jane had moaned to Lucy. And then had come the inevitable question, what am I going to do about Dillon? Chuck him simply because she'd met him too soon? When he was in every other way perfect? And, struggling as she was at the time with Teddy, Lucy had felt uncharacteristically livid with Jane for taking so much for granted, for not understanding how lucky she was. And for talking about it the whole bloody time.

Jane wasn't going to react well to the story of the Milestone Motel. It was going to make her feel more boring and predictable than ever, and realizing that, Lucy even considered not telling her about it at all — but she dismissed that straight away. It was inconceivable that something so huge was not going to be discussed with Jane, her closest, dearest friend.

Still, it was going to have to wait until the following week. Impatiently, Lucy drummed her fingers on her desk. She opened the door and saw that her floor was almost deserted. She looked at her watch and saw it was one o'clock, lunchtime. She thought about how the sales had just started, Selfridges, Fenwicks . . . There were ways of getting over the disappointment of Jane. She got up from her desk and slipped on her coat.

8

If she didn't care about him, what was she doing looking at his house? Or, more accurately, what was she doing sitting in her car in the dark, squeezed into a space almost directly opposite his brother's house, watching a man in a dinner jacket make his way along the street towards her, a girl in a glittery black evening dress trailing along behind him? The man stopped for a moment to let the girl catch up and Lucy watched him slide an arm around her waist and then they disappeared down the road behind her, the clackety-clack of the woman's sandals slowly fading to silence. Lucy turned back to the house.

She'd only been parked in the space for a few minutes — surely that didn't qualify her as a stalker? Anyway, she was having supper in the next door street and was lucky to find a space so close by. And she really wasn't there to see *him*, she just wanted to see the house again, sit out on the street and look at it, just for a few moments. She went to open the car door but instead wound down the window and breathed in the cold night air. It had stopped raining, but the look of the glistening wet pavement caught in the orange glow of the streetlights and the wet stone steps leading up to the front door that shone like silver were just the same as she'd remembered. Last time the door had opened under the weight of her gaze and Luke had come out on to the steps, Jude rushing to get out of the car to reach him. Now it was a shadow of a house, an empty space between its two brightly painted, brightly lit neighbours. She looked at the windows, three rows of two, black shadows within the dark blue, the faint reflection of the glass, saw that the downstairs curtains were undrawn and one of the sash windows was open at least a foot, so that anyone who wanted to pinch anything could have peered straight in. It looked empty and probably was, and staring at it inspired no feelings of excitement, longing or regret, no rush of blood to the head. If anything being there made her feel exposed and a bit silly, not so far away from the stalker after all. She unclipped her seatbelt; she should go.

But then, as if she'd worked some magic just by starting to move, a light came on in a downstairs room. She stilled, drawn to it like a moth, and then suddenly there was Jude coming into the room with Luke standing behind him in the doorway.

And it was a rush of blood to the head to see him again, moving around the room, looking so exactly the same and yet so unfamiliar too. At times during the week she'd struggled to picture his face clearly, and seeing it again now she wondered how she could possibly ever have forgotten it. Not just because it was such a strong, lively face, but because it was Jude's face, the face she'd held in her hands and kissed.

She watched him come to the window and stare out into the street, then turn back and say something to Luke. She saw Luke hold out a can of what looked like beer, Jude shake his head and turn back to the window, and she saw then that he was angry, was glaring out into the street, his hands clenched by his sides. She watched Luke move forwards, walk across the room to touch Jude lightly on the shoulder and Jude irritably shake him away.

She didn't want to see this. It was one thing to come back to look at an empty house and remember, but another to sit and watch them come to blows. She started to open the car door, planning on slipping past the window and out of the way, then changed her mind, turned on the lights and started the engine, went into reverse and began to edge backwards, wanting the car to hide her from their stare. And then her heart stopped because Jude's voice was now so clear and so close by that her first thought was that he'd seen her and was coming to get her, and she looked up to see him coming fast down the steps, just across the road from her, his long black coat slung over his shoulder, a bag in one hand and Luke just behind him.

'Leave me alone,' she heard Jude shout over his shoulder.

With a trembling hand she turned off the engine, flicked off the headlights, pulled on the handbrake and then, without consciously thinking what she was doing, undid her seatbelt and slid down in her seat until her head was level with the bottom of her window and half hidden by the steering-wheel. She could hear her heart pounding in her chest, could feel every muscle of her body tensing as she sat there, so still, keeping her eyes down because she knew that if she looked up it would be straight into Jude's disbelieving eyes.

Silence. Eventually she risked a quick glance out of her window and saw that Jude had paused on the bottom step of the house to turn back to Luke, who stood in the doorway, at the top of the steps of his house.

Start the engine. She must get away before he turned around and saw her. Because now that he was outside, what else was going to happen? She was a sitting duck, not even discreetly parked any more, but with the front of her car protruding out into the road. And what would Jude think but that she was a loopy stalker after all? Lucy cursed herself for ever coming here. And, having come, for getting into a space so minutely small that the only way to get out quickly would be to shunt the car in front and then reverse hard into the one behind.

Then things began to get worse. Jude turned his back on Luke and crossed the street towards her. He was walking fast, shrugging himself angrily into his coat as he approached, looking as if he might head-butt the next person who came close. No longer the dreamy, gorgeous Jude she'd known but far more compelling now.

'Stop!' she heard Luke call.

Go, Lucy begged him, shutting her eyes and slipping further down into her seat.

And then, just when she thought he was going to walk straight past her, Jude stopped right beside her car. Lucy winced and turned away, and then, when he didn't notice her, cautiously turned her head back and looked through the window at his jean-clad thigh, so close to her nose that she could see where the seam was white around the pocket and beginning to fray.

'Why?' Jude demanded.

'Because you can't just walk off. I want you to finish what you started. I want to know what you meant.' Luke was insistent, calling down the street. 'And I can't come after you or I'll lock myself out.'

'Stay there then.'

'Tell me, Jude.'

Walk on, Lucy begged.

'Lipton St Lucy,' Jude called back, as he moved down the street, and this time Lucy saw there was a new purpose in the way he was walking, a lightness in his step. 'Mum's party. Two weeks' time. I'll be there.'

'Stop, Jude. Don't do this.' Luke was still standing at the top of the steps. 'Think of Mum?' he called.

'Good one, Luke.'

'You're running away.'

Jude stopped abruptly. 'No, I have a job to do.'

'That's such crap.'

Jude turned around. 'Fuck you.'

For a moment Lucy thought he was going to go across the road and up the steps to hit his brother, but he stayed very still.

'Don't you tell me how I think, what I feel. You have no idea.'

'Then you tell me. Come back in the house . . . You won't, will you? Suddenly Aberdeen needs you.'

'You don't want to know what I think.'

'I know already. You want me to start behaving more like you, don't you? Pick up a girl like that one with the nose like a rabbit.'

Lucy uncoiled one clenched fist to bring her fingers slowly up to her face.

'That would be a start,' Jude agreed. 'That would definitely be a welcome change, if you think you could manage it. That would definitely lighten us all up.'

Lucy couldn't imagine where the punch in the words had been, but suddenly Luke was standing there at the top of the steps, looking so crushed and lost for words that she wanted to open the car door and fly up the stairs to him, spread her arms like wings to hold and protect him from Jude.

'I'm sorry.' Jude apologised immediately. 'I shouldn't have said that. I'm a bastard, you know that.'

'Is it too late?' Luke asked after a long time. 'Are you not allowed to change your mind?'

'I'll sort it out.'

'You won't. You'll go back to Aberdeen.'

'Forget about it,' Jude insisted. 'I'm not asking you to do anything. I've told you what it's like sometimes, that's all. And I shouldn't even have done that. My plane gets in at twelve, OK?' All the aggression had gone now

166

from his voice. 'I'll be with you just after lunch.'

'Fantastic, Jude,' Luke said flatly. 'I'll see you then.'

And in response Jude turned away, so that he seemed to be looking straight at Lucy without seeing her at all. At the last moment he glanced back at the house over his shoulder as if he wanted to say something more, but Luke had already closed the door, and so he slowly walked away.

Far from putting the Middletons to bed, as it were, new questions were now falling over each other to get to the front of Lucy's brain. Watching Jude walk away down the street, she wanted to climb out of the car and run after him, to grab his arm and tell him he had to go back to Luke, try to put right whatever was wrong between them. She wanted urgently to ask him if the girl with the rabbit nose was or wasn't her. And what it was he might he have changed his mind about. Even as she told herself that of course she wasn't the girl and he wouldn't have changed his mind about her, and whatever their fight was about, it was none of her business. She could wish them well, hope that the two of them would sort out their differences, that the party would be a huge success, binding up the wounds, but she'd never *know* because it was nothing to do with her and she would never see them again.

And yet, suddenly now, sitting there in the car, she *did* want to see them again. She wanted to see where they lived, what they ate, the clothes they wore, the way they lived. She wanted to meet the glamorous mother who pined for her son and who did or didn't drown her troubles with wine, and the father who spent all his days outside as far from the house as he could be. She wanted to know why Jude and Luke had fallen out and whether they would ever put it right again. Wanted to know but couldn't. She unclipped her seatbelt and got out of the car, locked the door and turned back to the house. Goodbye, she thought, staring at it one last time.

And then she turned away, walked away, following the route Jude had taken just a few moments before her, but immediately breaking left into Moreton Street, towards number 27, where her supper and her friends were waiting.

9

'It's a sweet little nose,' Jane told Lucy firmly as they sat outside Mr Wa's sushi bar at lunchtime, five days later, and in answer Lucy wriggled it gently.

'Although, when you do that . . . '

'Which I don't ever, do I?'

'You do, actually, when you're thinking hard.'

'I do not!'

Mr Wa himself interrupted her, bringing to their table the red Perspex bowls of endaname, and saucers of pickled ginger, wasabi and soy sauce, then laying down square red plates of sushi and sashimi. Passing their table again a minute later, he surreptitiously dropped them two unordered Japanese beers because, he told them, Jane and Lucy were his favourite girls. Every time they had lunch there — at least once a week — he'd arrange for something extra to arrive at their table.

Lucy picked up a piece of endaname and slid her teeth down it, popping out the green beans. 'He was not talking about me. I was not that girl.'

'Don't be sad,' Jane looked across at her in concern. 'I'm sure it wasn't you.'

'But maybe I want it to have been me.' Lucy sighed. 'Bugger him and bugger Teddy too. Stick to Dillon, Jane, whatever you do.'

Jane reached across the table to squeeze Lucy's hand. 'You didn't feel any of this until you went back to the house. You've been so cool. And I'm so envious. Don't spoil it now by wishing you could see him again.'

'It's more complicated than that.'

Jane put down her chopsticks. 'Think about everything that's happened to you recently.' She stopped. 'All of it's good.'

'You think?'

'Of course!' She paused. 'How can I say this without getting it wrong?'

'Try.'

Jane nodded. 'OK,' she said, 'I will. When I said I nearly lost you, I think I meant it.'

Lucy looked at her sharply.

'With Teddy, you moved out of reach so fast. I used to see you together sometimes and I'd think I don't know her, doesn't she realize how much she's changed?'

'But in what way?' Lucy demanded defensively. 'You could still talk to me, we still had a laugh, didn't we?'

'Yes, when Teddy let you out, in your new knee-length skirts and your sensible shoes.'

'Don't say that. If you felt it so strongly you should have told me. Why didn't you say?'

'Because I thought you were happy. And I didn't think it was right to try to stir you up.'

Lucy looked down at her plate, dragging a chopstick through a trail of soy sauce.

'I'm not criticizing you, Lucy. I'm just telling you how it was, for me. And I'm only telling you that because I want you to know how lovely it is to have you back.'

'I knew.' She looked up at Jane again. 'And I'm not angry with you, I'm angry with myself for taking so long to do something about it.'

Jane smiled in relief, raised her beer in salute. 'So thank God he wanted you to go up to his mum and dad for New Year.'

Lucy nodded. 'Thank God he thought *it simply wasn't fair to leave them on their own.* Because that was it, when suddenly I understood. Realized that I didn't have to go. I'd had that invitation from Julia Clegg for weeks, but I hadn't thought once about going. And then, I suppose I just thought sod it, sod him. And that was it.'

Lucy looked at her. Jane was wearing a cream wool coat and she had pulled the collar tightly around her neck so that her thick shiny auburn hair, newly streaked with dark red highlights and cut shorter than when Lucy

171

had seen her last, was curled around her face. She looked lovely and hugely sympathetic, but still Lucy wondered how much she really understood. Because to Jane it must have seemed the simplest thing in the world to walk away from Teddy, who, after all, she'd only been with for a few months.

Impatiently she scraped back her chair and stood up. Seeing Jane's concerned face, she nodded at the gas burner that was standing tall above them, like a parasol, barbecueing them hard. 'I'm hot.' She quickly undid her buttons and ripped off her coat.

'I thought you were about to walk out on me,' Jane said.

'Of course not!' Lucy sat down again. 'I'm far too hungry.'

Jane grinned back at her. 'I want to have sex with some gorgeous stranger in a Milestone Motel.'

'Jane, you don't,' Lucy exclaimed. 'Don't start on that again.'

'How many times?'

'What!'

She nodded. 'How many times did you do it?'

'That's a very personal question.'

'Which you can surely answer for me.'

'Why?'

'Because I'm thinking that if it was once

you were only doing it because you liked the idea. Twice and you two really had a good thing going. Three times and, quite frankly, Lucy, I'm a bit shocked.'

'Once,' Lucy said in a small voice. 'And we were out of the room again in an hour.'

'There you go. It's a good thing you're not seeing him again.'

Jane helped herself to a piece of sushi, poured over a little soy sauce, deftly picked off the salmon with her chopsticks and popped it into her mouth, then looked back at Lucy. 'I wonder if he had a girlfriend.'

'No, Jane. Listen to me, he might have done but that wasn't the problem. And anyway, if he did he wasn't going to tell me. Nothing in our real lives mattered that day. That was the whole point. He didn't want me to know anything about him. Right from the start, he didn't want to talk about his family or why he was working in Aberdeen. And he didn't want to find out anything about me, either.' She shrugged. 'He doesn't know how old I am, doesn't know where I come from, where I live, if I have a boyfriend. Doesn't know I have a fourteen-year-old brother competing in the National Swimming Championships next month. Doesn't know that my dad's thirty years older than my mum, or that they met on a ship sailing to New York,

173

doesn't know I . . . ' She stopped and smiled. 'Oh yes, he does know I trained as a vet and he does know that I'm a headhunter. But he doesn't know the name of the company I work for. He knows I catch the tube at Barons Court but not where I get off. He doesn't know about you or my other friends . . . And I barely know anything more about him.' She thought back to the weekend, sitting outside his brother's house in the rain. 'Well, I didn't until I sat outside his house on Saturday night. I know a bit more about him now. I know he's having a hard time with his rather sad older brother and that he's somehow hurting his mum's feelings. I think he's holding out for something she wants him to give up on.' Lucy heaved a huge sigh, running out of steam abruptly.

'He's stirred you up, made you catch a glimpse of a new exciting world you'd like to see more of. Take advantage of it. Let it take you somewhere new.' Jane shrugged. 'I don't know, go travelling, jack in your job. See the world if you're suddenly so restless here.'

Lucy looked at her, surprised. 'Are you talking about me or you?' She waited, but Jane didn't answer. 'Since we sat down here today you've not been right. And talking to me like that — something's happened, hasn't it?'

'Mmm,' Jane admitted, sighing deeply.

'Oh, God, Jane, tell me what it is! Something awful? Something exciting? Are you getting married? Are you pregnant?'

'Dillon's asked me to move to Australia with him. Three years, he says it would be, and more if we liked it.'

'Australia?' Lucy said in a quiet awestruck voice. 'That's a very long way away.'

'He's been offered a great new job,' Jane explained tonelessly, looking down at the table. 'And it is very exciting, even I can see that.' Slowly she raised her eyes to Lucy.

'And you don't know whether or not to say yes because you think this is it, if you say yes to this, you're saying OK, I'm ready to settle down with him.'

'And you know how I feel about that! I'm twenty-five. I can't help thinking there's still time for so much else.'

'We've talked about this so many times, Jane. You know how I feel, that you'd be crazy to lose him. That this is *grass is greener* taken to dangerous, dangerous lengths.'

'I know, I know. Of course I can see that too. And I love him and I don't want him to be with anybody else, ever. But, oh God. Call me a fool, self-indulgent, greedy, all the things I know I am, but I still can't look him in the eye and say yes, I'm coming with you.

And it's like this awful test. He's thinking that by hesitating I'm proving to him that I don't love him like he does me. And I do.'

'I can see why he thinks that. He's had to put up with it so many times before, too, hasn't he?'

'This is the last time. I have a week to decide. Dillon's going away on a conference all this week. And when he gets back I have to tell him what I'm going to do.'

Lucy nodded. She couldn't say what she should have said straight away, that of course Jane should go for it, that they were the best couple together she'd ever known, that they inspired her, made her see how good it could be, because she'd told her this so many times. And perhaps all the doubt that Jane expressed time and again meant something beyond her fear of commitment and insecurity, perhaps it did mean that she didn't love Dillon enough.

'You decide this one, Jane. Whatever I say, it's only what you think that matters.'

'I know.' Jane sighed, then reached again for Lucy's hand. 'The worst bit would be leaving you behind. How would I cope without you?'

'You won't have to cope without me. I'll be there, on the end of a phone. I'll come and see you, I'll email you. It won't be the same, but we'll still be there for each other, you

176

know we always will.'

She glanced down at her watch. It was late, past three o'clock, time to return to their respective offices, no time at all to talk through everything in the detail it deserved. And seeing the look on her face, Jane nodded and pushed back her chair. They stood up to go, both of them feeling that the lunch hadn't worked as well as it should have done. That for such close friends, they'd come unstuck, neither of them being able to say what the other really wanted to hear, both of them wishing they'd had a little longer to talk.

'Don't worry about Jude,' Jane said again as they reached Milton Street and the point in the road where they went their separate ways. 'He's sorted you out without you even realizing; just give it time and you'll see it's true.'

'And don't you worry about Dillon, either.' Lucy reached forward and pulled Jane into a hug, holding her tight. 'You know you had to arrive at this moment. Something had to force you to decide what you want. It's good that it's happened.'

Jane nodded.

'And we'll talk about it. We'll go out for supper — yes?'

Jane nodded again, turning away from Lucy and starting to walk away. 'And I hope

Teddy leaves you alone now. I hope nothing else happens.'

'Nothing is going to happen apart from him going completely crazy and demolishing my reputation in Barley & Bross, which he's tried to do already.'

But then, the following Tuesday morning, exactly a week since the drive down from Inverness, something did happen.

★ ★ ★

That morning Lucy walked into Barons Court tube station at eight o'clock, barely aware of what she was doing because she'd done it so many times before. She bought a paper from the same newspaper stand and read the headlines until it was her turn to push through the ticket barrier, keeping her head down and rerunning a conversation she'd just had on the phone with her mum about whether she was going to make it home for the weekend.

She collected her ticket and moved seamlessly to join another queue moving to the steps to the platform, one person in a sea of others. And then, just as she stepped on to the first step and looked back to her newspaper again, she passed a poster, an A3 sheet of dark green card with a cartoon car drawn in red at the top of it, seen out of the corner of her eye, and some words in bold black letters, taken in by a corner of her brain, so that she stopped, momentarily disconcerted, and looked up, wondering what it was that she'd seen. But then the tide of commuters was carrying her down onto the platform and she put it out of her mind and went back to her paper.

There was a train already waiting and she could see three or four empty seats in the carriage ahead of her. So holding her paper and her bag tightly at her side, she walked straight in, found a seat and sat down — and then in her head, she saw the poster again, the little red car at the top, and the words underneath, and she found herself whispering them disbelievingly, aghast that she hadn't taken them in properly before: *Lucy Blue, where are you?*

It felt as if everything inside her stopped. And then her heart began to pump again, leaving her lightheaded, as if she might be about to faint, and she stood up and turned to get off the train. But it was like one of those dreams where you're trying to run but can barely move at all, and even as she was forcing her legs forward towards the doors they were slowly closing in front of her, sealing her in, and then the train was starting to move, and then it was accelerating fast until it hurled itself headlong into the tunnel with a roar.

She clung to a pole, finding herself swinging and falling again against the door as it swept her around corners at breakneck speed, further and further away from the poster. She looked at her bewildered face in the juddering reflection and felt nothing but alarm, not that he'd tried to reach her, but that the poster would be gone before she could get back to it.

Whereas the District Line from Barons Court to Earls Court stays above ground, the Piccadilly Line takes you deep underground, and as she was swept on, and she began to think coherently again, she started to plan what she would do once she arrived in Earls Court, trying to remember if it was simply a question of crossing directly from one platform to another to take her back or whether she would have to climb to the exits and then turn back. At this time of day the trains would surely be only a few moments apart; either way she could be back in Barons Court in what, ten, fifteen minutes time? Surely it would still be there. It had to still be there.

Finally she felt the train start to slow down, and around her other passengers left their seats and joined her to face the door. Lights from the platform appeared through the windows, and finally, with a hiss of air, the doors opened and Lucy left her carriage, slipping through the crowds of people, following the signs for the westbound Piccadilly line, hearing her harsh breathing as she pushed and dived her way past people, people everywhere, briefcases and rucksacks and feet. She had only to cross from one platform to the other but she could feel the hot air blowing up from the tunnels, telling her that a train was approaching, and still the people in front of her hardly picked up speed, so that when she finally reached the platform she was skating across the polished floor, long-jumping on to the train just as the doors shut again behind her.

Surely only five minutes since she'd left Barons Court station? Surely nothing could have happened to it in such a short time? She kept her head down, gritting her teeth, unable to look at anybody, unable to bear any distraction. He would have left her some way of contacting him, wouldn't he? And she'd answer him, wouldn't she? Whatever she'd said to Jane, whatever she thought about not wanting to see him again, he'd tried to find her; she had at least to find out why, what it was he was wanting to say.

Finally the train pulled into Barons Court station. She was back above ground again now, and this time as the doors opened she was aware of the cold air as she walked quite calmly up the few steps and was back where she'd begun, just in front of the ticket hall.

And the poster had gone.

She knew it was true but she couldn't accept it. She could see exactly where it had been, pinned above the tube map. She could even see a tear of green paper left behind whenever whoever had pulled it down. But still she thought perhaps she'd got it wrong, that she'd walked into a different part of the station, that she hadn't retraced her steps in exactly the right way. She paused for a moment, trying to get her bearings, waiting for that moment when she'd realize where she'd gone wrong, but of course the moment didn't come because this was exactly as it should be, this was where she walked in from Palliser Road every morning. It all looked exactly the same as it did every morning of every day that she went to work.

She walked over to the wall where the poster had been, reached forward with her hand and touched the square of torn dark green paper and a piece of sellotape.

She placed her hand flat against the wall. It had gone, and it felt as if this were proof, if ever there was, that fate did not want the two of them together after all. Trying not to let the sense of anticlimax overwhelm her, she told herself how the right thing to do now had to be to get on the next train and put him, even temporarily, out of her mind.

But there was someone behind her, she could hear their breathing, and she spun around, for one crazy moment thinking that it was going to be Jude. But it wasn't, it was a girl, coming through the ticket barrier to stand close beside her considering her, head on one side, thin and pretty with dyed red hair and very pale skin and piercing blue eyes.

'Who are you?' Lucy asked.

'I'm Aileen Richards, Lucy Blue.' The girl grinned. 'It's you, isn't it? I could tell it was you from the way you touched the wall.'

She was looking Lucy critically up and down, obviously trying to decide if she warranted such an effort on her behalf, and Lucy wished she was wearing something more original and romantic, something more deserving of the poster than tights and a long blue coat.

'But it's gone,' Lucy mumbled.

'Lucy Blue.' Aileen Richards shook her head and smiled. 'Are you blind?'

Lucy turned around. Was he really there, hiding behind the ticket machines, about to jump out at her with a bunch of red roses? She looked, feeling sick with nerves, but there was nobody there. And then the girl took her arm and led her back through the ticket machines away into the middle of the ticket hall, where she stopped and started to look slowly around at the walls, and then she caught Lucy's eye and smiled again and looked again, and unsure whether she was looking for another poster, or even still looking for Jude, Lucy followed her gaze, staring round the shiny limegreen tiled walls, that in all the time she'd been using the station she'd never noticed before.

And suddenly, leaping out at her, Lucy saw the posters. All of them dark green, all of them with the little red car cartoon at the top, all of them saying the same thing. There were three of them stuck to the tiled wall in a line just in front of her, another over the top of a tube map. She turned again and saw two more, one above another, right in the entrance to the underground station, positioned so that she couldn't possibly miss them as she walked in. But she had.

She looked back to the girl and found herself starting to laugh. 'Thank you so much.' She walked to the nearest poster and read again *LUCY BLUE WHERE ARE YOU?*, saw that there was a telephone number beneath it, ripped the poster off the wall and held it in her hand.

'So how did he lose you?' the girl asked curiously, back at Lucy's side. 'Did he lose you on the train? Did he get to Barons Court station and think *Sugar, where's that Lucy Blue got to?*'

Smiling at the thought that it could be so simple, Lucy shook her head and read the poster again, touched that he could have gone to such lengths to find her.

'You do like him, though?' the girl asked curiously, shoving little white hands into her pockets. 'I haven't been persuading the London Underground staff to leave them up for nothing, have I?'

'Did you do that?'

'Of course! It's so romantic, what he did for you. But you are pleased to be found?'

She turned back to her distractedly. 'Yes, Aileen, I am. But I can't believe he's done this for me. It doesn't make sense.'

'It's the loveliest thing I've ever seen. Not that I ever saw *him*. I wish I had.'

Lucy held the poster close against her.

'You realize he's the one,' the girl said wistfully. 'You do know that, don't you?'

'Perhaps!'

'What do you mean?' the girl cried, outraged. 'Anyone who does that for you

. . . He's definitely the one.'

'Shut up!' Lucy said, laughing now. 'You don't know what you're saying.'

'I don't need to know any more. You're going to make that call, that's all that matters. And when you find him you'll see I was right.'

She held out her hand. Lucy found herself gripped hard. 'You'll see,' she said again. Then she smiled at Lucy once more and was gone, slipping back through the ticket machines and disappearing out of sight.

Lucy found herself walking slowly out of the station, following the road for a few hundred yards until she came to a wet bench on a patch of muddy grass and sat down. The poster trembled in her hand as she held it out in front of her and keyed the number into her mobile.

'Hi,' said a voice after the second ring.

She tipped back her head and smiled at the sky.

'It's me,' said Lucy.

10

For the second time that day, Lucy leapt for a train. This time she left the platform with a good three feet to spare, and forced herself through an opening just a few inches wide, only to be greeted on the other side by a crush of soggy, steaming, irritable bodies, none of them remotely pleased at having their last few centimetres of space invaded by yet another thoughtless, pushy passenger.

She wriggled forward, aiming for a space just in front and to the left of her, about one foot square, where, if she stood on one leg, and kept her head bent at ninety degrees, she reckoned she'd be able to wait out the rest of the journey home. She looked up and caught the eye of a girl staring back at her disapprovingly, swinging on the end of a pole with a briefcase wedged between her ankles. Lucy gave her a what-a-hell-hole-this-is kind of smile but the girl scowled and immediately looked away.

If I told you what I'm doing tonight, maybe you wouldn't toss your head like that, Lucy wanted to say. Then you'd understand why I had to catch this train.

She looked at her watch and saw that it was nearly six-thirty. She'd known she was crazy to try to get home and change before she went out again to meet him, but she had to go home. She wanted to be out of her work clothes when she saw him and she needed just a few moments in her flat, alone, time to gather herself up before she saw him again, to quickly dry her hair from the rain, to go through her wardrobe, take deep breaths, persuade herself that she could cope with anything he might throw at her.

She'd spent almost the whole day thinking about what that might be, and then just as she was about to slip unobtrusively away there'd been a call from Greta Dolland, picking her moment to announce suddenly that she wasn't going to take the Stillman Sound job after all. And Lucy had had to swing into action and put Jude out of her mind, so that she'd ended up leaving the office half an hour later than she'd planned and with only seconds left to change her clothes before she'd have to leave again.

How mad was she still to be trying to get home first? It would have been so much simpler to have gone straight to the bar, which was what Jude imagined she'd be doing, the reason he'd picked Meat, a restaurant bar in South Ken because he'd thought it would be easy for her to reach by tube. But she'd order a taxi from the flat. If she was lucky it would only take ten minutes to get to the bar, and that way she'd add on twenty minutes to her time at home, plenty of time to get changed.

She'd wear jeans, she thought, as the train pulled to a halt in Earls Court station and then went very quiet, leaving only the disconcerting ticking sound that told her it was not about to leave again in a hurry. She clamped down on the rising feeling of panic in her stomach, ignoring it, thinking about Jude. He wasn't about to choose what he was going to say depending on what she was wearing, after all. He knew what he wanted her for. But what could it be, she thought again for the hundredth time, how could she think it was completely out of character, when the truth was she hardly knew him at all. Even so, he'd have to explain why he was going back on everything they'd agreed. Come to think of it, why he was even still in London? Hadn't he said he'd be back in Aberdeen by now?

She'd got no further on the phone, he'd sounded pleased that she'd called but cautious too, and so to-the-point that she hadn't liked to question him. He'd asked only if she'd meet him and when she'd said yes and had suggested that evening — she'd figured the shorter the time he left her wondering, the better — he'd mentioned a bar and restaurant in Arundel Street in South Ken that she'd never heard of, and had asked her what time and she'd said seven-thirty, and all he'd said then was *Good. See you then*, and had gone before she could even say goodbye. Hardly the grand romantic reunion she'd been expecting.

Forty minutes, she thought as the train finally arrived at Barons Court station. And then she'd find out what was going on.

On the street outside, she saw that the rain had got harder still. She paused for a moment in the dry of the station, wondering why it was that whenever she met Jude it had to be snowing or pouring with rain. And then she turned up her collar and ran into the street, shielding her head with her arm and leaping over the puddles.

She reached her block, unlocked the front door, ran dripping up the stairs and opened the door to her flat, undoing the buttons of her coat at the same time, pulling it off and leaving it in a damp heap on the floor, slipping out of her shoes, pulling her jumper over her head. Standing in her bra and pants, she rang three taxi companies before she finally found one free to pick her up and then, when the cab was finally booked, she walked through to the bathroom and stepped into the shower, rubbing shampoo into her head and tipping back her face to the rush of hot water. Minutes later she was sitting on the floor of her bedroom drying her hair, then she put on some make-up and pulled on her clothes. And by seven-fifteen she was ready to go, looking out of the window impatiently, waiting for the taxi.

When the intercom buzzed, she didn't even register that it was strange she hadn't seen the taxi arrive. She moved from the sitting-room to the hall and picked it up.

'Hi, I'm coming down,' she said.

'Lucy?' said a voice, Teddy's voice. 'I'll wait down here then.'

'No,' she gasped, leaping away from the intercom.

And then the anger pushed her forward again because Teddy was not going to do this to her. How could he possibly have known to come around now? She'd told nobody, not even Jane, that she was seeing Jude that evening.

She leaned back to the intercom. 'What are you doing here, Teddy?' She made her voice sound normal, calm.

'What do you think? I've come to see you.'

'No, but that's such bad timing! I'm going

out, any minute now.'

'Lucy, I wanted to apologize. How I behaved . . . It was intolerable. I wanted to tell you face to face.'

'Thank you, Teddy, but I'm going out. Why don't we get together at work tomorrow, we could go out for lunch if you like.'

'You must be very desperate to get rid of me if you're offering to do that. Where are you going, anywhere nice?'

She shook her head, wondering what she was to do. Not just now, but for every day that followed too.

'Let's talk tomorrow, like I said. I really don't have time now.'

'Five minutes of your precious time.'

'But there's no point,' she couldn't help crying out in frustration. 'There's nothing to say.'

'How do you know that if you don't talk to me? Lucy?' He waited but she didn't reply. 'I'm not going to let you go out until you do.'

This was Teddy as he used to be. Insistent, not stopping until he'd trapped her into a corner and made certain she'd do what he asked.

'You are not going out without seeing me. You owe me that. At the very least you owe me that.'

'I owe you nothing,' she hissed, and

192

slammed the receiver back into its cradle.

Immediately it buzzed again and furiously she picked it up.

'You owe me that,' he insisted furiously.

She waited.

'Lucy . . . Who are you seeing? Is it him?'

Her heart sank. Now she could see him waiting there all night.

'Perhaps tonight you might find out his name.' She heard him kick her door and alarm rolled through her. Perhaps now he'd go further, force his way upstairs?

'Let me in.'

'No, Teddy. I will not let you in.'

'Then I'll huff and I'll puff . . . ' He started to laugh, and she imagined herself still in her flat an hour later, calling the police, watching from her window as he was dragged away. And then his laughter stopped abruptly and she heard the unmistakable sound of the taxi pulling up beside her front door.

She dropped the receiver back in its cradle, ran across to the window and looked down at the street, and with disbelief she saw him turning towards the taxi with a newspaper shielding the top of his bare head from the rain as he opened the door with the other hand.

'No! Wait!' she shouted. She turned away from the window, reached for her coat and her bag and her keys, and was out of the flat in just a few seconds, running towards the stairs.

But even as she descended them, clattering down as fast as she could to the front door, she heard the taxi's engine start to change, moving from a rumble into gear and then the inevitable awful sound of it moving off. She opened the front door to see it heading away fast, rainwater curving out from its wheels as it cut through the puddles, a figure, unmistakably Teddy, sitting tall in the middle of the back seat. And she thought, wretchedly, how she'd told the cab firm where she was going and that there was surely no chance at all that Teddy wouldn't now be heading there too.

It was seven-fifteen. No chance of booking another cab. She'd have to hope she found one on the street, in the rain.

All around her people were running for cover. But Lucy walked on, down her street, passing the tube station and walking out on to the Cromwell Road, surprised by how much better it felt to be outside and walking, rather than trapped in a tube, or waiting restlessly in her flat for a cab. What could Teddy do? What had he ever actually done but bluster and shout? He'd controlled her by suggestion, not action; he'd shouted at her once or twice in public, enough to make her nervous of it happening again, but he'd never done anything physical. And if he was there, waiting for her in Meat, Jude would be there too, and so would a crowd of other people. How bad could it be? Or perhaps Teddy wouldn't be there at all. She hadn't ever had him down as the particularly courageous sort. He'd arrive at the restaurant, perhaps, look inside. But then, more than likely, he'd walk away . . . Wouldn't he?

And meanwhile, there was Jude, waiting for her. He was the one, the girl had said; how much better that she was walking to him through the rain. Weren't the most romantic reunions always in the rain? *Breakfast at Tiffany's, Cinema Paradiso, Singin' in the Rain.* Perhaps he'd be waiting for her outside Meat, and at the sight of her, wet as she was, he would open his arms and hug her tight, all explanations unnecessary after all.

Five minutes later, she wasn't so sure. The rain was too cold, numbing her cheeks and sliding down her neck and under her warm clothes, soaking her hair and sending dissolving hair mousse running into her mouth whenever she took a breath. And she was suddenly ravenously hungry too, images of hamburgers and chips pushing aside even those of Jude. She walked on, sidestepping

195

the puddles, and all the time the seconds ticked away and she had to wonder how long before he gave up on her.

And then, when there was only five minutes to go before she was due to meet him, the orange light of a taxi magically appeared in front of her and she charged out into the road, madly waving her arms so that it barely had time to stop before it ran her over. She climbed in, apologizing for the pools of water she was bringing in with her, and breathlessly told the driver where she wanted to go.

★   ★   ★

Ten minutes late, she stood in the street looking up at a blue neon sign flashing Meat. With her heart in hands, she pushed through the door into a large dark T-shaped room, with a long bar running all across the back wall and tables and chairs lining each narrower side. It was dark, lit only by pencil-thin strips of electric-blue light that ran around the tops of the navy-blue walls.

People sat together chatting at the bar, or eating at the tables, and she took a few seconds to look around slowly and swallow the relief that Teddy wasn't there among them. Then disquiet began to build because she had to acknowledge, with bitter disappointment, that Jude didn't seem to be there either, certainly hadn't materialized at a run the moment she'd appeared in the doorway.

She scanned the bar for a second time, the chocolate leather and blue glass bar, with a mirrored wall running across its back. There were two or three couples in the middle and two solitary men standing like bookends at each end, both of them with their backs to Lucy and the doorway, one short and blond, one tall and dark-haired, neither of them Jude.

She turned to the rest of the room, trying to see the faces of the people sitting at the tables, thinking surely he hadn't given up on her? Not so fast, not after such an elaborate ploy to track her down? She looked at her watch again. She was fifteen minutes late, barely enough time for Teddy to have got in before her, let alone time for him to have deduced which man was the Scottish bastard who'd pinched his girl, and *persuaded* him to leave.

A waitress appeared at her side, a butcher's apron tied around her waist, but Lucy mumbled that she was looking for someone and edged closer into the room, searching even more carefully, peering into all the dimly lit corners, the strange blue light making it hard to distinguish anyone clearly, but seeing enough to know that everyone sitting down was with someone else, and that Jude wasn't there.

And it was only then that she walked forward a few more paces and scanned the bar for a second time. And this time met the eyes of the tall dark man who'd turned now and was looking at her, looking for her. And looking back at him, she finally acknowledged what she'd sort of known from the start but hadn't been able to accept. That Jude wasn't anywhere in Meat and never had been. And that the man who'd caught her eye, who was now walking towards her, full of purpose, as if he knew what her reaction would be and wanted to catch her before she fled, was his brother, Luke.

11

Lucy knew exactly what she should do. And yet she stayed, rooted to the ground, and waited for him to come to her, swamped with disappointment and with the knowledge that somewhere along the way she'd been made to look a complete fool.

'I needed to talk to you,' was the first thing he said, stopping in front of her.

And she was surprised that he wasn't even attempting to apologize, that it didn't even cross his mind that maybe she might not want to listen to him.

'I take it he's not coming?'

'No.'

'He never was?'

'No.'

'So you put up the posters?'

'Yes.'

She nodded. 'Then I'm going home.'

'No, you're not.' He shook his head. She'd have found him rather intimidating if anger hadn't been boiling up inside her. 'You can't,' he insisted. 'I have to talk to you.'

'Get off me.' She shook off the hand that had dared to touch her arm. 'You give me the creeps. You and your creepy posters.'

'No,' he spluttered, jerked into life by her words. 'It was the only way I could find you.'

'*Lucy Blue, where are you?*' she spat out furiously. 'You deceitful bastard. Making me call you like that, letting me think you were Jude. What were you *doing*?' She'd spoken his name aloud and immediately there he was in front of her again. And it was so hard to accept that she wouldn't be seeing him after all. In the course of the day she'd fast-forwarded to this moment a thousand times, had imagined him so clearly, how he would kiss her, his eyes alight with the excitement of finding her again. And now, she thought, glaring back into Luke's dark unsmiling eyes, she'd got this, this twisted, heartless man who bore no resemblance whatsoever to his lovely younger brother. She looked at the hard line of Luke's mouth, his high wide forehead and dark springing hair, at the uncompromising look on his face, and found herself taking two steps back from him.

'I had to be sure you'd come. The only way was to mislead you.'

'Why? For a game? Some joke you're planning?' Even as she said it she knew it wasn't that. No one as full of purpose as Luke was ever going to play a joke. 'Didn't you think I'd care?' She was aware of the rasp in her voice, loud in the little room, people starting to stare. She shook her head, dropping her voice again. 'No, you — ' she paused briefly, searching for the right word, 'you *egotistical* man, you know what? Forget it. I *don't* care.'

'Jude doesn't even know I'm here.'

'So what? Is that meant to make me feel better or worse?'

'Better,' he insisted.

'It doesn't.'

He nodded, raking a hand through his hair. Belatedly it seemed to occur to him that stage two of his plan wasn't going quite like he'd expected it to, and that some degree of soft talking was necessary after all.

'But you're so wet,' he said, looking her critically up and down. When she didn't respond, he shrugged impatiently. 'OK, aren't you hungry? Thirsty?' He peered closer at her face. 'Oh, for God's sake.' The sweet talk ended abruptly. 'Stop being so damned stubborn. Stay for one drink, and then I'll take you home.'

'I've already shared a lift with your brother and that did me no good at all,' she snapped back. 'And whatever it is you want to say, every single bit of me is saying don't hear it, that the Middletons are not good news. Steer well clear of them. I came here tonight against all my better instincts, and I was wrong.'

'You make it sound as if we're a couple of psychopaths.'

'I wouldn't be surprised.'

'Don't be ridiculous.' He sighed heavily, gazing around the room for inspiration, found none, and turned impatiently back to her again. 'Look what I've done to find you. Doesn't it count for anything? Won't you lie awake at night wondering what on earth it might all have been for?'

'I'll never think about either of you ever again.'

'I don't believe you.' He leaned towards her, clearly now as irritated by her as she was by him.

'I don't give a damn.'

'Why come if you didn't care?'

'I nearly didn't.'

'Stop it!' Luke cursed, making her jump. 'Why won't you listen to me? Once I found you . . . ' He shook his head. 'Why didn't I think what a major disappointment I'd be?'

'I have no idea.'

She turned away, towards the door.

'Just fancied a bit of room service, did you, in your Milestone Motel?'

She stopped, turned slowly back to him. 'Fuck off.'

'I want you to listen to me, Lucy.' Then, belatedly, he saw the hurt on her face. 'Lucy, I'm sorry.' Desperately he scrunched his hair in his hands. 'I didn't mean that, I'm not trying to taunt you, bringing that place up again. I'm sorry if it makes you so uncomfortable that I know all this about you.' Now he was speaking much more quietly and gently. 'I've been behaving badly.'

She looked at him.

'I'm rude and insulting. No wonder you don't want to listen to me.'

'This is the charm offensive now, is it?'

He shook his head. 'No, I mean I really have been behaving like an arse.' He folded his arms again. 'But what if I'm here to tell you that you were right to come, that he does really care about you? What if I can explain why he can't tell you himself?' He went straight on. 'You know what? I'm going to tell you, right now, whatever you say. I'm going to tell you standing here if you won't sit down.' He paused. 'And my feeling is you want to listen. I don't think you're quite ready to walk out of the door, after all.'

That was the moment to go, but, of course, she couldn't bring herself to do it.

'The first, most important thing, Lucy,' Luke said steadily, 'is that Jude does badly want to see you again. He talked about you an awful lot on the way down to Oxford.'

She shrugged, as if she couldn't care either way, even as her heart did a great flip of pleasure at his words.

'And if you'll listen I'll tell you why he hasn't told you himself.'

She shifted from one foot to the other, hitched her bag back over her shoulder, self-preservation still insisting she should go, curiosity making her stay, then looked up at him again.

'He was relieved to get out of the car and I was relieved to see the back of him,' she told him. 'We may have liked each other at the time, but we both knew it wasn't going to turn into anything more.'

'But don't tell me you two didn't care,' he insisted. 'Because I know that's not true — at least I know it's not true for Jude. If you could have listened to him after you'd gone, you'd understand why I'm trying to talk to you now, because there's so much more to know about Jude. And if you'll let me, I'll tell you what I mean. Nothing scary. Nothing awful,' he added hastily, seeing the sudden dread on her face. 'Just some things I think you'd be glad to know.'

Finally he'd got to her, and he knew it. He stood there quietly, waiting for her to tell him so, and as if to tempt her further at that moment the door from the kitchens swung open and a waitress appeared with a sizzling roast chicken on a wooden tray, with two wooden bowls of thin French fries perched on either side of it. Despite herself Lucy felt her stomach rumble, and tried to remember when she'd last eaten. She watched the tray make its way across the room to a couple sitting at a table at the edge of the room, and the girl picked up a chip in her fingers and bit off the tip.

'Are you hungry?' Luke asked immediately. 'Why don't we have something to eat? Come on, Lucy, it's the least I can do — buy you some supper while you listen to me.'

'OK,' she agreed, thinking what a good idea it sounded, but ashamed of what a complete pushover she was.

Instantly he sprang into action, grabbing a waitress, then steering Lucy, frogmarching her, across the room to an empty round table and two chairs in the corner. He helped her out of her coat and handed it to the waitress, pulled out her chair and practically pushed her down. He sat down opposite her, and while around them the bar buzzed with laughter and chat, and before they'd even talked about drinks or food, barely before Lucy had settled herself into her chair, he took a deep breath and started to talk.

And the first thing he told her was how, just over a year ago, Jude had been in a car accident and the girl he'd been with had died.

Luke was right. His news punched her in the stomach and changed everything. And as she listened, as Luke explained how Jude had picked the girl up at the station to bring her home, how she'd flown back from her parents' home in Italy to join them all for a second Christmas in Oxfordshire, Lucy slumped in her chair with the shock of what he was saying.

'What was her name?' Lucy whispered.

'Gabriella.'

'Was it Jude's fault?'

'No.'

He sat back, waiting for her to take it in, and she looked away, unable to hold his stare, and sat quietly, trying to imagine how it must have been for Jude but knowing she could come nowhere close. Then she looked back at Luke, lost for words for him too.

He saw her stricken face and leaned towards her, full of concern.

'I know it's a shock.' He looked at her kindly. 'But I had to tell you. We couldn't have talked about anything else until I'd got it out of the way.'

She could see a waitress making her way towards them, the same one who'd caught

206

her eye earlier, in her long white butcher's apron, coming through the swing doors from the kitchen with menus in her hand and a smile on her face, and Lucy willed her away, thinking not so soon, we've only just sat down. How can we hear about the dish of the day after Luke has just told me that?

'Can I interest you two in any drinks?'

Luke turned to her. 'Two minutes?'

The girl nodded and was gone.

'Sitting here, in a place like this,' Lucy looked around the room, 'I can't believe I'm hearing something so sad.'

'I'm sure.'

But of course, no longer a shock for Luke and for Jude. They had to be carrying the knowledge of what had happened with them for every minute of every day, into whatever they were doing, wherever they were and far more acutely than she ever would.

And it was as if Luke hardly needed to tell her any more, because she'd seen the consequences for herself. How guilt had made Jude leave the Navy. How the loneliness of Aberdeen had become so attractive. How he could hardly bring himself to talk about home. How missing Gabriella had become such a part of Jude that it was there even when he'd been joking and laughing and sweeping Lucy off her feet. How easy it must have been to let Lucy go again, when all his thoughts had still been focused on somebody else.

And meanwhile, back in Oxfordshire, the whole happy Middleton family was slowly being broken apart. She'd seen him and Luke at each other's throats, after all, as she'd sat in her car in the street outside the house in Notting Hill.

'It's over a year ago now.' Luke was speaking again. 'It's a terrible cliché, I know, but Jude needs to move on.'

So that was why Luke had found her. It was his mother's birthday in two weeks' time and meanwhile Jude's misery was grinding them down. Time to find the girl Jude had talked about, the girl who perhaps might make him forget. After all, Luke had no doubt reasoned, how much longer was Jude going to take? Didn't he see he had a responsibility to the family to pull through now? She could almost hear Luke's voice telling Jude just that, wondered if that was what he'd been telling him when she'd watched them arguing outside the house in Notting Hill. He was the older brother, used to pushing Jude around, and now he was getting impatient. Yes, he'd have told Jude. *It was awful. Yes, Gabriella was a lovely girl.* Perhaps he'd even argued that Jude had to move on because *it's what Gabriella would have wanted*.

'I understand you'd like him to be happy again,' she said, carefully picking her words. 'I'd like it too. But surely he's got to be happy on his own before he's ready to meet someone new? Don't bully him into something he's not ready to do.'

'But he told me,' Luke insisted, 'all about you. Just by talking about you he was the happiest I've seen him. He was lit up by you, Lucy.'

Could it really be true? Could she really do that for anyone? And what did she feel if it was? She looked down at the table. She felt complicated and confused, flattered but panicky at the pressure it put her under.

'I hardly knew him.'

'But you knew how you felt?'

'I suppose, but . . . I don't want to have to persuade him. Jude and I,' she shrugged, remembering he had heard it all anyway. 'Despite everything that we did, at the time, I . . . It sounds so silly but it was like a fairytale day. I thought it was all to do with the snow.'

'The snow?' he repeated.

She heaved a deep sigh, aware that it wasn't just the shock of what Luke was telling her that was making her feel as if she might pass out.

'Are you all right?' He shook his head, staring at her worriedly. 'Lucy, you need to eat something.' He caught the eye of a waitress and almost immediately hot crusty French bread arrived at their table, then butter and knives and forks and thick linen napkins.

She broke off a piece of bread and ate it gratefully, then ate another piece smeared with butter, then smiled at Luke and he grinned back at her.

'I'm coming back to life now,' she said through a crumbfilled mouth, and stopped. 'Oh God, Luke, I'm sorry. What a terrible thing to say.'

'No,' he reassured her. 'It really doesn't matter.'

'What I should have said is if I'm coming back into Jude's life. If he cares as much as you say he does, then I should be certain that I want him and I'm not.' She swallowed the last of the bread, wiped her mouth with her hand and looked at him seriously. 'I hardly know him, Luke. And it wouldn't exactly help, would it, if I met him again and then I turned him down? We had an amazing time together. And yes, he's a very attractive man and that has a lot to do with why it happened. But that doesn't mean it's going anywhere. I don't think I ever thought it was love at first sight.'

'And when you thought it was him who'd put up the posters, how did that make you feel?'

'Confused, because I didn't think he cared enough. We never seemed to be on that level. But then I understood I'd probably got him wrong, that neither of us had given the other a chance to be how we really were. And he was showing me now . . . ' She looked at him, rubbing crumbs away from her mouth. 'The most romantic gesture of my life, and it was you.'

'Forget about it,' he said briskly. 'How about love at second sight? Given what you know about him now. And there'd be no secrets between the two of you any more. Couldn't that happen?'

'But, Luke.' She felt better now, and something was occurring to her that surely should have been the very first thing she had thought of. She couldn't believe how stupid she'd been not to think of it before. 'Of course it can't work like you're saying it might. You're saying come back and make my brother happy, but the fact is, he's still in love with Gabriella.'

'No.'

'And you shouldn't be trying to rush him,' Lucy insisted. 'Jesus, a year, it's not exactly long. And in any case, surely it's up to Jude to

211

know when he feels ready for somebody else? Who are you to tell him how long he needs to get over her? Maybe he never will. I can understand it's uncomfortable for you all, and time's pressing with the birthday party coming up and all that,' she paused, 'but what are we thinking! Of course it won't work. I can't believe you're even trying to put us together again.'

'Listen to me, Lucy,' Luke interrupted, then added in a rush, 'You've got it wrong. Jude was not in love with Gabriella. I was. She wasn't his girlfriend. She was mine.'

★   ★   ★

For the second time Lucy felt physically winded by his words, shocked that she'd got it so wrong. How could she have been so wrong?

'Oh, Luke,' she said, her voice choking on his name. She reached for his hand, but he flinched and pulled it away.

And now, for the first time, he was losing his cool. It was as if he'd been able to keep everything perfectly together as long as he wasn't the subject of their conversation, but now that they were talking about him she could see that he could hardly bear to talk, all the loneliness and battered spirit that she'd imagined for Jude there in Luke's sad dark eyes. How can it be true, she thought miserably, that everything I've just been thinking and feeling and saying about Jude is really about you?

'I'd have gone to meet her myself,' he said, talking calmly enough but unable to keep his hand from gripping the edge of the table as he spoke, 'but she caught an earlier train and I wasn't home. So Jude went instead of me. She must have thought it was brilliant, she was going to see me a whole hour earlier than she'd thought she would.'

'I'm sorry,' Lucy repeated the same useless words.

'Thank you.' And then he looked back at her squarely in the eye. 'But the point of telling you this is to explain why Jude has to have his life back. I want him to stop feeling guilty whenever he sees me. I want him to be with you, if you'll make him happy, if you want him. I'm this awful, malevolent shadow, hanging over him, stopping him meeting someone, bringing them home. I want him to feel free to walk into the kitchen at Lipton St Lucy and introduce his new girlfriend to Mum and Dad and me. But he thinks he can't, not while I'm still half-dead with grief.'

'Did he say that?'

'Yes, his exact words, in the middle of a

fucking awful row last weekend.'

'And are you half-dead with grief?' she whispered.

'Don't ask me that.'

'I'm sorry,' Lucy said hastily, looking at his dark head as he bent to unfold his napkin and spread it slowly on his lap. Of course you are, she thought. I don't even need to ask. It's there in every word you say, every look you give me. It's there in your black eyes, in the way you flinch if I touch you, in the way you're so fiercely determined that your little brother should be freed of it, even if you can't be. And she thought of the lengths he was going to, to help Jude, and wished desperately that there was a way to help him too.

'And so you thought if you found me, delivered me back to Jude, that that would somehow make it all better?'

'Something like that,' he agreed. 'I want to prove to him that I mean it when I say I don't blame him and that I don't want him to suffer because of what I'm going through. It would be good for all of us if Jude, at least, was able to move on. And I think the fact that I've gone to all these lengths to find you will have an impact on him. It has to.'

'I do understand.'

'I'm sorry if I snapped at you then, but I'm not very good at talking about her.'

214

She looked away, and understood better than before how impossibly hard it had to be for Jude. 'And you really think it could work?'

Luke shifted in his chair, and then surprised her again with a smile. 'I wouldn't be here otherwise, would I? I think it would be wonderful. Honestly Lucy, more than anything you have to believe that he was completely bowled over by you. I think I had the full thirteen hours' worth of your conversation replayed back to me over the weekend in Oxfordshire.'

'Oh God, no.' She grimaced. 'Not all of it, please.'

'No.' He gave an embarrassed half-laugh. 'You're right. Perhaps not all of it. But what I'm trying to say is that you must know that this has come from Jude's heart. I want it to work for that reason more than all the others.'

'Any other reasons?'

He grinned. 'What, apart from the fact that he's never shown any taste before?'

'Oh, great,' she laughed. 'Sell him to me, why don't you?'

He shifted in his seat. 'Have you anything to lose? Is there someone in your life already?'

'No,' she said. 'Definitely not.'

'Thank God for that.' He stretched back in his chair. 'And thank you, too. I really didn't think you were going to stay.'

She laughed. 'Because you gave me the creeps, didn't you?'

'I don't think I'll ever forget it.'

'I'm sorry.'

He grinned back at her. 'You're forgiven, just.'

Inexplicably she found herself starting to blush.

'So,' she said brightly, twisting her napkin in her hands. 'When were you thinking I would see him again? I suppose he's back in Aberdeen now?'

'I've been wondering about that . . . '

'Oh no, not another plan?'

'Yes, another plan,' he said apologetically. 'Can you bear to hear it?'

But the smiley waitress was back at their table, explaining their choices. A half leg of roast lamb, rib of beef or roast chicken. Potatoes, fried or dauphinoise.

'I'm guessing you're not vegetarian?' Luke said, looking at her across the table, and she shook her head and smiled back at him, feeling suddenly a bit shy at the prospect of a whole meal with him, now that the reason for them to be there together was out of the way.

They ordered chicken and chips and another bottle of wine.

'Cheers,' Luke said, clunking his glass against hers when the waitress had left them

216

alone again. 'So, what are you doing the weekend after next?'

'Could I be meeting Jude?'

He nodded. 'My plan was that you should come to my mother's birthday party. Black tie, bit of music, bit of dancing, it will be big and noisy enough for you and Jude to get lost in it together. I think it would be perfect.'

Lucy took a great gulp of wine, feeling the kick of excitement course through her as she swallowed. The thought of seeing Jude again made her feel warm and jittery. But go to the party? Meet him with his family all around him? If it worked, Luke was right, it could be perfect. She could see herself in her pink dress, dancing with him cheek to cheek, him looking unbelievably gorgeous in black tie. But what if it was a disaster? Surely meeting him again amid a crowd of others would make it even worse?

'You could come down in the morning,' he said reading her thoughts. 'Lucy should come to Lipton St Lucy in the morning. Don't you think it's fate that you have the same name? That you're here with me now? That I'm bringing you home?'

She blushed, remembering the conversation she'd had with Jude about her name and the name of his village as they lay on the hotel bed together. But Luke didn't notice her discomfort. He leaned towards her, his eyes bright, his face that had once seemed so hard now alight and warm and full of enthusiasm. 'Don't you think it's perfect?'

'You are a romantic,' she said, looking away.

'About this I am,' he nodded, unabashed. 'I feel as if you were meant to come into our lives. In my head you've become our talisman.'

'No.' She shook her head. 'Too much pressure, Luke.'

'It's all right, I'm joking, sort of. If you and Jude don't work out, that's fine. I just want him to see you again. I want him to see I meant what I said.'

She nodded.

'So perhaps you should turn up at Lipton Hall in the morning before he arrives? Meet my mother and father, if you want to, and I'll be there, and as soon as Jude arrives at the house I'll talk to him, so that by the time you see him he'll understand that you haven't just turned up uninvited. Otherwise,' he frowned, 'I think he might give you a bit of a hard time.'

'Of course he would. He'd hate it. He'd think he was being stalked.'

'And he's stubborn, and he won't like

being set up, especially by me. But trust me, Lucy. It will all work out. Once he's realized why I found you for him, once he sees what a leap of faith you took, he will be so chuffed . . . It's the most flattering thing in the world. And then you could celebrate finding each other again, have fun, watch the fireworks.'

'Fireworks?'

'Fireworks. My father doesn't believe in doing things by halves.'

'It all sounds terribly grand. I'll be terrified.'

He smiled, realizing that, implicitly, she'd said that she would come. 'I'll look after you.'

And he would, too. She knew already that she could trust him to do that. But what about Luke himself? Wasn't all this the wrong way around? Shouldn't Jude have been looking after Luke? I'll tell him, she vowed. We'll work on Luke together. We'll find someone to make him happy again too.

'Jude will behave himself, you'll see.' Luke rolled the stem of his wineglass between his fingers, considering her. 'And if he doesn't . . . then he doesn't deserve you.'

'Thank you.' She laughed, awkward again, and she picked up her glass and downed the rest of the wine. No more, she told herself, immediately feeling it take effect. But then she looked back at him again, unable to resist. 'I have to ask, Luke. What sort of girls does he usually go for? Are they so different from me?'

'There have been a disproportionate number of blondes,' he said carefully. 'Tiny little blondes . . . and they're usually allergic to dogs. And they always have very long hair.'

'Personalities, Luke?'

'Not so far.'

'You're so disapproving. Do you tell him what you think of them?'

'If he asks.'

'What, marks out of ten? Look at the moustache, that one had a nose like a rabbit, that kind of thing?'

He stopped in surprise, his glass of wine half-way to his mouth. 'What did you say?'

'That one had a nose like a rabbit.'

He put down his glass. 'Which one did?'

'I don't know which one it was.'

'How do you know any of them did?'

'Just a guess.'

It was satisfying, in a reckless kind of a way, to see how far she'd thrown him. But even with the wine loosening her tongue she knew that she wouldn't go any further and that she shouldn't have said anything at all.

He let it go. What else could he do?

'I suppose we talk about a few of them.' He winced. 'And OK, I know it's incredibly

220

pompous to say and you must never tell Jude, but what I'm trying to tell you is that Jude's girls have always been of a type and they're nothing like you.'

And why did she care? Why was she so pleased to hear he thought her different?

'Food,' she said decisively. 'Where is the food? I have to eat.'

She turned away from him, searching the room for a waitress, and saw Teddy making his way towards their table. His face was pink with sweat and wet with rain, his hair and his suit soaking, and he was breathing hard, his eyes darting between Lucy and Luke.

'Whatever he says,' she hissed urgently to Luke, catching his sleeve, 'you must not believe him. Please.'

'Who?' he asked in surprise, then followed her gaze and saw.

'Hello, you two,' Teddy said with a tight, fixed smile, crouching down between them and wiping his face with his hand. 'I thought I'd find you here. I gave you a head start, Lucy, I've been hanging around outside. Sorry I'm a bit wet.' Then he held out his hand to Luke. 'Lucy didn't tell me your name. Pleased to meet you . . . ?'

'Luke,' Luke introduced himself, grasping the damp hand.

'And I'm Teddy. No doubt Lucy's told you

221

nothing about me at all.' He turned to her. 'Lucy, close your mouth. I can see all your food.'

Luke pushed himself back from the table.

'Who are you?' he demanded.

'How about I pull up a chair and explain?'

'No,' Lucy groaned.

Was this to be the pattern now? Teddy appearing like a spectre at the feast whenever she was with another man? And yet, at the same time, looking at him standing there blustering and soaking wet, seeing the wild look in his eye, she felt responsible, and miserable too, that he could be behaving like this because of her.

'Oh, I think I should explain.' Teddy turned back to Lucy. 'Because in all your excitement I think you might have forgotten to mention me.' He balanced his hands on their table, then looked up again at Luke. 'And I think Scottie here should know that while you two were busy driving off into the sunset together, I was lying in bed waiting for you in your flat, half out of my mind with worry. I'm Teddy,' he said, and his lips twitched at the shock on Luke's face, 'Lucy's boyfriend. At least, I was. I've probably scuppered my chances now.'

'Please, Teddy,' Lucy said desperately.

'Please what?' he demanded. 'Please go? Please don't make a scene? Please don't tip this glass of wine over his head?' He tapped it with a finger, making it sing. 'Please don't tell Luke here what an untrustworthy bitch he's having dinner with?'

And she heard what he said and realized just how much had finally changed after all. That although Teddy could threaten, and might indeed do just what he said, she could turn away from his words. She *had* cut loose and he couldn't get to her now. She was still concerned about the kind of scene he had in mind, embarrassed by the fact that Luke was watching it all, but it was not as it used to be. Now she could hold her ground.

She turned quickly to Luke, who hadn't moved a muscle. 'It's OK,' she told him calmly, 'it's OK. Let me deal with this.'

'If you can.'

And then she moved back to Teddy. 'What are you doing this for? Why are you here?'

'Because I'm a little pissed off, Lucy. Can't you tell? And I want you to leave your delicious dinner, and Luke here, and come with me now because I want to talk to you, and you refuse to talk to me, and this seems to be the only way to get your attention.' He waited, but she didn't move. 'And if you don't come with me now, I'm going to make even more of a scene.'

'Make a scene then. Tip the bottle over,

throw the chairs around. Get arrested. What good is that going to do?'

'It might make me feel better.'

And at that point Luke stood up, towering over Teddy who was still crouched down, level with Lucy. 'I want you to leave us alone,' he told Teddy. 'Up and out. Right now.'

And immediately Teddy rose to his feet too, turned to Luke, who was still a good head and shoulders taller, and defiantly clenched his fists, looking up at him aggressively. And Lucy could see it all playing out in front of her, the swinging punch from Luke that would send Teddy sprawling on to the table among the chicken and chips, wineglasses smashing, everyone starting to scream.

'Get out.' Luke said it calmly and with easy, quiet authority.

'I'll get out. But Lucy is coming with me.'

'No, she isn't. She's going to finish her meal.'

'Yes, I am, Luke,' Lucy interrupted softly. 'I have to go with Teddy.'

All the uncertainty and doubt that Teddy had sought to create was there suddenly on his face, and she hoped so badly that she'd be given another chance to explain.

'We've talked enough, haven't we?' she pleaded. 'I've said yes, completely yes. You know I'll do it.' She saw the hesitation still there. 'And I haven't misled you about anything at all, please believe me.' She turned away, reached for her coat.

She could see the waitress coming towards their table now, with a tray of food, knives and forks wrapped in white linen napkins, a fresh bottle of wine. How badly she wanted to stay with Luke and share their meal together. They'd had so little time. But now Luke was standing to meet the waitress, explaining that he wouldn't be staying either, reaching for his wallet.

Lucy slowly did up the buttons of her coat, and Teddy, knowing that he'd won for now, stood there quietly watching her.

'Will you be all right?' Luke asked, coming between her and Teddy and standing close beside her, full of concern. 'You're not frightened of him?'

'No.'

And so, reluctantly he stepped aside to let her go.

'Thank you, Luke,' she said. And she looked back at him one last time, as Teddy took her by the arm and steered her away then out through the doors and into the street.

'You humiliated me in there,' he said as soon as they reached the pavement outside.

'Made me look a fool.'

'You did that yourself when you came in to find me. And it was awful, Teddy!' She shook her arm free. 'How could you?'

'Because I thought I wanted you back. I thought I didn't want to lose you. I thought if I fought for you, you'd realize how much I cared.'

'You thought?' she said bitterly.

They were walking slowly down the street, going anywhere. She watched people hurrying along on either side, saw the pavement shining pinks and reds and golds from the lights of the passing restaurants and shops.

'And then, when I saw you in there, with him . . . ' Teddy gave her a tight smile, of relief and triumph. 'I realized how cheap and insignificant you are and that I didn't want you after all.'

'So why didn't you leave?'

'Because so far this has all been about you and what you want. And nothing at all about me. I thought it was time to redress the balance.' He stopped walking and turned to her, and Lucy saw something wild in his eyes and wondered if she'd been wrong to walk so freely out of the restaurant and away from the security of Luke.

She looked away from him and saw that the street, after being so crowded with people entering and leaving the restaurants around Meat, was now almost deserted.

'Our relationship only worked when I did exactly what I was told,' she said, trying to sound brave and firm. 'And now I can't be like that any more.'

In answer she felt his hands suddenly gripping her shoulders hard, felt herself being walked across the street and shoved up against a wall.

'And I am telling you not to speak to me like that!' he insisted, inches from her face.

'Let go of me, Teddy.'

'I am telling you to listen because I do not want *you*. Understand? Is it clear? I do not want *you*.'

He gripped her head in his hands, reached forward and kissed her hard on the mouth, then stopped, only inches from her face. 'Goodbye, Lucy.'

Lucy stood there, arms at her sides, looking at him, making no attempt to push past him and run away, still so calm, because she had almost known from the start that this was where everything between them had been heading, ever since their relationship had first begun. That there would be an end and that Teddy would desperately need to control it. And in a strange way she was glad to be confronting it at last.

'Is that all you wanted? Just to feel as if you'd won, this one last time?'

'Maybe.' He patted her cheek with his hand. 'This way I am not being tipped out of your flat into the rain at three-thirty in the morning. I am not being interrogated by Zoe. I am not being forced to talk to you via intercom because you're in such a hurry to reach that arsehole back there. Now, *I* am telling *you* how it is and *you* are standing here and finally *you* are listening. And when *I* am ready *I* will walk away.'

'You're crazy.'

'No, I'm not. Crazy would be wanting you back and I certainly don't. I probably won't even have to set eyes on you again — we didn't before.'

She would see him again, she knew she would. They'd probably find themselves sharing a lift together the very next morning. But she didn't care, she knew she could bear it, because after all that he'd said, she knew now it was finally over.

After he'd gone, she waited for a few moments more in the dark doorway and then moved back into the streetlight and looked around. She turned back the way she thought they'd come, unsure about how far they'd walked, wondering if she could see the entrance to Meat there in the distance and if

228

there was any chance at all that Luke would still be waiting for her.

As she walked hesitantly back, she realized that she and Teddy had not moved so far from the restaurant. She turned a corner and straight away she could see its glowing blue sign lighting the street. And there, standing beside the doorway, Luke was waiting for her, and even as she was telling herself she'd hardly got the right to do it, she was moving forward quickly, straight into his arms, and she let him hold her tight, closed her eyes to the warmth of his body against her cheek, feeling the relief wash through her and then the tears start to spill.

'I shouldn't have let you go.'

'No.' She shook her head, keeping it buried so that he couldn't see her cry. 'It was the best thing.'

'Poor Lucy. He didn't want to lose you, did he?'

She shook her head.

They stood there together for a few moments more and then she felt his arms loosen and he gently let her go.

12

The following evening, Lucy was sitting on the sofa in Jane's sitting-room with Jane's dog Pablo curled up beside her as she looked at Jane's photographs of the Lake District and worked her way through a bowl of pistachio nuts.

'Dolly the sheep,' said Jane, passing Lucy a photo of Dillon's mother, who was standing square on, feet planted firmly, giving the camera a glassy smile.

Lucy took it and studied it more closely. 'But look at her face. I think she's feeling nervous of you, Jane.' She meant it too — Dillon's mother's eyes were wary and the smile was trembling around the edges as she stood, in her bottle green Guernsey jumper and her tweed trousers, a light silk scarf knotted carefully around her neck. 'I expect you were being horrible.'

'Not all the time.'

'How much?'

Jane rubbed her face, looking just a little uncomfortable. 'Most of the time I was nice, but occasionally I got a bit irritable, I suppose. I know she thinks Dillon's getting a raw deal with me. No breakfast in bed on a Sunday morning, like she gives Robin. She was dying to do it for Dillon too, but couldn't quite bring herself to come into our bedroom with the tray. She asked me if I'd like to prepare one together one morning *for our boys.*'

'And you put her straight?'

'Of course.'

'Poor Dolly. Poor Dillon too. Why shouldn't he get breakfast in bed?'

'He can. He does, when I've not been told to do it by his mother.'

'Jane,' Lucy admonished. 'It was only a few days.'

'And most of the time I was very nice. Dillon never complained.'

'But you say they're so thoughtful and sweet to you.'

'They are — bought me a dustpan and brush for Christmas.'

Lucy moved on to the next picture, which was one of Dillon and Jane sitting together, arms round each other's shoulders.

'Look at the two of you! This is what matters.'

'Robin took that one.' She picked it up off the table. 'When we were having lunch the day we were coming back. It was freezing, but we all agreed we wanted to eat outside.'

231

And watching her face, listening to the wistful note in her voice, Lucy was so sad for Jane that she had to force herself not to touch her, not to say anything, because after so many years together her instincts were good, and she knew that at that precise moment Jane was holding herself together and did not want to break down.

She looked at the photo again, at the way Dillon was smiling at Jane with such pride in his face, such delight that she was standing next to him.

'I'm wound up about Australia,' Jane said defensively. 'We hardly talked about anything else. Robin and Dolly don't think we should go. But then, Robin's seventy-four and of course they don't want their only son moving across the world.' She gave a sad laugh. 'I don't think I want him to, either.'

'Three years isn't a lifetime.'

'But it is. This is me saying yes. I'm with him for the rest of my life.'

'And what's most bothering you most? Is it simply the fact you've never tried anyone else?'

'I know it's hard for you to understand,' Jane replied darkly. 'But I can see myself in a few years' time, married to Dillon. And I fear that one day I'd be really, really stupid . . . '

'That's the fear everyone has. What will we

be like in years ahead? Knowing you won't both feel the same as you do now, but hoping it'll be even better, not worse.'

'Stop talking about it then.' Jane leaped to her feet in agitation.

'Poor Jane.' Lucy looked up at her from the sofa and grabbed her hand. 'This is horrible for you, I know. And I'm trying to be helpful, being the voice of reason, but I understand what you mean. For God's sake, I don't know what I'm doing either, do I?'

Jane squeezed her hand and let it go. 'So will you go to his party?'

'I did tell Luke I would, but it would be easier if I knew what I was letting myself in for. If I was going somewhere I knew.'

'Luke's on your side.'

'Yes,' Lucy agreed. 'Of course. And I like him very much . . . and I trust him . . . I mean he's . . . ' She faltered, aware of the colour rising in her cheeks. 'I wouldn't go there without him.'

Jane looked at her sharply.

'What?' Lucy asked defiantly. 'I can say that can't I? It doesn't mean anything.'

'You tell me if it does.'

Lucy shook her head. 'Of course not, and stop smiling at me like that, Jane. Stop looking like you've got everything all worked out, because you haven't.'

'You like him, don't you?'

'No,' Lucy cried. 'Of course I don't.' She stopped for a moment. 'And if I thought I did, I'd have to bury it again, wouldn't I? What else could I do?'

'It depends what he wants.'

'Jane! Don't even go there. Don't tease me as if this is all one big game. It's not. It's so important that I get this right, for Jude and for Luke. I know just what Luke wants and it's certainly not me.' She paused. 'If I go to the party, it'll be to see Jude, not Luke.'

'Oh, bloody hell, Lucy.' Jane laughed, sliding an arm round her stiff frame, as Lucy sat hunched uncomfortably on the sofa. 'Teddy did turn up at the wrong moment!'

'And definitely don't mention him.' She pushed herself back on the on the sofa. 'I'm sure I imagined it. I'll see Luke again and I'll wonder what I was thinking about.'

'And if you do, we'll forget you said anything. But you do see you have to go? You do realize that, don't you? There's no question about it. You absolutely have to go to their party.'

'Don't you think I should know what I want to happen when I get there?'

'Nothing has to *happen*. You've agreed to see Jude, that's all. To *see* Jude,' she repeated. 'Not jump straight back into bed with him.

That's not the deal you made. From what Luke told you, all he needs is for you to be there.'

Lucy dropped her head in her hands. 'And am I allowed to say that perhaps I will still jump back into bed with Jude? That I'm still hoping if I see him again, I'll realize that's all I want to do.'

'Of course, because that would be the perfect happy ending, wouldn't it?'

Lucy stood up restlessly. 'Oh, Jane, what am I going to do?'

'You can come and talk to me while I get us some supper.'

Lucy followed Jane through into the back of the flat, where in daylight the kitchen looked out on to a pretty rectangle of lawn and terracotta pots. Jane reached behind the sink and dropped the blind, and Lucy went over to the scrubbed pine table pushed up against one wall and pulled out a chair, watching Jane pick out parmesan cheese and pancetta from the fridge, then put water on to boil for some pasta, then reach for a handful of fresh thyme from the windowsill.

Whatever Jane liked to think and to say, seeing her here, pottering around, moving to the cutlery drawer to find forks and spoons, reaching up into the cupboards to pull out a couple of plates, there was no doubt in Lucy's mind that Jane had to stay with Dillon. Not because cosy domesticity so suited her but because she was so clearly happy to be there with all the touches of Dillon about the room. His muddy trainers by the back door, a hooded sweatshirt laid across the back of one of the kitchen chairs which, instead of moving out of sight, she slipped on herself, rolling up the sleeves. Jane was happy, but she couldn't seem to see it for herself any more.

'We'll go and check out the house,' she said suddenly, spinning around, knife in hand and looking at Lucy as if it was the simplest idea in the world. 'We could go on Saturday. I love snooping around houses, and Pablo would like a nice country walk. We can look up Lipton St Lucy on the map and work out which one we think their house is. There can't be that many to choose from. It would be fun, wouldn't it? Let's go!'

'We can?'

'Of course!' Suddenly Jane was uplifted again. 'We're not exactly talking about an overnight flight to Australia. It's an hour away, two at most. We could find some lovely country pub for lunch.'

'Because, of course, darling, we only ever eat out.' Lucy laughed. 'Heaven forbid we buy some sandwiches and eat them in the car for a change.'

'Whatever. We could eat our sandwiches, walk Pablo, check out the house and come home. It would be so easy. Of course we have to go.'

'But they might see us. I've already stalked my way around their London house and got away with it. I can't imagine doing it again.'

'No one will know. And if Luke saw you? So what? Anyone would understand why you were there. It's huge, what he's asking you to do. And you're contemplating staying with them all on the strength of what, one brief conversation with him?'

'And thirteen hours and a shag with his brother.'

'Oh, yes. That too.' Jane laughed. 'So we'll wrap up in our Barbours and green wellies and we'll look just like everyone else. Put a big hat on and a scarf around your face and even if he does see you he won't know who you are.'

★   ★   ★

So the next day, Saturday, a week before the Middletons' party, with Lucy driving and Jane navigating, Pablo at her feet, they sailed out of London at about ten-thirty in the morning on a cold, windy, blue-skied day, accelerated over the Hammersmith flyover, exhilarated by the lack of traffic, and picked up the M40. Less than an hour later they were following the tiniest of undulating turnabout lanes that plunged and climbed through the Cotswold hills. And barely before Lucy had had time to feel panic-stricken at how close they were getting, they found themselves making their way down one final steep-sided lane, following a white-painted signpost to Lipton St Lucy, and then they were there, in the centre of a clutch of five or six tiny stone cottages and a church.

The road forked in front of them. Straight ahead it wound on up into the hills, and to the right it circled around an old stone war memorial. They pulled up beside it and Lucy turned off the engine and listened to the silence, wondering if their arrival had been noticed by anybody, but there was nobody in sight.

She looked towards the perfect, turreted church, following the line of the path that wound between great clipped boulders of yew towards the nave, where centuries-old lichen had splashed the dark stone creamy white. And then she looked at the cottages, with their stone mullioned windows and tiny front gardens, their thatched roofs bending almost to the ground, but even by the greatest stretch of imagination there was no way any of these could be Lipton Hall.

'But this has to be the right place,' said Jane, looking at the empty hills all round them.

'Then where is the house?' Lucy murmured back.

'And why are we whispering?' whispered Jane.

Lucy started the engine and backed the car until they could rejoin the road, but as they set off again it was clear that they had immediately left the village — more a hamlet — behind them, and that if Lipton Hall was in Lipton St Lucy, and Lucy was sure that Luke had said it was, then they had to have missed it. So they turned in the entrance to a field and made their way slowly back to the war memorial. And it was then that Jane noticed another lane branching off from the road just before they reached the cottages, with an old wooden signpost that said *Nether Lipton Gated Road*.

'This is where it'll be,' Jane said confidently.

'How do you know?'

'I can feel it in my fingers and in my toes.'

Lucy turned down the gated road and almost immediately, and unsurprisingly when she thought about it, they came to a closed gate.

'Do we drive through?'

Jane shook her head. 'No. This is where we start walking. The house will be somewhere down there and a gated road is a public right of way. Dogs, kids, ramblers, you can be sure they're used to people passing all the time. Lucy,' she insisted, seeing yet more doubt on Lucy's face. 'Stop it! You used to do that look with Teddy. You're coming with me now. This is what we planned, remember?'

Jane clipped Pablo on to his lead and they set off, side by side, their breath unfurling in the cold clean air. They opened and closed the first gate and walked on, and Lucy was aware that the wind had dropped and there was a silence and an absolute stillness all around them. She looked to her right, across empty meadows, recognizing the remains of the medieval ridges and furrows that meant, hundreds of years later, the field still rose and fell in deep, perfectly symmetrical ripples. And then she felt rather than heard Jane gasp beside her and she turned and looked to her left and saw that they'd found the house.

It sat behind tall cedars that spread out across its lawns, built of the same weathered gold stone as the village cottages, long and low and beautifully symmetrical, serene and dependable, as if nothing bad could ever have happened there.

'Oh, wow,' breathed Jane. 'Please marry him so that I can come and stay.'

'Listen!' Lucy said, laughing. 'Can you hear that?'

From an open upstairs window came a heavy drum and bass.

'Now I really like him,' Jane told Lucy with satisfaction.

'Please don't start dancing.' Lucy moved away.

Jane walked to catch her up. 'But that can't be Jude's music. He's not here, is he?'

'Perhaps it's Luke's?'

'Isn't Wagner more his style?'

Lucy laughed ruefully. 'I have sold him to you well, haven't I?'

'Perhaps it's the mother, dancing in her bedroom with a bottle of gin?'

'No! Don't say that. It was only the tiniest thing Jude said in the car. I'm sure she's great.'

'Very defensive, Lucy.' Jane caught her eye, teasing her. 'That's a good sign, it shows you're feeling very committed to the whole family.' She turned back to the house. 'And who wouldn't be, because that house is enchanting. Grade II at the very least, seven bedrooms, wouldn't you say?' She swung slowly around, looking out across the empty fields. 'And *idyllically* situated on the edge of the village, amid the most *wonderful* Cotswold countryside.' She looked back to Lucy. 'Price on application but definitely worth investigating further.'

Lucy walked on again, leaving Jane a few paces behind her. Jane's merry quips were not what she wanted to hear, because the truth was, seeing Lipton Hall had done just what Jane had thought it would do. It had made everything snap almost painfully vividly into life. As her eye followed the straight gravelled drive to the wide oak front door, she could picture it opening, Jude and Luke emerging amid a crowd of barking, excited dogs, talking and laughing, their voices carrying on the still air. She saw them walking to the end of the drive, then turning back expectantly to the house, waiting for someone else. And then she could see Gabriella appearing hesitantly in the doorway, long black hair tied back in a plait, huge Penelope Cruz eyes breaking into a smile at the sight of the two of them waiting for her.

How unbearably sad it was and how inadequate it made her feel, to think of the three of them together like that. She barely knew Luke, she'd almost forgotten Jude, and yet she was being fired into this wounded family having been given what was surely an impossible task. Luke, in his misery, could so

242

easily have misjudged Jude; what if he'd heard only what he wanted to hear?

She looked back to the house again, this time imagining how it would look at night, on the evening of the party, lights on in every room, shining out into the dark garden, a steady stream of cars winding their way up the drive, glamorous women emerging in silk and taffeta, the men handsome in black tie. Would she really ever find herself inside that house with them all, standing there in her pink dress, Jude beside her, his arm around her waist, steering her around the guests?

She turned away, walking past the house and towards the barns, built of the same old stone. There were stables with a row of horses looking out at them. She wondered if Jude could ride, and thought again how little she knew about him.

'How do you feel?' Jane demanded, catching her up and taking her arm. 'Does it make you want to face the music . . . disco or maybe a little bit of jazz? Perhaps they'll have a band?' She caught the woebegone expression on Lucy's face and squeezed her arm sympathetically. 'It doesn't, does it? It makes you want to run away and hide?'

'Because it's so daunting,' Lucy insisted. 'I look at their house and it makes me feel even worse.'

'You wimp.' Jane smiled at her.

'I know I am.' Lucy bowed her head.

'So call him.'

'What?' Lucy's head snapped back up again.

'Now. Tell Luke where you are. Tell him you need to talk to him. Sort out the details.'

'No, no. I couldn't.'

'You could.' She breathed in the cold air. 'Being here, seeing where you'll be coming back to. It's made it all real. You have to call him. You need to make plans. If he's in, you could talk about them now.' Jane reached into Lucy's pocket and pulled out her phone. 'Call him.'

'But I should know what I want to say.'

She took her phone and weighed it in her hand, feeling as if she was about to leap not so much off a diving board as off the side of a mountain. Beside her, Jane bent down and undid Pablo's lead and immediately he streaked off down the lane. Then she stood up again and looked at Lucy.

'Call him.'

'Walk with me for a moment first.'

They walked on, picking up speed and quickly leaving the house behind them.

'This began when you went into that Milestone Motel with Jude. And now you've got no choice but to see it through. And you're not scared, you're strong now. You want to know what happens if you don't walk away but you go inside — just like when you walked into the Milestone Motel.'

'You make it sound as if I have nothing to lose, but I do. Being here . . . ' Lucy opened her arms, stretching out towards the bare winter fields on either side. 'I can feel it. There's lots more going on that I know nothing about. I know I could hurt them and they could hurt me. It's not just a question of being daring or not. There'll be consequences.'

Jane suddenly stopped again. 'Call Luke now.'

'Don't make me.'

'It's like me and Dillon. Once the momentum starts to build you can't take time to decide what to do. You have to get on with it.'

'So have you decided what to do about Dillon?'

'Call Luke,' Jane said determinedly. 'And then I'll tell you about that.'

Just then, swinging around the corner towards them came a galloping black spaniel and two small boys on very big bikes, riding side by side, very fast, all three of them aiming directly at Lucy and Jane.

Lucy and Jane stopped abruptly in the

centre of the lane, no time to dive out of the
way, no time to do anything but stand and
pray and then, with a skid and a heart-
stopping wobble, both boys managed to
divide around them and then were gone,
cycling away, shrieking with laughter. Far, far
away, Lucy could make out a couple of
figures, could hear their cries on the muffled
air.

'Tom! Jack! You've gone too far! Come
back! Come back!'

Have you, Jane? she thought. *Can you
come back? And have I gone too far. Can I
come back now?* She put her hand in her
pocket and brought out her phone, searched
for his number, waited, bent around the
phone, then slowly turned and walked away
from Jane, back the way they'd come.

And Jane could tell from the way Lucy's
back suddenly straightened exactly the
moment that the phone had been answered
and she waited, anxiously, for about ten,
twenty more seconds, as Lucy walked further
and further away from her up the road,
picking up the pace so that for a moment
Jane had to wonder if she was being
abandoned there and then, if Lucy had even
remembered she was still with her.

And then Lucy's call was finished and she
was swinging around, her face alight.

'I think it's going to be fine.' She came running back to Jane. 'He was a little surprised that we were here, but pleased too. Now I'm so glad I called him.' Lucy paused. 'What's wrong? Why are you looking at me like that?'

Jane came forwards, took hold of her arm. 'You're all sparkling. I think you know exactly who you're coming back to see.'

'No, please don't tell me that. It's not true at all. I'm pleased he wants me back here, that's all. He's hurt and sad. He doesn't want anyone. Truly, I'm coming back for Jude. I am, I am.' She bit her lip. 'But he's insisting we come to the house ... now. So, you'll meet him, if you want to ... ' Lucy's enthusiasm slipped away as she took in the doubt on Jane's face. 'I told him you were here with me. Is it OK that I said yes?'

'He needs to see you, Lucy, not me.'

'No, both of us, of course!'

'But I'd be in the way.'

'You wouldn't be. Jane!' Lucy caught her arm. 'You being here with me makes all the difference. You being here made it happen. I'm only here because of you. You have to come too. Now that he knows we're outside his house, we don't really have any choice.'

Jane shook her head.

'What's the matter?'

'I'm thinking. Pablo's not had much of a walk. And I could do with some time to myself, and so could you two . . . I could come and find you later on.' Jane looked down at her feet. 'Do it my way, Lucy, please.' She turned and gave an ear-splitting whistle for Pablo, then walked away from Lucy, shoulders hunched.

Lucy jogged after her and slid her arm around her shoulders, pulling her to a halt.

'Are you all right? What's wrong?' Because Jane was suddenly crying, in great heaving sobs, and Lucy looked at her in alarm, then pulled her close and hugged her tight. 'Jane?'

'I don't understand what's made me cry. I was fine and then . . . '

'I don't understand.'

'I can't talk about it now. Luke's waiting for you.'

'He can wait.' Lucy shook her head, dropping the phone into her pocket. 'Are you crying about Dillon? Jesus, Jane. When were you going to tell me?'

'Today. Now. After we'd sorted this out.' She gave Lucy a wobbly smile. 'I told him last night. He's going to Australia without me.'

'Can you change your mind?'

She shook her head. 'I don't want to. And I was going to tell you about it in the car but then I couldn't. We were thinking about you

248

and being here . . . ' She turned away. 'I didn't want to talk about him.'

'But it's Dillon!' Lucy couldn't help herself crying at her, even as she knew it was the last thing Jane wanted to hear. She took hold of Jane's oilskin-clad arm, wanting to shake it. 'You believe leaving him's the only thing you can do. I was so worried that it would come to this, and now it has and it's so awful. Australia would have been your big adventure together. You were so lucky . . . '

'You really thought so, didn't you?'

'I still do.'

Jane stopped abruptly and stared hard at Lucy, her face set. 'Changing countries won't sort it out. I don't love him enough. How come you can't see that?'

They'd reached a second gate and she angrily wrenched it open and let it slam shut behind them, the metallic crash echoing out across the fields. Then she stopped. 'We're going the wrong way, aren't we? You're meant to be meeting Luke.' And she immediately turned round again, opened the gate and led them both back through, Lucy following quietly behind.

'He's definitely going without you?' Lucy said in a little voice as Jane again set off up the lane without her.

'Yes.'

'And Robin and Dolly?' She'd caught up again now, striding as fast as Jane. 'Has he told them yet?'

Jane shook her head.

'I'm so sorry,' Lucy said desperately. 'I'm so sorry I didn't realize how you really felt. That I didn't understand better and help you, because it must have been so hard.'

Jane finally slowed down and then she turned to her. 'You were telling me what you thought I should do. And I don't blame you for that. But look at my face and you'll see I'm OK, because you know what, I'm so *relieved*, Lucy, you have no idea. I could hardly bear to tell him but . . . ' she looked down at the ground, 'now I'm free, for better or worse.'

'Is he all right?'

'I think he will be. I don't think he was even that surprised.'

Lucy nodded, still wanting to cry out to her, *But it's so sad. Whatever you say to me, I still think you're wrong.* But she really knew Jane was right. She'd only been seeing what she wanted to see.

They walked silently down the lane towards Lipton Hall, only the sound of a lone crow cawing on the top of a telegraph pole breaking the peace, and all the time Lucy was waiting for the moment when Jane would

250

start to pour out her heart. She was so used to Jane talking to her about Dillon, telling her how she felt, asking her what she should do, involving Lucy in every detail of their lives together, that this silence between them felt horribly unfamiliar and awkward. And then she realized belatedly that this was how it was — that now, after all these years, there was nothing more to say.

'Isn't it silly? I only started to cry . . . ' Jane gave a big sniff, 'because you looked so happy.'

'Scared you mean!'

'No, you're happy.' She gave Lucy a smile. 'You know what you've got to do. And I'm better now.' She wiped her eyes again. 'Do I look awful?'

Lucy shook her head. The truth was that Jane's was one of those enviable faces that could cry and cry with barely a visible sign, her skin was just as pale, her eyes just as clear, no telltale blotches on her cheeks.

'Good,' she sniffed again, 'but I'm still going to walk for half an hour. Then I'll meet you.' She turned agitatedly and gave another whistle. 'Pablo!'

'I don't want to leave you now.'

Jane shook her head. 'Honestly, Lucy, I want you to.' Already she was sounding stronger, brighter. 'I need to have a walk on my own. Here is just the perfect place to do it. When I come back to the house to find you I'll be a different person, you'll see.'

'Where's your dog?'

'I'll find him.' She pointed back down the lane, smiling now. 'Go on, Lucy, before Luke comes looking for us. Back to the house now, back to the house, there's a good girl. Stop dithering,' she added sharply, when Lucy still didn't move. 'You know you want to go.'

Lucy nodded and turned away, and then she heard Jane cry out and spun round again to see that Pablo had finally appeared and was making his way proudly back across the field towards them with a cock pheasant in his mouth. The bird, alive but perhaps not so well, had one wing fluttering wildly as it fought to free itself from Pablo's jaws.

'Here, Pablo, here!' Jane yelled at him.

'Drop it,' Lucy commanded and Pablo abruptly changed direction and galloped up to her, then stopped at her feet, the pheasant jammed in his mouth, wagging his tail.

'Not me, you stupid fool of a dog! Go and give it to your mistress.'

'No, give it to her.' Jane shrank away. 'Sort it out Lucy.'

'Drop it!' Lucy commanded, striding over to him. 'Drop it, Pablo!'

'You're the vet. You've got to sort this out,

make the bird better,' Jane insisted.

Lucy grabbed Pablo by the muzzle and forced open his mouth, which only made Pablo adjust his grip and hang on harder, whereupon the bird set up a sustained flapping of its one free wing, making Jane shriek and leap away in fright.

Lucy moved towards Pablo again, who immediately leapt away, and then her heart stopped because there, coming down the road to meet them, was Luke.

She glanced quickly back at Jane. 'Get Pablo to drop the fucking bird. Luke's here.'

'But I daren't.' Jane practically wept at her. 'Luke's here.'

Lucy marched over to Pablo and jammed her fingers into his mouth, prising his jaws apart. 'Drop it, Pablo!'

The bird dropped limply to the ground and Pablo sat beside it, guarding it, ears cocked, watching it intently. Lucy could feel Luke at her shoulder and she turned to him first anxiously, then unable to stop herself smiling at the sight of him.

'Is this your dog?'

'No, it's hers.' She pointed an accusing finger at Jane, who immediately came forwards with an outstretched hand.

But for the moment Luke ignored her, picking up the pheasant and swiftly breaking its neck. As the pheasant set up a sustained flapping, Luke held out his other hand to Jane. 'Hello.'

Lucy watched Jane step warily around the beating wings and reach out and take hold of his hand.

'If you let your dog run loose,' he said, letting go to scratch Pablo behind the ears, 'that's what will happen. You should keep him on a lead at this time of year.'

'Yes, yes, of course,' Jane said, seriously. 'One less to shoot tomorrow, what a terrible shame.'

Luke laughed, then he turned back to Lucy. 'I was thinking about you. Isn't that strange?'

'I hope you don't mind we came this morning?' she asked him, not sure whether or not to kiss him hello, suddenly feeling very polite.

'Mind? No! I've been waiting for you to call, hoping that you'd call,' he corrected himself, 'hoping you were OK.' He seemed not to care in the slightest that Jane was standing beside them, listening to everything he said, but even so Jane turned and walked away, out of earshot.

'No more hassle from Teddy?'

She shook her head and smiled at him, suddenly relaxing. 'But I dream about the chicken and chips.'

'We'll Meat again, perhaps?' He stopped abruptly. 'I'm sorry, did I really say that?'

She laughed. Luke nodded over to where Jane had wandered, a few yards away, and was staring down at a brook that ran parallel to the lane.

'Is she all right?'

'You saw us?'

'I was in the lane. She was crying?'

'She'll be fine. She's better now.'

He called over to her. 'Jane, would you like some coffee? Why don't you come back to the house?'

Jane turned back to them, not coming forward, standing a little awkwardly. 'No, I think I'll walk Pablo, at least to the end of the lane.' She fished out the lead from her coat pocket and swung it in front of them. 'On the end of this, of course. Pablo,' she commanded, without a pause, 'over here!'

Eyeing the lead, Pablo slunk reluctantly over to her.

'I'll give you half an hour,' she told the dog. 'And that's it. It's too cold for any longer.' Then she turned back to them, gave Luke a grin and a wave. 'We think we worked out which is your house. I'll come and find you soon.'

13

Luke held out his hand. 'Come with me?'

'Sure,' she nodded, slipping her hand into his, and felt again that immediate connection with him, as if she'd woken up after years of being asleep.

They walked across an immaculately tidy yard towards a low stone building.

'Come and meet our old ladies.'

She raised her eyebrows at him questioningly, but she had a good idea what he meant.

'They're all in calf, not that any of them are due yet. That's why we're keeping them close by.'

She waited as he heaved open the door, still holding her hand. They went inside and he switched on a light and she stepped cautiously after him, to find herself in a warm dark space with low raftered ceilings, looking into the soft, liquid eyes of about forty Friesian cows.

But you're holding my hand was all she could think. *Surely you shouldn't be doing that.*

The cows were divided from Lucy and Luke by a low metal rail with diagonal struts that they could stick their heads through to reach their food on the other side, and they were knee-deep in golden straw, several of them lying down.

As Lucy and Luke entered the barn, a few of them turned away; most of them simply carried on slowly chewing and looking. To Lucy, they all seemed completely blissed out.

She moved forward cautiously.

'Let them sniff you,' Luke said quietly, finally dropping her hand. 'They won't bite.'

'No?' she whispered back. 'Really?'

She walked forward a few more paces, then slowly dropped on to her haunches and stretched out her hand to the nearest cow, who tossed her head and snorted at her warily and then stepped cautiously forwards, nudging at her sleeve with a very wet nose, back and forth, back and forth, before starting to lick the back of her hand with a scratchy and extremely long tongue. Lucy slowly reached up to rub the cow's broad forehead.

'Hey, Luke,' she said in a low voice, 'you know how to show a girl a good time.'

'Oh, you'd be surprised, Lucy Blue.' She looked up and saw that he was standing directly above her. 'Remember, please, that you were the one that called when I wasn't expecting you. I do have jobs to do here, you

257

know. I can't stop just because you decide to turn up on my doorstep.'

She smiled and stood up, wiped her hand on her jeans and looked around the barn. 'So is this what you do? You're a farmer?'

He shook his head. 'Kind of, but not really. Dad's the hands-on farmer here. He hopes I'll take it over one day, when he's about a hundred and ten and I'm eighty-six. But in the meantime I work in the same world, only more in theory than in practice.'

'Meaning?'

He came over to her and stood by Lucy's side as her new friend continued to reach for her sleeve.

'I'm an agronomist.'

'I'm so sorry.'

'Shut up,' he smiled. 'I work at Imperial College. I'm studying wheat, specifically the best sort of wheat to grow in Africa, where, as you know, they don't get enough rain.'

'That's wonderful. How come I didn't think to ask you that before?'

'Because we had other things on our minds, I suppose.'

She couldn't think how to reply, couldn't even turn away, and for a long moment it seemed neither could Luke.

'And you love it, presumably?' she said eventually. 'I'm thinking headhunting isn't perhaps so rewarding.'

'I love the travelling. I get to spend a few months of the year in Africa.'

'Everyone must miss you so much while you're away.' What on earth had compelled her to say that?

'Do you think so?' He sounded amused. 'I'm not sure all my family would agree with you.'

'No. Probably not,' she gave him an awkward smile, 'knowing what an *egotistical man* you are.'

She turned away from him self-consciously, looking around the barn. 'So, what needs doing around here? Shall I roll up my sleeves and get on with some examinations?'

His lips twitched just short of a smile. 'So you'd know how to do that, would you?'

'Can't be that hard.'

He walked behind her and vaulted easily over the low bars dividing them from the cows, landed gently and then walked slowly among them, slapping them gently on the rump to push them aside so that he could get a closer look. 'I'm not usually here at a weekend.' He glanced up at her. 'You and Jane were lucky to catch me.'

'That's not what we were setting out to do.'

He grinned back at her. 'Humour me, Lucy.'

'So, why are you here?'

'My parents are away so I said I'd come down, keep an eye on everything.'

'And that's what you're doing now, is it, casting an expert eye?'

'Don't sound so doubtful. I'm giving each of these cows a sound and thorough health check. I might look as if I'm not paying them much attention but that's not the case. Not that you'd know.'

'That's where you're wrong, actually, because I trained as a vet.'

She laughed at the startled expression on his face. 'So, just pass me an apron and a pair of wellies. When are this lot due? March? April?'

He came back to the rail and rested his arms on it, looking up at her with a smile. 'You're full of surprises, aren't you, Lucy Blue? If you're a vet, what are you doing headhunting in London?'

'Career change, but I like to think I could come back to all this again one day.'

Again she felt herself staring at him, felt herself move closer.

'There's another thing Jude didn't tell me about you.'

She stepped back again. Saying Jude's name was as if Luke had physically pushed her away. 'So,' he went on briskly, 'they're all looking good, wouldn't you agree? And now, if anything goes wrong on the night of the party, we'll know who to turn to.'

'Let's face it,' Lucy couldn't stop herself adding darkly, 'if there's trouble at the party, I don't think it'll be this lot causing it.'

He didn't answer, just climbed back over the rail then snapped off the lights, returning the barn to its wintry gloom, and she dropped under his arm and stepped outside.

'Lucy?'

'Yes?' She turned to him quickly but his face in the darkness was completely unreadable.

'You're definitely coming back? You still want to see this through?'

'What do you mean?' She stopped, feeling herself go light-headed and giddy. 'Are you saying you don't think I should any more?'

He shook his head. 'I want you to come back.' And then he stopped and added deliberately, 'For Jude.'

'Then I'll be there,' she told him. 'After all you've told me, everything you've done for me, for Jude, how could I be anywhere else?'

14

Clutching her overnight bag in one hand and a bunch of hyacinths in the other, Lucy staggered down the carriage, just about managing to keep on her feet as the train rocked and rolled its way towards Lipton St Lucy station and then, with a long, thin squeal of brakes, finally pulled to a halt.

She reached for the door of the carriage, opened it, then stopped, unable to make herself step down. She felt weak, wobbly and sick with nerves. Why was she here? How would she feel when she saw him again? And then almost as if someone behind her had impatiently shoved her forward, she found herself jumping down on to the platform.

Straight away she saw him, looking for her at the wrong end of the train. And she was completely unprepared for the sight of him. *Oh God*, she thought, watching him, watching for her, peering so hopefully, pushing back his dark hair impatiently, turning this way and that as he sought her out. *This isn't how it's supposed to be.*

For a moment she stopped, unable to walk forward because she wanted to run, throw her arms around him but eventually he turned in the right direction and saw her and then he stopped too, and waited as she walked stiffly towards him.

'Hi, Luke,' she said, and stretched up and gave him a quick peck on the cheek.

'For a moment then I thought you'd decided not to come after all.'

She shook her head, but just as she was about to step away from him again, he reached out for her, gathered her up in a great bear hug and pulled her hard against him, and she felt herself breathing in the warm scent of his body, felt her legs disappearing beneath her. It was as if now that she'd allowed herself to acknowledge how she felt she was giving free rein to her body to react as it wanted to.

'I thought you might have changed your mind.'

But I have. Oh God, I have.

He held her away from him. 'Nervous of seeing him again?'

'Yes.'

'Remember you're his *golden girl*.'

Remember why I am here.

She shook out her flowers. 'Look at these.'

'Oh, you shouldn't have done. Thank you.'

'You know they're not for you.'

'I suppose I guessed they weren't for me.'

He seemed high on her being there. But how could she know why? Perhaps it was just because, by the sheer force of his will, everyone and everything was finally fitting into place.

He took her arm, picked up her bags and pointed her towards the steps leading out of the station.

'Thanks for coming to pick me up,' she said, trying to match his mood, trying to sound happy and normal and unfazed. 'How's everything back home?'

'We're all OK. So far, Mum's only burst into tears once and Dad not at all.' She looked at him uncertainly, unsure whether or not he was joking.

When they reached the station car park he took her bag, dropped it in the boot and opened her door. And then they were leaving the station behind them, turning right into a little lane, immediately dropping over a humpbacked bridge and disappearing into a tunnel of leafless trees.

'How far to the house?'

'A few miles.'

She sat quietly, the hyacinths wrapped in pink tissue paper damp on her lap, watching his big hands on the steering-wheel. She looked at his face, the leanness of his cheeks, his high cheekbones, the way his dark wavy hair sprang up from his forehead and how his wide brown eyes with their thick dark fringe of lashes stared unblinkingly at the road ahead. At first she'd thought it was a hostile, angry face. She remembered thinking how unfair it was that Jude was so beautiful in comparison to Luke, but now she thought it was an inspiring face, full of strength and purpose. And she wondered again what the hell she was going to do.

She looked out of the windscreen at the frost-swept fields, so beautiful, cold and grey, imagining the great house waiting for her at the end of the journey. How on earth was Jude going to react to finding her in his house, waiting for him? Had she been crazy ever to believe there might have been enough between them to set up a future together?

'How long is Jude staying for? Did he say?' She had to say his name. She was aware of her foot tapping frantically against the floor of the car. She looked across at Luke, and watched his smile slip away.

'That depends if you give him something to stay on for . . . '

She flinched at the cold tone in his voice. 'I'll come up with something,' she said, biting her lip.

He stopped at a tiny T-junction, waited for a car to pass and then pulled out, taking them down another tiny, twisting lane, high hedges on either side. 'I'm sure you will.'

'What's the matter?' She turned to him in surprise. 'Why did you say it like that?'

'I didn't mean to say anything in any particular way.'

'Because this is exactly what you wanted, remember?' she said. 'You planned this. Now you're making me feel as if you wish I wasn't here.'

'Don't say that, Lucy. Stop thinking this is all about you.'

'I'm sorry, but I'm sick with nerves about seeing Jude again. I really want to get this right, for you and for me. And this is probably the last chance we get to talk before he arrives.'

Still he didn't reply, just drove silently, staring unblinking at the road ahead. And then she understood. And as soon as she'd thought it, she cursed herself for not taking a taxi and finding her own way to Lipton Hall, because of course this had to be the same way home that Jude and Gabriella had taken almost exactly a year earlier. No wonder Luke had gone so quiet. Perhaps they were driving the very same stretch where the accident had happened?

She glanced across to him, saw his hard face and thought how he had to be thinking about Gabriella, as he surely must do every time he drove this way. If only he hadn't been out walking when she had called. If only she hadn't caught the earlier train, it would have been him rather than Jude who had come to meet her. And the car that had met them so catastrophically would have safely passed by a good half-hour earlier.

And then, she thought, looking miserably down again at the bunch of hyacinths in her hands, it would have been Gabriella sitting beside him in the car, Gabriella he'd be bringing home for the party. She looked at him, imagining herself for just a moment in Gabriella's place, how it might feel to have him turn to her, his face happy, soft and loving. She imagined them laughing, talking non-stop, filling each other in on their time spent apart, Luke sliding his arm around her shoulders and pulling her close, and she saw how stupid she'd been to read something into their moment in the barn, how unlikely it was that Luke had been even remotely aware of how she was feeling then. A year, that was all it had been.

'He hasn't arrived yet. He said he'd be with us by lunchtime.'

'What?' She was startled to hear his voice.

'I'm saying you've got a little time to settle in.'

She nodded. *Good,* she was supposed to say, wasn't she? *How excited I am to be seeing Jude again.* But she couldn't bring herself to say it. The truth was that in the last few days, whenever she'd tried to remember what Jude looked like, she had hardly been able to bring his face to mind. 'Whatever happens, you will make sure you talk to him before I do?'

'Of course I will.' He paused, then heaved a giant sigh. 'Lucy, everything is going to be just great. At least, far better than you're expecting.'

'I'm so nervous I can hardly think straight.'

He nodded, misunderstanding. 'I tell you, Jude will be fine. More than fine, he'll be over the moon.'

They bounced over another bridge, climbed a hill, and mile upon mile of undulating Cotswold hills rippled out below them, as far as she could see. But then, immediately, they were plunging down again, the road twisting and weaving through more woods and bringing them out into a tiny village of heart-stoppingly sweet houses, all built of the same rich gingerbread-coloured stone. She saw a duck pond, the village church, signs for the school, and then they were out the other side, climbing again, meeting the same lane she'd driven down with Jane. Luke slowed down once more, indicated right, and they turned again, down a lane so narrow the car could barely slip between the high banks on either side, and she recognized the same little crossroads with the old stone war memorial in its centre. And her heart gave another giant leap as she realized that they had arrived. Luke turned right into the gated road, the gate open this time, and there, waiting for them, was Lipton Hall.

'It doesn't look real,' she said in a whisper, stunned at the sight of the house transformed for the party.

It had been one of the most beautiful houses she'd ever seen, and now it took her breath away. Great swathes of holly and tiny white fairy lights had been built into a spectacular arch around the old oak front door, and all around the garden the majestic clipped yew trees were also covered in lights that glittered and twinkled in the grey daylight and were only going to look better once darkness fell.

He nodded briefly, taking them over a stone bridge and into the drive that cut in a straight line between the smooth flat lawns to the front door of the house, but instead of parking there he drove them around to the back, pulling up between a Range Rover with blacked-out windows and a convertible Porsche with the roof down.

'You've got other people staying?'

He glanced across at her. 'One or two.'

'Friends of yours?'

'Sort of.' He shrugged.

Some of the surprise she felt must have shown, because he reached across and took her hand. 'I'm sorry this is so hard for you, Lucy. I know you think I'm completely certain about what I'm doing but I'm not. I'm sitting here too, wondering what the hell I was thinking bringing you here, to face everyone, believing that you, who hardly know us at all, can sort us out in just one night. But there's no going back, is there? We have to let it happen now.'

She nodded, taken aback by his admission, and sat there silently, aware of his eyes on her face, her hot sweaty palm pressed against his but not wanting to pull it away.

Then coming out through the door to meet them appeared two handsome black Labradors, bounding out towards the car in ecstatic welcome, and behind them a tall, stunning-looking woman, with long dark grey hair swept loosely up into a clip, wearing velvet slippers and a long white nightgown and hastily throwing a jewel-bright shawl around her shoulders.

'My mother,' Luke said, 'who evidently hasn't found time to get dressed.'

His mother, Suzie. Nothing like Lucy had imagined her to be. She came forward, opening the passenger door for Lucy. 'I'm Suzie,' she said, leaning in and giving Lucy a warm smile. She reached out a hand to help her out of the car and Lucy caught the wink of the largest diamond she'd ever seen.

Luke got out of the car too and Suzie turned to him. 'And before you say anything rude, someone's used up all the hot water.' She had a musical, tremulous voice. 'So I'm having to wait for the immersion heater to make me enough for a bath.'

Lucy went to hand her the flowers but had them knocked out of her hand as both dogs decided to jump up at her at the same time.

'How absolutely lovely of you,' Suzie said, pushing the dogs away with her foot. 'Get off them, Parson, get off them, Wiggins.' She picked the hyacinths up one by one, along with the various pieces of soggy pink tissue paper, then bunched them together again and sniffed deeply. 'How wonderful.'

'I'll take Lucy upstairs, show her where she's sleeping,' Luke said from the back of the car, where he was lifting out her bag. 'Then you can interrogate her properly.' He swung the bag over his shoulder and, without stopping to see if Lucy was following him,

271

strode into the house, the dogs following eagerly.

Suzie stared after her son.

'He's not told me anything about you at all,' she said, springing back to Lucy, her eyes now bright and warm. 'I didn't even know you were coming until this morning.'

'I'm sorry.'

'Heavens, I didn't mean it like that. I'm delighted.'

'Good.' Lucy grinned at her, relaxing for the first time since she'd left London.

'Have you known Luke long?'

'No.' She wanted to explain a little, but somehow guessed Luke wouldn't want her to . . .

'Mum!' Luke demanded through the open door. 'Stop that. Lucy, come inside.'

Suzie rolled her eyes at Lucy, and led the way through the kitchen door. Lucy followed her into the room and immediately caught the smell of something burning.

'Oh, Christ,' said Luke, seeing the look of alarm on Lucy's face and going straight to the Aga, where smoke was curling up around the edges of one of the half-opened ovens. He grabbed a tea-towel and pulled out a tray.

'Shit!' Suzie said, making Lucy laugh. 'Shit, shit, shit. I deliberately left the door open so I wouldn't forget them.' She took another towel and wrestled the tray out of Luke's hand, then took it over to the sink and shook it, releasing a shower of blackened crumbs.

Suzie turned, catching Lucy's eye, and grinned at her, sensing an ally. 'Croissants,' she explained. 'Would you like one?'

'I'm taking Lucy to her bedroom,' Luke insisted.

'Oh are you?'

But Luke was in no mood to be teased. 'If Lucy wants something to eat, she can brave it when I've shown her where she's sleeping,' he said sharply.

'Whatever you say, darling.' The fun had vanished from Suzie's face now. She walked over to the breadbin, turning her back on the two of them, lifted out a craggy rock of bread and silently started to cut a slice.

'We've got caterers for this evening, thank God. Never ever eat anything homemade here if you can possibly help it,' Luke told her as they left the kitchen. 'It's a golden rule.'

'Shhh, she'll hear you.'

'No, you don't understand. It's *her* golden rule.'

He led Lucy into a flagstone hall with an inglenook fireplace at one end, a fire already lit and burning brightly, throwing shadows around the dark beamed walls. Lucy barely had time to take it in before Luke disappeared again, leading her up an ancient oak staircase. They arrived at the top of the stairs and moved onto a wide landing with bare oak floorboards and a shining suit of armour standing guard at the far end, with a crown of silver tinsel and a dog lead hanging off one arm.

'This one goes for walks then, does he?' she laughed as they passed him by, but Luke immediately pulled the lead off and slung it around his neck instead.

Partly in response to his silence, she defiantly veered off course towards the windows and looked out. She could see across the garden towards the gated road where she and Jane had stood. She remembered being out there, looking in, and now she was inside looking out, and for the first time since she'd arrived she felt a tiny kernel of excitement growing deep inside her, and an inexplicable confidence that she was in the right place after all.

A moment later Luke came to stand beside her and they looked out together across the frosty fields, towards some dark woods and a hill in the distance with a tiny little church perched on top.

'You were horrid to her,' she told him, very, very aware of how close he was.

He looked sideways at her. 'It's how I am

with everyone. Haven't you realized that yet?'

She laughed nervously, aware of her heart thumping in her chest, and she leaned forward on the wide oak windowsill in front of her, staring out of the window again but this time taking in nothing at all. Then he touched her shoulder with his hand and she stopped, frozen, then turned so that she was facing him and, looking up at him, thought for one ridiculous, heart-stopping moment that he was going to kiss her.

'That church is very pretty,' he said, nodding towards the window. 'You should get Jude to take you to see it this afternoon.'

'But — ' she began, staring up at him stupidly. 'Luke?'

'What?' He let her go and stepped back from her.

She was going mad. Imagining all the time that he was about to kiss her, pull her into his arms, crush her against him, tell her how ridiculous it was to think she could have anything more to do with Jude.

She turned away. 'Will you show me my room?'

He nodded, then took her to the end of the landing, turned right into another smaller corridor with doors on both sides and opened the first to reveal her bedroom.

She followed him in, finding herself in a large square panelled room with dark red linen curtains and wide oak floorboards covered with rugs and with the same heavily beamed walls. Luke brushed past her and dropped her bag on to a huge white bed in the centre of the room.

'Bathroom's through there.' He nodded towards another doorway. 'I hope this will be all right for you. Prince Charming's next door, so I thought this would be the appropriate bedroom for you.'

It hurt, and she suspected it was meant to, too.

'Do you want to unpack? Have a wash? Hang up a dress?'

She sighed, then walked over to the bed and sat down.

Luke moved over to a cupboard in the wall. 'There'll be hangers here, somewhere.'

'Shall I come down with you again now?'

'No rush. Stay here, sort yourself out. I'll come and find you downstairs.'

Now he looked so tense she thought he'd ping if she touched him.

'Lucy?'

'Yes?'

'I don't want you to tell my mother what's going on.'

She slumped again. 'Oh, for God's sake, of course I won't.'

She jumped off the bed again, walked over to the window and found she was looking down to where they'd parked, to the three cars standing in a line just beside the kitchen door.

'As I said,' Luke said, watching her from the doorway, 'Jude's bound to be late.'

She didn't turn round.

'And as soon as he gets here, I'll talk to him, before he sees you. And then he can come and find you.'

And my role in all this will be over. Lucy almost heard him thinking it.

She didn't reply.

'You can find your own way down, can't you?' he said and when she didn't answer he quietly left the room.

15

After Luke had left the room, Lucy turned back to the bed and sat down heavily on it, imagining how it would feel to see Jude arriving, to look out of the window and watch his dark head emerging from the car. What would she say to him? How could she explain why she was there when she didn't know herself any more? She imagined the moment when he saw her, and then, after that moment, every possible outcome seemed awful. How likely was it that she'd take one look at him and fall for him once more, when the only person she could think about at all was Luke?

She should leave, she thought. She should avoid what was undoubtedly going to be an excruciating reunion. So what if her presence here proved something to Jude? She could do that *in absentia* — Luke could regale Jude with the whole exciting story of how he'd tracked her down and too bad she'd ended up making a dash for it before the final chapter. Suzie Middleton could act as witness. Yes, Luke had indeed picked her up from the station and brought her here. And then all the Middletons could live happily ever after ... And Lucy could go back to London, forget about them all. All of them but Luke.

Luke, Luke, Luke. She closed her eyes and breathed out his name. How had he managed to take over her thoughts so completely? When had it begun? You were aware of him right from the start, the voice answered in her head. It began right back to the very first time you laid eyes on him, when you dropped Jude home, but you're only facing up to it now.

At this thought, such crushing despondency overwhelmed her that she flopped back on the bed and covered her eyes with her hands. Nothing like this had ever happened to her before. She'd always despised people who talked of unrequited love. What was the point, she'd asked, not understanding until now that that had nothing to do with it. But now she did understand. She understood that she would stay, see the evening through, simply because being near Luke was better than being away from him. To go through the awfulness of her reunion with Jude was a price worth paying if it meant staying close to Luke, even though she knew that all Luke wanted her to do was fall into his brother's arms, not his own.

She went to her bag and got out the pale

pink dress that she'd worn to the party in Inverness. The only dress she could have chosen for this night, unblemished and still lovely despite having been rolled up in her bag for hours. She wondered if Jude would remember her describing it as they'd lain together on the bed in the Milestone Motel, remember what he'd said about undoing the non-existent buttons. She remembered how she'd kissed him, how exciting it had been to be with him then. Perhaps . . . was there any chance that to see him was all she needed to make her fall for him again? Was there any possibility at all that everything she thought she was feeling for Luke was bound up in the confusion and uncertainty of being here, and in her fear of how Jude was going to react when he saw her again?

She took the dress over to the cupboard, feeling the soft, stretchy fabric heavy in her hands. She hung it up and immediately it slithered off the hanger and fell to the floor — very symbolic, she thought, picking it up, looking at how the sequins shone softly in the light. She hung it up a second time and shut the door on it.

She left the bedroom, heading for the staircase that would take her back downstairs, then changed her mind and followed the landing in the opposite direction instead, wandering down the long corridor, looking through the windows as she went.

At the far end was a huge planter of white hyacinths, sitting on a very beautiful little table that looked at least five hundred years old. She walked over and touched the stiff flowers, breathing in the sweet, heady scent and thinking how they put her own meagre bunch to shame. Then she walked on again, randomly turning left through an open archway and into another long hall, more rooms to the right and the left. It was a huge house, she was beginning to realize, wondering how she would ever find her way back to the kitchen.

Now she came to a heavy velvet curtain, dark red and trimmed with tiny embroidered birds, all different colours, and with beaks of silver thread. She pushed her way through and wandered on, past a rusting watering can sitting incongruously beside a bedroom door, and peeped around the corner to see a lion skin spread out across the floor.

'It jumps up at you when you go through the door,' a voice said at her shoulder.

Lucy spun around to find a girl standing close behind her, with fluffy blonde hair and wrapped in a fluffy white towel, holding a hair-dryer and looking at her with unabashed interest. 'There's a hot-air vent under the floorboards that switches on and off automatically. It absolutely terrified me the first time, but there, I've warned you now.' The girl stuck out a hand. 'I'm Sophia,' she said with a flash of white teeth. 'And I'm guessing you're probably Lucy?'

'Hello.' Lucy smiled, rather disconcerted that she should be known by name. 'I'm sorry. Is this your bedroom?'

'Absolutely not. I wouldn't sleep in there if they paid me.' The girl, Sophia, adjusted her towel and Lucy looked down at her bare feet. 'I've just been having a bath, getting hot water before everybody else uses it up. There's never enough in this house. If you're wanting to have one too, make sure you get it in early.'

'Thanks for the tip.'

Sophia stared at her again, not hostile but not particularly friendly either. 'Why don't you come and talk to me while I get dressed?'

It was more an order than a question and, without waiting, Sophia set off down the corridor. Lucy followed her rather uncertainly, trying to get over the surprise of finding her there, telling herself it was a huge house, probably stuffed full of pretty girl guests wandering around in towels, all with bleached blonde hair and spectacular tans. She guessed she should be thinking how nice it was to meet one of them.

She followed Sophia into another gigantic bedroom and the girl skipped across to her unmade bed and leapt up on it.

'So . . . I know your name but that's all,' she said to Lucy, who was still standing rather awkwardly in the doorway. 'Luke is being very secretive about you.'

Lucy laughed warily. 'God knows why.'

'I have to be honest, I'm *dying* to know why!' Sophia exclaimed. 'He wouldn't even let me come to the station with him to pick you up. He told me to stay here and wash my hair.' She rubbed at her wet hair. 'Which was perfectly clean as it was. He can be such a bossy, can't he? But I always find I do what he says.'

Lucy nodded uncertainly.

'Still, I've found you now.' She winked at Lucy. 'So, spill. Who are you? Why couldn't I come and pick you up?'

Lucy didn't want to be rude. God knows, she could do with making a friend before the party, but this girl was so inquisitive and in-your-face. 'Probably because he's only got two seats in his car?' she ventured.

'Oh yes, I forgot that.' Sophia paused, then immediately came back at Lucy again. 'But it still doesn't explain who you are. I'm a very old friend of the Middletons and I've never heard of you. And I went through the guest list a couple of weeks ago with Suzie, checking to see who hadn't replied, and you weren't even on it.'

She tucked her feet under her and sat cross-legged on the bed, looking at Lucy expectantly.

'I'm a last-minute addition,' Lucy replied, knowing she sounded defensive. 'That's allowed, isn't it?'

'I suppose,' Sophia said. 'But I think I'll keep an eye on you, all the same.'

How could she respond to that? Lucy watched the girl slip back off the bed and walk over to her chest of drawers, the top of which was completely hidden by various pots and potions. She picked up a bottle of body lotion and tipped some out on to her hand, then let her towel drop to the floor, leaving her completely naked, and began to rub cream into her thin arms and legs.

So who did she have her eye on? Lucy wondered. Was it Luke or Jude?

'You know,' Sophia said, turning back to her, completely unbothered by her nudity, 'I just can't decide what to wear.' She put the lotion back on to the chest of drawers and wandered over to a cupboard, taking out an armful of coat-hangers and cellophane.

'Jeans, perhaps?' Lucy suggested. 'Something warm?'

'No, I mean tonight. I've brought three.' She rolled her eyes as if to say what a pain it was, having so many lovely clothes, then held the cellophaned bundle out in front of her, not that Lucy could see anything. She imagined tiny, wispy, backless, frontless dresses, looked again at the girl's long blonde hair and decided she was probably after Jude.

'Perhaps you should wear all of them, one on top of the other?'

'Oh, don't be silly.' Irritably, Sophia disappeared back inside the cupboard again.

Lucy gritted her teeth. 'I'm sorry,' she said. 'It's just that Luke's waiting for me downstairs. He'll be wondering where I am.'

'You hope,' said Sophia from inside the cupboard, and then she looked around the side of the door, eyes bright with mischief. 'Yes? You do realize there's no point lusting after him?'

'I don't lust after him.'

'Of course you do. Everyone does.'

Why was she blushing? And in front of this dreadful girl who'd now come out of the cupboard and was looking at her almost pityingly.

'No, I'm here with Jude,' Lucy said impulsively, regretting it immediately.

'You're not!' Sophia was hanging on to the cupboard door. 'Please don't tell me that!'

'I'm sorry,' Lucy said hesitantly, wishing very much that she hadn't.

'And that's why Luke thinks you should be downstairs, because Jude's about to arrive, isn't he?'

'That's right.'

Sophia saw the distraction in Lucy's eyes, the clear desire to get out of the room.

'Please?' she begged. 'Stay for just a second?' And before Lucy could respond she dived back into the cupboard, pulled out a pair of jeans, knickers and a T-shirt and kicked some boots out on to the floor with her foot. 'Tell me more.' She hopped on one leg as she pulled on the knickers. 'Because I have to know . . . Are you serious? You know you're nothing like his usual girls, nothing like me! And take that as a compliment. Oh Lucy!' Abruptly she sat down on the bed and looked her in the eye. 'There's no point me pretending. I'm gutted.' She laughed at herself sadly. 'I thought this weekend I could have been in with a chance. He's been away so bloody long — I haven't seen him for almost a year.'

She made Lucy feel more awkward than she could bear. *Have him*, she wanted to cry. *I don't care.* And she was tempted to tell

Sophia the truth, that Jude didn't even know she was going to be there. That she was a fraud, that the whole undertaking was a complete sham. But loyalty to Luke and a dogged determination to see it through, at least for a few hours more, gave her strength. Sophia, sweetly honest as she was turning out to be, would have to be hurt.

'I met him at New Year.'

'At a party?' Sophia had stopped trying to dress and was hanging over the top of the cupboard door again.

'Something like that.'

'So, *is* it serious?'

'No.'

'Serious enough for you to be here now, though. You must be so excited about seeing him again!' Sophia gazed at her with big sad eyes and Lucy thought what a masochist she was. And yet how she'd been in similar situations herself, when every question is agony and yet not knowing is even worse.

'I don't suppose you understand the significance of all this . . . ' Sophia went on. 'Last year, it was terrible.'

'Yes, I know.'

'But clearly Jude's feeling better. And I suppose, because, buried somewhere, I do truly have his best interests at heart, I have to say that's good news. Oh God,' she sighed theatrically, 'I don't mean it at all.'

'I'm sorry,' Lucy said weakly, wishing she was anywhere else, but Sophia hadn't finished with her yet.

'Luke? Luke?' she suddenly shrieked, looking over Lucy's shoulder towards the doorway. 'Is that you?'

Immediately alarm swept through Lucy and she spun around to see that yes, Luke was walking down the hallway towards them. He peered in through the bedroom door and shielded his eyes at the sight of Sophia.

'Luke, get out of the room!' Sophia said immediately, walking away from the cupboard to ensure he got a good look. 'Can't you see I'm practically naked?' Luke stepped back again, so that he was standing shoulder to shoulder with Lucy.

'Don't do that in front of my father,' he told Sophia, 'or he'll have a heart attack.'

'Of course he wouldn't. He'd love it.' She reached for the towel and pulled it back around her body. 'There. You can take your hand away from your face now.'

'I was just going downstairs,' Lucy said.

'And I was just saying she had to stay and talk to me.' Sophia looked from Lucy back to Luke. 'I was saying she wasn't allowed to leave the room until she told me *all* about

Jude. I can't believe you, Luke. Why didn't you say?'

The smile was wiped from Luke's face. 'You two have been making friends fast,' he said.

'Lucy was just saying how excited she is about seeing him again. She's spent the whole time watching out of the window to see if he's arrived yet.'

Still standing close beside him, Lucy looked at Luke for the first time. 'I was actually saying that I needed to get downstairs because you'd be wondering where I was.' She could hear the defensiveness in her voice.

'But Jude's not arrived yet, has he?' Sophia said immediately. 'I'm sure we'd have heard the car.' She walked across the room to her window.

'No. Sorry, Lucy, no sign of him yet.'

Now she couldn't bear to look at Luke. What must he be thinking? That she'd tossed out the information like a bit of gossip that didn't matter to her at all? That she'd callously been passing titbits of her time with Jude to the one person who wouldn't want to hear?

She shrank back from the doorway and immediately Sophia came across the room and put her arms around Luke's shoulders.

'I'm making a great effort to be pleased for both of them. You are pleased for him, aren't you, Luke?' she asked, staring up into his eyes. 'You do see that it's great he's met someone? One of the Middleton boys has to be snuggled up with someone tonight, after all.'

'How do you know it couldn't be me?'

Lucy froze.

'Is that an invitation?' Sophia laughed, arms still draped around his shoulders. 'You know I'll be free.'

And Luke was smiling back at her.

'Lucy,' Sophia whispered, not breaking the gaze she was still holding with Luke. 'Would you mind? I think I need a private word with this lovely man.'

From being so impatient to go, now Lucy felt weighted to the floor. *Please, Luke,* Lucy begged him silently, *just say no. Tell her you want me to stay. Tell her that you badly want me to stay.*

Instead, Luke walked out of Sophia's reach, made his way across the room and sat down in an armchair by the window. Then he turned to Lucy. 'Why don't you go downstairs and find Mum?' he said dismissively. 'I'm sure she said she needed some help with the flowers.'

Lucy stared back at him, terribly hurt.

'That's a good idea, Lucy,' Sophia said encouragingly, verbally shooing her out of the room. 'Luke and I will come and find you soon.'

'Perfect,' Lucy said. 'I'll see you down-stairs.'

She stalked out of the door and off down the hall and heard the bedroom door close behind her. Fine, you fuck-wit, she thought savagely. Shag her for all I care, if you're not quite so *half dead with grief* after all. She found herself in front of the red velvet curtain again and ripped it aside, furiously trying to think which was the way back to her fucking bedroom. Damn it, why did people have to live in such stupidly huge houses? She didn't want to be wandering around these endless corridors, she wanted to find her bedroom so that she could close the door and bang her head against the wall in private.

She turned around and walked backwards, trying to see everything as she had done when she'd first walked in. But it didn't help. She turned round a second time, opened another door at random, turned a corner and found herself in a pale blue drawing-room, still and quiet, with a desk in one corner looking out over the garden and long windows looking out into the gardens. At least there was a staircase at the far end that would take her downstairs.

She started to move towards it but then realized that she couldn't face the thought of Suzie Middleton. She didn't want to talk to anybody, she wanted to sit on her own and think. She went over to one of the pale blue silk-covered sofas, sat down, put her hands on her knees and looked down at the floor.

She sat there for a few moments until the pain in her heart subsided and was replaced with sick determination not to let Luke, Jude or Sophia get to her any more. She would complete her task, and whether she ever saw Jude again after the night ahead didn't matter. This evening she was going to forget about Sophia, she was damned well going to kiss Jude right in front of the pair of them. Show Luke that he was just as invisible to her as she was to him.

She heard footsteps ringing out across the wooden floor, and looked up to see Luke. He sat down opposite her, stretched out his long frame and smiled. 'What were you doing in there?'

'I got lost,' she said. 'I was trying to find my way downstairs and I bumped into her. Would you mind showing me the way down? I was going to help your mother do the flowers, wasn't I?'

'I mean, what on earth were you saying?' Luke didn't move. 'I thought that was supposed to be our secret?'

'I'm sorry. It just burst out of me.'

'Yes, Sophia can have that effect on some people.'

'But not on you?'

'No, rarely on me.' He grinned. 'But I suppose it can't matter too much. She'll get over him. And you mustn't worry about Sophia, she's a drama queen. She'll have forgotten him by tomorrow.'

Lucy nodded.

'I didn't expect her to find you so fast.' He was looking more gently at her now. 'I should have warned you she was hunting you down.'

'I suppose I should have kept to my quarters.'

'Out of harm's way.' He ran a hand through his hair. 'Sophia was explaining to me how it was time I moved on.'

'With her?'

'I could do worse. If you're with Jude, perhaps I should help her drown her sorrows.'

'Depends what you're looking for.'

'Everyone keeps telling me I should be having fun. If everyone else is having such a good time, perhaps I should be trying to do the same.'

'Then I expect Sophia's your girl.'

He leaned closer. 'But I'm not looking for fun.'

She stared at him and saw the soft, sad look on his face, and suddenly he was rising up out of the chair, taking two steps towards her.

'Lucy,' he said urgently. 'He's my brother. After all we've done and everything he said to me, you can't dismiss him before you've even seen him again. Remember how it was between the two of you last time you met. How do you know it's not going to be like that again?'

And at that moment Suzie called up the stairs. 'He's here, he's here!'

Suddenly dogs were barking, doors were slamming, there was the sound of feet running across the hall below them.

'Luke!' Suzie shouted urgently up the stairs. 'He's here, for God's sake come down.'

'Does she know?' Lucy asked in surprise.

'Some of it, just a little.' He turned back to her. 'I'm going to talk to him, warn him that you're here.' He leaned forward and kissed her briefly, chastely, on one cheek. 'OK?'

Then he was gone, and she could hear him running down the stairs. She walked to the window and saw a taxi pulling up outside the front door, and her heart was beating, beating, beating, waiting for the moment when she would see him again.

But there, instead of Jude, was a sweet-faced, grey-haired old lady, climbing carefully out of the back of the taxi as Suzie came running around the side of the house, exclaiming, 'Felicity! It's you? Why didn't you call us from the station? Someone would have picked you up!'

On shaky legs Lucy returned to her chair, hoping Luke would come back for her. And she waited for long enough to know that he wouldn't.

★ ★ ★

Back in the kitchen she found Suzie and Luke chattering rapidly.

'Darling,' Suzie said as she saw Lucy arrive. 'Come and have a coffee.'

'And darling,' she turned to Luke, laying her hands on his shoulders, 'go and help the Butler and Rodd men bring in the wine. They insist they can do it themselves but there must be twenty cases.' She smiled at him, adding in a stage whisper, 'They look really old. I don't think they'll manage on their own.'

'Sure,' said Luke, glancing uncertainly across to Lucy.

'Don't you worry, Lucy can look after

herself,' said his mother briskly. 'Take the white down to the cellars, it's cold enough down there, but leave the red in the dining-room. Stack it up below the window. And you could put all the extra champagne in the cold room.'

Suzie waited until Luke had shut the kitchen door behind him and then turned back to Lucy. 'And you can help me finish the flowers.'

She clearly wanted to talk to Lucy alone. She led her out of the kitchen, through the hall, gliding ahead of her like a ghost, still dressed only in the long white nightgown. She took them out of the house, along a little cloister, and then through a door at the far end that opened into a wonderful, long rectangular room with angels painted on the ceiling, and floor to ceiling windows running all down one side.

'Wow,' said Lucy, looking around. She turned to Suzie and raised her eyebrows. 'The ballroom?'

'Yes.' Suzie smiled. 'Isn't it a waste? We only use it about once a year.'

'For parties?'

'We used to, yes, lots of lovely parties. We've had one every New Year for the past twenty years. But,' she put her hands up to her cheeks, and closed her eyes, 'not this year.

Not after Jude's accident.' She opened her eyes again. 'And now look at us, three weeks after New Year and what are we doing, we're having a party. I wouldn't have agreed to it but James absolutely insisted. I don't know why. I'm going to be fifty-four, for God's sake. Since when has that been cause for celebration?' She drew her hands slowly down her face and let them fall to her sides. 'Yes, if I'm honest, I like the chance to have my two boys home again and I like decorating the house and I enjoy choosing the flowers and the food.' She shook her head. 'But guests? And dancing? Alcohol and merriment? I certainly don't think I want any of that. I think how absolutely awful of us to be having a party on what's practically the anniversary of Gabriella's death. I'm looking around at all of us today and I can't help thinking what on earth are we doing? It feels so horrible, as if it happened yesterday.'

'Perhaps a party at this time of year is a good way to remember her,' Lucy ventured. 'You're all together. You're talking about her . . . '

Suzie shook her head. 'James doesn't talk about her at all, of course. And he absolutely adored her. Thought she was the prettiest girl he'd ever seen. Luke talks about her a lot. And Jude shouts about her, when he's feeling particularly angry with the rest of us.'

'Oh,' said Lucy, flinching at Jude's name, then added clumsily, 'I haven't met James yet.'

'You will. He'll be in soon. He's around the farm but I know he'll be wanting to get back for Jude. Because do you know, last year Jude came home the grand total of *once*, for Sunday lunch, didn't even stay the night. But we've done better with him this year, New Year, and now here he is again.' She smiled briskly, moving across towards the far end of the room. 'One good reason for having a party. We tempt Jude home.'

Lucy followed her to the far end of the room, where the wall was entirely taken up by a huge mirror, painted white and very plain, but with armfuls of pine and holly lying on the ground beneath it.

'I'm worried about seeing him again too, you know,' Suzie said unexpectedly, taking a chair and carrying it over towards one of the windows. 'We had such a bloody awful row the last time.' She stood up on the chair and reached along the curtain pole to pull down the remains of a yellow balloon tied to a piece of dirty, cobwebby string. She climbed down again and carried the chair back to the side of the room.

'He can't see that by behaving as he does,

he makes it so much worse for everyone else, especially Luke.' She looked at the balloon distastefully. 'I think we had these at Luke's twenty-first. So, why are you nervous about seeing Jude again? Has he been beastly to you, too?'

'No,' Lucy said, 'not at all. It's just . . . ' She paused, wondering whether Luke would mind her saying so, but unable to resist Suzie's interest. 'I'm here to see him, but he doesn't know it yet.'

'Oh, bugger,' said Suzie, crumpling slightly. 'And there I was thinking you were here with Luke.'

'Oh no,' Lucy said defensively. 'Not at all.'

'I thought it was too good to be true. And, to be honest, Luke did insist that you weren't.'

'I'm sorry,' Lucy said sadly.

'Can't be helped. And I must say I wondered how much longer Jude could last without a girlfriend.' She stopped. 'Now that sounded very rude, didn't it? What I mean is he's not a loner, Jude. He doesn't much like his own company, he needs to be the centre of attention.' She stopped again. 'Now, that was rather rude of me too, doesn't make him sound very nice at all. And of course he is. Terribly nice.' She shook her head. 'Ignore me. I should keep quiet. *You* can talk to *me* while we finish these wretched flowers.'

Lucy had imagined fresh flowers, to be artfully plonked into vases around the windowsills, but instead Suzie led her across to a couple of cardboard boxes. Lucy bent down, lifted the lid of one of them and peered curiously inside. Then she dipped in her hand and carefully brought out a flower with the wonderful loose floppy petals of a peony, on a long string with many, many others. They were all different colours, some pale olive green, others a dark crimson, the one in her hand a beautiful dark violet, all made out of some sort of stiffened linen and wire, and at their centre was a tiny lightbulb in the shape of a seed pearl.

'Where did you get them?' Lucy said, wonderingly, touching one of the centre petals with her finger, seeing how they had been stiffened to keep the flower in shape. 'They're so beautiful.'

'I made them.' Suzie emptied the box on to the floor, gathering the long strings of flowers up in her arms and taking them over to the mirror. 'There are a hundred and fifteen.'

'How long did it take you?'

'Years,' Suzie laughed. 'I began when I was pregnant with Luke. But the most difficult part was finding someone who could put the bulbs in and get the lights to work. I ended up discovering a place in Shrewsbury.' She turned to Lucy. 'So now they can flash, dazzle or twinkle depending on your fancy.'

They worked quickly together, Lucy lifting and holding the branches of pine and Suzie artfully twisting and tying them on to the mirror, then together they picked up the armfuls of flowers and began to arrange them among the pine branches.

And suddenly Suzie started to talk about Gabriella again, the words beginning hesitantly and then picking up speed until they began to pour out of her, running away with themselves, and although Lucy knew that she had to have said it all before, could sense that she was the type of woman who talked easily and openly and who would undoubtedly have had many friends prepared to listen, still it was as if she was saying every word for the first time. And as if, in the year that had passed, the agony of that night had hardly lessened for her any more than it had for Luke or Jude.

She said how she couldn't breathe the smell of wood-smoke without thinking about that day. How she couldn't bear to hear church bells, because they had been ringing as the police car turned into the drive. She described the slow agonizing seconds when she'd first registered the awful fact that Jude was nowhere to be seen, how Luke had answered the door.

And then she told Lucy how, when Luke had heard what had happened, he'd turned back to Suzie and James. And seeing Luke's face, at first Suzie had thought Jude was dead. So that when he'd said Gabriella's name she'd felt such a wave of sick, guilty relief that she had had to turn away so that Luke couldn't see her face.

'What about Jude?' Lucy whispered.

'He wasn't hurt, although he'd have preferred it if he had been. It wasn't his fault at all, but of course that doesn't make the slightest bit of difference.'

As she spoke, Suzie bent to pick up one of the last branches of pine and then seemed to give up on it. She let her knees give way and sat down heavily on the floor. And Lucy silently dropped down too, so that they were both sitting facing each other, cross-legged, surrounded by the remaining branches and flowers.

'We could cope with grief. God knows we've learned that over the years, but guilt is a different one, isn't it? One year on and I feel we're falling apart. What happened was a terrible thing and Gabriella was the loveliest girl in the world and I'm not for a second trying to get my family to forget about her, but the guilt that Jude carries around with him is breaking us up. He's dealing with it far worse than Luke. Luke's bereaved. It's understandable that he's taking his time to grieve for Gabriella, but Jude's lost. And he's lost who he was. There's no room for the person he used to be any more. His job used to be to make us all laugh.' She gave a cry, half laugh, half sob.

'I'm so sorry for you all.' Lucy swallowed hard.

'And of course he can't do that any more. And when I saw Luke sitting in the car with you just now, smiling and holding your hand, I thought, at last Jude is being set free. And I can't tell you what it was like.' She put her hand on her heart. 'My lovely boys. I felt this wonderful, blessed relief. Because if Luke could sit there outside the house holding your hand, I thought it meant that Jude would be freed . . . that everything was going to be better.'

'Everything is going to be better. Jude will be free.'

Suzie wiped her eye. 'I shouldn't have said that, should I? About Luke holding your hand.'

'Of course I don't mind,' Lucy lied. 'I'm here because Luke thinks I can help.' She gave Suzie a rueful smile. 'And he was holding my hand because he wanted to reassure me.' Now was not the time to confess all the doubts, the longings, the complications that ran through her visit that day.

'But I don't really understand, Lucy. You said that Jude doesn't know you're here?' Suzie looked at her quizzically. 'Forgive me for saying so, but when I last saw Jude, and it was only a couple of weeks ago, he was in such a filthy temper, and was so battered and angry with everyone. I really don't think there was much room in his head for a girlfriend. If he doesn't know you're here — '

'Luke asked me here,' Lucy interrupted. 'He tracked me down because he believes that the only reason Jude didn't come to find me himself was because of the guilt. Jude told him,' she shrugged awkwardly, 'that there *was* room in his head for me. And so Luke has asked me to come here. It's his way of pushing Jude forward, trying to make sure he moves on from all this.'

'Luke has done that for him?'

'Yes, Luke found me. We had met each other on New Year's Day, that night when the two of them arrived here so late? Jude and I had spent the day driving down together from Inverness.'

'Go on,' Suzie encouraged her gently.

304

'We'd decided, both of us, that we wouldn't see each other again. But then, on the way up here, I suppose, Jude told Luke about meeting me and how he wished . . . I don't know exactly what he said. But, Luke didn't want Jude to lose me because of him. And it was such an amazing thing to do, wasn't it? I couldn't turn Luke down, could I? I wanted to come. I wanted the chance to see Jude again . . . But now . . . ' She looked at Suzie, listening so intently, caught the flicker of anticipation that told her that Suzie perhaps knew exactly how she was feeling now. 'Jude's lucky to have him as a brother and he should know it.'

Suzie picked up one of the flowers by its centre bulb and twirled it between her fingers.

'Jude has always broken everything Luke loved,' she said carefully. 'And Luke has always had to reassure him that he doesn't mind. I know it sounds awful to compare Gabriella's death with a broken toy, but it's true nevertheless. When they were little Luke used to have to lock his things out of Jude's reach, but he'd still always find them. And yet it's always Jude we have to reassure.'

She put down the flower in her hand and looked sharply towards the door. 'Hello, Sophia. Feeling lost?'

Lucy turned to see Sophia standing in the doorway at the far end of the room.

'I was wondering where everyone was. Have you seen Luke?' She must have caught the wary look on both their faces. 'But he's busy, is he?'

'No, darling, not at all. I think he's waiting for Jude to arrive, that's all.'

Sophia nodded, clearly too restless to stay; or perhaps intuition played a part after all, and she realized she'd butted in on a conversation she wasn't to be included in. 'I think I'll go and find him anyway,' she said, turning away from them abruptly. 'Keep him company, perhaps.' She looked back at the two of them. 'The room looks gorgeous,' she added as an afterthought. 'I'll see you both later.'

'Poor girl,' Suzie said, after she'd gone. 'She's a little lost today, isn't she?' She stopped, saw the guilt on Lucy's face and smiled. 'Now I'm going to say something else I probably shouldn't say. But somehow I don't think you'll mind.'

'What's that?'

'That she's far better suited to Jude than you are. Don't you think they're two of a kind?'

'No!' Lucy cried. 'You really shouldn't be saying that to me.'

'I can. I can say whatever I like.'

'So what else then, might you say?'

Suzie looked at her carefully.

'I could say that when he was younger, Jude was completely out of control. He made us laugh and we loved him for it but we — usually Luke — always had to pay for it. A few years ago he borrowed Luke's car and drove it into the bottom of our lake, but it was an accident and Luke would get it on the insurance, what was the big deal? With Gabriella, however much it was an accident too, in a way it fitted with everything that had gone before.'

'So you *do* blame Jude after all?'

'No, but I am saying that before the accident Jude was as charming and as selfish as it's possible to be and we've all grown up looking out for him, and looking after him, Luke especially, and if there's any doubt in your mind . . . about anything at all . . . ' Her eyes were on Lucy, and her stare made Lucy think *She knows everything.* 'Don't ever think that Jude isn't plenty strong enough to cope, because he is . . . ' She paused. 'Look at you all,' she said eventually. 'Trying to do the right thing.'

'But *trying* to do the right thing is *doing* the right thing, isn't it?' Lucy insisted.

Suzie gave a little laugh. 'We'll have to see, won't we?'

She stood up, picked up the last remaining branches and stuffed them into the empty cardboard boxes. Then she closed the lid and turned back to Lucy. 'I liked talking to you and I'm so pleased that you're here. Luke was right to bring you. I think you'll be the making of us.'

'I'm not sure he wanted me to talk to you quite as much as I did.'

'Probably not.' She smiled suddenly at Lucy. 'But he is used to it, you know. He calls me the great interrogator, but I don't think he really minds. He knows I like to talk to people. But you . . . ' she touched Lucy's shoulder gently, 'have talked and thought enough. You should stop worrying now, just let it all begin. In the end, you're not going to be able to control what happens next, even if you think you can.'

She carried the box out of the ballroom and led the way back through the hall to the kitchen. She opened a door to a scullery and disappeared inside, and Lucy went over to the kitchen table and sat down at a chair.

When Suzie reappeared, without the box, she lifted a saucepan off a rack above the Aga and filled it with milk from the fridge.

'I'll make us some lunch,' she said decisively.

Out of milk? Lucy wondered.

'Coffee, coffee,' Suzie sighed, seeing her face. 'I mean I'll make some coffee. We'll have lunch when Luke appears.'

Lucy stretched to look out of the window. It had to be getting close to the moment when Jude would appear too, and Luke was nowhere to be seen.

'He'll get to him, don't worry,' Suzie told her, seeing the tension in her face. 'Butler and Rudd have gone, and as Luke's not here with us now, he's probably outside. Don't you worry, he won't let anything distract him. He knows how important this is. After all he's done to set you up, he's not going to blow it now. He'll be outside somewhere, listening out for the car.'

Suzie passed her a mug of coffee and found a plate of biscuits and they sat down together at the kitchen table.

Above her the kitchen clock ticked.

'Where could Luke have got to?' said Suzie after a long pause. 'Now I'm getting worried too.'

Lucy shook her head. 'As you say, I'm sure he's outside, waiting for the car.'

And at that moment the kitchen door opened and her heart stopped because there was Jude standing in the doorway, all alone, looking weary and very handsome, with dark shadows beneath his eyes and two days' worth of stubble on his cheeks. And Lucy found herself frozen to her seat because he hadn't noticed her at all.

16

He walked into the room in the same familiar cashmere coat and scarf, holding a bag in each hand. He paused there for a moment without coming forward, staring across the room to his mother, sitting so still at the kitchen table.

'Aren't you going to come and say hello?' he asked, dropping his bags and holding out his arms.

Suzie leapt to her feet.

'Of course, darling,' she said, reaching him and hugging him tight. 'How are you? How was your trip down?'

'What's the matter?' He kissed her cheek, then held her back from him so that he could look at her face. 'Why are you talking in that funny voice?' And then he looked at her again, saw her unease. 'What's wrong?'

And then, finally, he came further into the kitchen and set eyes on Lucy.

He stopped dead, his eyes widening, the smile dropping from his face. And seeing nothing but shock and absolute dismay in his cold blank stare, all Lucy was aware of was the sound of the blood roaring in her ears, so

311

loud that it was drowning out everything else in her head, everything that might have told her how to explain what she was doing there, sitting at his kitchen table, when Luke so clearly hadn't got to explain it to him first.

'Lucy?' he croaked.

'Don't say anything,' Suzie cried.

He turned to his mother incredulously. 'What do you mean *Don't say anything?*'

'Oh, Jude!' Suzie literally wrung her hands. 'I mean, let Lucy explain. I mean, please don't say anything horrible.'

But Lucy couldn't explain. She couldn't think how to start, so she sat there stiff and still, red with guilt and embarrassment, while Jude walked across the room until he was standing directly in front of her.

'Explain, Lucy,' he said icily. But then, before she could begin, he went on. 'Tell me what you're doing here. Because, as far as I remember, I didn't send you an invitation. I don't think I even told you where I lived.'

'Stop!' Suzie insisted. 'That's enough.' And she positioned herself between the two of them like a referee in a boxing match. 'She's here to see you.'

Out of the corner of her eye, Lucy glimpsed Sophia standing in the doorway, her mouth open in shock. As Lucy caught her eye, Sophia gave her a little, helpless thumbs-up.

Jude turned back to his mother. 'Oh, she's not here to see you? Or the dogs? Or Luke, perhaps? She's here to see me, is she? Yes, Mum, thank you. I think I might have worked that out for myself.' He turned back to Lucy, his face flushed and angry. 'What is it you want from me, Lucy?'

Lucy pushed back her chair, making a terrible screech on the terracotta tiles, and slowly stood up.

'Jude,' she said, her voice wobbling. She clung on to her chair for support, then reached out her hand. 'Please, for God's sake, stop talking to me like this.'

He deliberately turned his back on her and walked over to the Aga, where a large saucepan sat bubbling furiously. He lifted the lid and peered inside.

'I'm not boiling your rabbit, if that's what you're worried about.' Lucy snapped at him, and she heard a hysterical giggle burst from Sophia at the other end of the room.

'Then what *are* you doing?' he asked, dropping the lid back again.

'Don't speak to her like that,' Suzie cried. 'Lucy's very nice.'

'Stay out of this, Mum,' Jude snapped. 'You know nothing. I can't imagine what crap she's been spouting but I'm telling you, this girl is weird, and seeing her here, sitting in *my* house, in *my* kitchen, drinking coffee with *my* mother, is fucking weird too. How did you find us, Lucy? How did you get here?'

'I'll tell you,' Sophia declared, coming into the room. 'Luke picked her up from the station.'

And then the kitchen door opened again and Luke walked in from outside, took in the scene in a second, first looked quickly to Lucy and winced and apologized all in one glance and then turned all his attention to Jude.

'OK!' he cried, walking across the room as Jude swung round, looking as if he might be about to punch him. 'One major cock-up clearly not averted.' He took Jude's arm and held on to it tightly. 'How did I miss you? I've been hanging around outside the house for the last hour and a half and yet I didn't see you arrive?'

'Tell me this isn't true, Luke,' Jude told him. 'Tell me you didn't bring her here.'

'Yes, I did.'

'But why?' Jude demanded. 'You must be mad.' He turned back to Lucy. 'What did you say to him?' he demanded, practically spitting the words into her face. 'How did you get him to do this?'

'Lucy did nothing. I invited her here because I wanted her to come to the party. And I'll tell you why if you stop shouting and behaving like a complete twat.'

Lucy could hear Suzie's voice rising in a quavering wail. 'Yes, Jude, remember who she is. It's *Lucy*, the girl you met on New Year's Day.' As if by reminding him, she would make it all better. *Oh, you mean it's that Lucy!*

'Have you looked at her once? Look at her now, look at her, you stupid, stupid man. See her face, see what you've done to her.'

At first, Lucy had felt terrible shock and agonizing hurt that Jude could behave like this, that no memory of their time together was softening his treatment of her now. But seeing him turn his poisonous glare on Luke, anger flooded through her, giving her strength. So this is what you're really like, she wanted to shout, wanting to punch him in his pretty-boy face. This is the man we've all been agonizing over for so long! He was the reason she was here, feeling more miserable than she'd ever done before, and she strode over to him, elbowing Luke aside and glaring up at him.

'I want to boil your head in the saucepan, let alone your bloody rabbit,' she told him furiously. 'You presume everything and you know nothing. Your family loves you.' She was shaking. She could feel deep uncontrollable shudders running through her. She would get out of this house, soon, soon, she told herself. It was nearly done. 'That's why I'm here, because they asked me to come, for you. Because Luke had some stupid idea that it might help you to see me again. I only came here because of Luke and you don't deserve him as a brother. And you certainly don't deserve me.'

Jude looked as if he'd been turned to stone but it didn't stop her. She leaned even closer to him.

'Look at me,' she commanded and he dragged his eyes to hers. 'Listen to me. You know what?' She spoke slowly and clearly, enunciating every word just a few inches from his face. 'Everyone has spent too much time worrying about *what will help Jude.*' She nodded into his startled face. 'Run away to your oil-rig, that'll make them worry about you, and it's worked hasn't it? Brilliantly well. You got exactly what you wanted, everyone spending all their time worrying about you, your mother, father, especially Luke.' She shook her head in frustration, turning to Suzie, who stared back in wordless shock. But she couldn't stop. No one else in this family of pussy-cats was going to tell him the truth if she didn't. 'How ridiculous is that, Luke having to worry about you? What about you worrying about him? Surely he's the one who's lost the most? You should be the one lifting him up, not pulling him even further down. And if that means being strong, *being here*, being positive, that's what you should be doing. Running away is what a self-pitying loser . . . '

'Stop!' Suzie commanded her, rising out of her chair. 'Who the hell do you think you are?'

Lucy looked at her furious face and abruptly ran out of steam, all the anger vanishing, so that she felt only crippled with embarrassment.

Suzie walked closer to Lucy.

'How dare you speak to us like that?' she demanded, eyes flashing with anger. 'How dare you walk into this house and tell us how to live our lives, talk to us about our grief, our private, horrendous grief, as if you can have *any idea* of how it's been. How dare you criticize my son? How dare you tell me how I should have behaved? Do I know you? Do you know us?

'But in the ballroom, when we talked, I thought you understood.'

Suzie glared at her unblinkingly. 'You have no right to speak to us in this way, in our own house. How dare you?'

'You're right,' Lucy said falteringly. 'It was a terrible thing to say. I'm so sorry. I'll go. I'll pack my bag. I'll walk to the station.'

She turned away from them all, fumbling as if she couldn't see, and moved across the kitchen to the door.

'Lucy?'

It was Luke, taking hold of her arm. 'Don't go. Please wait for me . . . ' But she shook her head, shaking her arm free, unable to look at him, unable to bear to look back at any of them again.

On the other side of the door she bumped blindly into Sophia, who stepped in front of her, forcing her to stop. 'Wait,' Sophia insisted. 'Stop.'

Lucy looked up at Sophia with dead eyes.

'I didn't realize . . . that Jude didn't know you would be here.'

'Is that all you're bothered about? That now you've got free rein to do what you like?'

'No. Don't be ridiculous, of course that wasn't what I meant. Everything you said in there, it had to be said. It's what we've all been thinking but nobody could say it but you. I'm glad you said it. They need you, all of them. This is what they've become. Don't go.'

Lucy laughed bitterly, shook her head. 'At least you know Jude won't want me now.'

'Do you really think I'm so superficial?'

Lucy stopped abruptly, snapping briefly out of her misery. 'Of course I don't, I'm sorry.' She took Sophia's arm. 'I've been feeling awful for you the whole time I've been here.'

'You shouldn't have done, it wasn't your fault. I've wanted him all my life but I know I'm never going to get him. I've had years to get used to it.'

'Somehow I don't think I'm about to get him either.'

'Do you really want to?'

Despite desperately wanting to go, Lucy stopped and stared at Sophia.

'So stay and be brave,' Sophia told her. 'Don't run away. Don't be a wimp. Stand up to Suzie and Jude. Jude's behaved like a pig. Let him come back and apologize — he will, when he's realized just how much of what you said was true. And Luke? How can you think of running away from Luke?'

'The truth is I can easily think of running away from all of them.' Lucy stopped, fighting back tears. 'It was difficult enough before, waiting all the time for Jude to come home, but now that he's back . . . ' She shook her head, walking away, towards the hall and the stairs to her bedroom.

Once in her bedroom she threw her bag on

the bed, then opened the cupboard, gathered her dress up in her arms, picked up her shoes, and swept her make-up, washbag, nail varnish and hair-drier off the chest of drawers beside the bed and into the bag, chucking the dress and shoes in on top. She zipped it shut, picked up her coat and slipped it round her shoulders, took a deep shuddering breath and closed her eyes. A couple of minutes, that was all it had taken. Another five and she'd be gone. Free of the lot of them.

She sat down heavily on the bed. Free? Free wasn't the word. Wherever she went she wouldn't be free at all.

17

Lucy walked back into the kitchen to find Suzie waiting for her alone. She immediately took Lucy by the shoulder, steering her to a chair, and Lucy sat down, staring at Suzie warily.

'I'll take you to the station.'

'I'm so sorry I said all that.'

'There's a rule that you clearly don't know. It says that mothers are allowed to criticize their children, but nobody else can. Luke says it was good for Jude. He's with him now. Perhaps you might talk to Luke again before you go?'

'Why?'

'Because he made me promise not to take you to the station until you had. And Luke's done nothing wrong, and he's done an awful lot right, and I think you owe him that and I think you owe it to me too.'

Lucy nodded, and immediately Suzie's face cleared a little. 'Thank you.'

'Luke's plan rather backfired, didn't it?'

Suzie gave her a wry smile. 'Or perhaps you being here has had exactly the effect Luke wanted it to. It's forced everything into the open, after all.'

She got back to her feet and picked up their two empty coffee cups, then went across to the Aga and opened one of the ovens, half-heartedly waving aside another cloud of smoke. 'Are you sure you won't stay for lunch? You must have heard how a meal at Lipton Hall is always an experience? And it is a quarter to two.'

'You want me to? You can face having me in your house?'

'Just about,' Suzie said, cocking her head to one side like a bird. 'I've enjoyed most of the conversations I've had with you today.'

'I would like to talk to Luke.'

Suzie nodded. 'Jude was deeply sorry, Lucy, once he'd got over the shock. It might make you feel better to talk to him too before you go?'

'I was meant to be a nice surprise for him. Surely if any part of him felt anything for me at all, he wouldn't have behaved like that?'

'Jude is extremely sensitive about being made to look a fool.' Suzie lifted the lid off one of the saucepans and peered inside, then jumped back in surprise. 'And he felt trapped by us all, so he behaved like a complete pig.' She picked a wooden spoon out of a pot beside the Aga and prodded cautiously, leaning well away from the saucepan as she did so. 'But I know he'll be feeling terrible

322

about it now. Trust me, once Luke has finished with him, he'll be wishing he'd never been born.' She turned to Lucy. 'Luke can be rather good at making people feel like that.'

So can you, Lucy thought, watching as Suzie picked up a sieve and took it over to the sink, then went back for her saucepan, staggered over to the sink and tipped the contents through the sieve. Dark brown lumps the size and consistency of horse droppings plopped steadily out of the pan in a cloud of steam.

'That looks good,' Lucy said with a tired grin.

'It'll be fine once it's mashed.' Suzie stopped, listening intently. 'They're coming back now.' She gave Lucy a smile of reassurance. 'Nearly over.'

But it wasn't Luke who came through the door into the kitchen, it was Jude. He walked over to Lucy, still sitting at her chair, and crouched down at her feet. Suzie seemed to melt into the corner of the room and disappear.

'Luke's told me everything,' he said, dropping his head.

She sat there, looking down at his dark hair, and then, slowly, he looked up at her again. 'You're free to boil my head if you want to.'

'I think your Mum's used up all the saucepans.'

'It wasn't me, Lucy,' he said, trying to take her hands in his, but she pulled them out of his grasp and sat on them. 'I can't believe I behaved like that. I'm more sorry than I can begin to tell you. Can you ever forgive me?'

He looked up at her sorrowfully, and when she didn't reply he said, 'No, of course you can't. Why should you?'

'I knew you'd be surprised,' she offered. 'I knew it would be a shock. And Luke was meant to get to you first, to explain. But Jude, how could you have thought I'd do that? Track you down like some creepy stalker? You know what we said, how we left everything in London. You might have known I wouldn't have followed you here without a good reason.'

'Now I know why you're here, of course I understand. But when I walked through the door I can't tell you what a surprise it was. And you know as well as I do, we hardly knew each other at all.'

'So you had to presume . . . '

'Yes. No. Oh, Lucy . . . Of course I didn't have to. Of course I could have rushed up to you and said how fantastic it was, is, to see you again. Don't think that I don't wish I'd done that now with all my heart. I can't bear that I behaved like that, to you.' He pushed himself away from her knees and sat heavily down at her feet. 'Is there anything I can say or do that might make you stay? Please.'

She hadn't expected him to be so nice, and the sincerity in his words took her aback, so that yet again she felt the certainty evaporate, leaving doubt and confusion in its place. She wanted to stay . . . but was that simply because she could hardly bear to tear herself away from Luke? Luke who'd not reappeared and perhaps didn't even care any more whether she stayed or went. She wanted to go because to stay here with Jude, now, still felt like a sham. And yet she wanted to stay . . . and Jude wanted her there, Suzie wanted her there, and to insist that she was driven to the station, to leave under such a cloud, seemed perhaps unnecessarily petulant, not really her style.

'I need to get out of the house for a bit,' she told him quietly.

'Sure, sure, I understand. Let's go outside, walk somewhere, drive, anything you want to do, I'll do it. Let's go now.'

'But what about your lunch? Suzie's been cooking a welcome home special.'

'Then we have no choice. Lives depend on it. We must go right away.'

He grinned at her, climbed back to his feet

and held out a hand. 'Come on. You've got your coat on. We'll go for a walk and a talk and then, if you still want me to, *I'll* take you back to the station.'

She nodded, starting to feel better. 'Down the lane and back again?'

'Wherever you want.'

'And then, I could come back to the house to say goodbye to Suzie and Luke?'

'Absolutely. No problem at all.'

* * *

And so, with the two dogs, Parson and Wiggins, oblivious to the tension and running ahead joyfully, Lucy and Jude opened the back door and stepped out into the cold winter afternoon, walked around the side of the house and down the gravelled drive, crossed the bridge and turned left down the gated road.

They walked to the first gate with neither of them saying a word and then Lucy, hesitantly, began to speak.

'I came here with my friend Jane just over a week ago. And we walked down here as I tried to make up my mind what to do about you.'

He nodded. 'Don't make me feel worse.'

'You deserve it, you know.'

He turned to her, seeing from her face that although she wasn't joking, she wasn't completely serious any more either. 'I'm still surprised you had to be quite so angry. I wasn't threatening you, was I?'

'You were very threatening in the kitchen just then.'

'Yes, I'm sorry about that.'

'Is that what you think? That I'm a loser?'

'I think it's wrong the way you make them tread so softly around you. And I meant what I said about you needing to look after Luke.'

'You think so?'

She nodded.

'It's very strange, hearing you talk about everyone this way. When I left you last, you didn't know them at all.'

'I do understand.'

'Luke seemed to think you needed looking after too.'

'He was angry with you. He wanted this to work.'

'Do you like him?'

'Of course.'

'You've spent time together?'

She shrugged. 'Supper, when he told me about you . . . A coffee.'

'Fancy him?'

She flinched. 'Don't ask me that.'

Jude turned in surprise. 'Forgive me, Lucy,

I was teasing you, that's all.'

She looked down at the tarmac, kicked a stone with her foot. Then looked back at him again.

'I'm sorry, I was messing around. Getting used to you being here, that's all.'

'I think it was a strange thing to ask.'

'And I apologized.'

They walked on slowly, matching strides, and came to a T-junction in the road where a lane wound up into the hills to the church. Get Jude to show it to you, she remembered Luke suggesting as they'd looked out at it through the upstairs windows of the house.

'Shall we see the church?' she asked him.

'Sure, we can do whatever you want.'

Then he looked doubtfully at her feet, at the trainers she was wearing. 'Although perhaps we should go the long way around, stick to the lanes, it's a little further.' He looked up at the grey skies, heavy with rain. 'But it's not raining yet and we're in no rush, are we?'

They skirted around the fields, the brook on their left, a light breeze in the air, and as they walked she found comfort in the rhythm of her steps and began finally to relax. They turned right, into the wind. She could see the church, shielded by trees at the top of the hill. She was aware of him looking at her, considering her, getting used to the sight of her walking there beside him.

They strode on up the hill towards the church and she could hear his breath coming harder as she pushed on faster and faster, feeling the muscles in her calves beginning to ache with the steepness of the slope. And then she had to stop, and she swung round and looked back down the way they'd come towards the house, tiny as a dolls' house now, in the valley below them. Jude came and stood beside her, then touched her arm and led her to a fallen tree-trunk and she sat down beside him.

He turned to her and opened his mouth to speak.

'Don't apologize again.' She found herself able to look at him calmly now, and the relief on his face made her smile.

'Actually, I was going to move on to the thank you for coming bit now. And then I was going to ask you . . . before I blew it all by behaving like Mr Angry, how you were feeling about seeing me again?'

He should have said *before Luke got in the way*.

'Scared, and intrigued, I suppose, because we hardly know each other. And it was a strange time, our long drive, wasn't it? A million miles away from a place like this.'

He took a deep breath. 'It's probably the last thing you want to hear,' he said in a rush, 'but I have to tell you even so, even though it's probably much too soon. I always wanted to see you again. I thought you were great. I wished, very much that I would see you again. Is that so bad?'

'No. But I'm surprised.' She looked at his face, staring at her full of hope. 'It all seemed very clear at the time.'

'But that was your fault,' Jude said immediately. 'I knew, or I thought I knew, how you felt about me. You seemed very clear. I'd got you sorted too. I thought I knew exactly what you were like, what you wanted. I couldn't see you because of Luke. You didn't want to see me anyway. It seemed very simple. That was another reason why it was such a shock, finding you in my kitchen . . . '

He waited expectantly and she knew what he was asking her. How did she feel now? And the truth was that everything she thought she knew and felt and believed was spinning round in her head, uprooted and out of control. And there was Jude, labouring under the misapprehension that it was all about getting her to forgive him for what he'd said in the kitchen . . . But poor Jude, what else was he supposed to think?

'The truth is, I hardly know you, do I?'

330

What was it he was hoping for now? Could he possibly believe that she'd turn to him as they sat together on the tree trunk and confidently tell him that it would all be all right, kiss him maybe, here on the hillside, in this wonderfully romantic spot he'd brought her to?

And in spite of all the doubt, she was tempted to do it, to blot it all out simply by kissing Jude. After all, here was a man, such an attractive, handsome man, sitting beside her and telling her in a heartfelt way just how much she meant to him. Someone she'd once been so close to, had shared so much with, someone she'd once sat beside for thirteen hours, someone she'd felt good enough about to walk into the Milestone Motel with. And meanwhile, back home, there was Luke, who still seemed only to see her as a means to an end, who was difficult and still full of grief, who'd never said anything to give her hope, probably with no space in his life for her at all.

Was it so bad, to be tempted? Not for long, not with any commitment to the future, just for as long as the party lasted, because she wasn't going to leave now. She'd realized that almost as soon as they'd started to walk, that she was going to stay.

Beside her, Jude rose to his feet and held

out his hand. 'Don't let's talk about it any more now. Let me show you the church.'

She stood up, wishing she could respond as she knew he wanted her to, that she could be happy now, could turn to him and begin again.

They walked up a grassy path with a post-and-rail fence separating them from fields on either side, through an ancient wooden lychgate and into a churchyard. They walked between the headstones and she looked ahead to the beautiful little golden-stone church. She heard the distant whinny of a horse, carried to them on the wind, and Jude lifted the latch of the door and waited for her to go in first. She stepped inside, into the silence, breathing in beeswax polish and a faint smell of lilies, and left Jude and walked on down the tiny tiled aisle. Her footsteps were loud on the floor as she walked between the simple wooden pews, black with age, then looked up at the wonderful stained-glass windows that threw in a clear gentle light. *In memory of the dear infant Mary*, she read.

Then she turned back to Jude, still standing in the doorway, watching her quietly. And as she met his look he came forward to meet her.

'It's OK, everything's going to be all right.'

If he'd been awful earlier, he couldn't have

been nicer now. And yet, as he took her in his arms and held her close, she still felt deceitful and troubled, the serenity of the church making it feel all the more wrong that she was here with him, unable to say what he wanted her to say. When Jude suggested they move on, she nodded quickly and they left the church, carefully shutting the door behind them, and she felt grateful for the wind in her hair, the openness of the sky.

As darkness began to fall, the rain came too, and they walked bareheaded back along a lane with high-sided hedges and down through fields of sheep, and as they neared the house again, she finally turned to him. 'Of course I'll stay.' And in response he slipped his arm around her, and this time it felt natural to fall into the fold.

They reached the gated road again, the house looming up on them, and just as they reached the last bend in the lane he touched her arm and stopped.

'What?' she asked. And in answer he pulled her into his arms.

'I said I'd forgiven you.' She looked up at him, half smiling, half scared. 'That doesn't mean you can get too close.'

'I want you to know how happy I am that you're here.' He smiled into her eyes, not making any move to release her. And then he leaned forward and brushed his lips against her cheek. 'How good it is to see you again, even more gorgeous than I remembered.' His eyes were full of intent and she looked back at him, her cheeks burning. What was she doing, letting this happen? How much more trouble was she setting up for herself now? But if Luke couldn't tell her he wanted her, Jude certainly could.

'Is that all right?' Jude asked, his arms holding her still.

'Yes,' she smiled. And she looked up into his eyes and this time he held her look and she thought she saw something like triumph in his smile. And then he dipped his head and kissed her again, this time softly but on the lips, and despite thinking so badly of herself, hearing a voice shouting in her head that she was deceitful and was behaving so badly, still it was lovely and she couldn't stop herself kissing him back, caught in the moment, remembering the past.

18

Lucy opened the kitchen door and cautiously looked inside, and Suzie spun around from where she was washing up.

'You're staying, aren't you?' she asked, though it was barely a question. 'Of course you are.'

'Yes,' Lucy agreed, smiling rather sheepishly. 'I'm too easily influenced, aren't I?'

'Thank heavens you are. I'd have been absolutely miserable if you'd insisted on going home.' She came over to Lucy and started undoing the buttons of her coat. 'Have a cup of tea. It's only an hour and a half before everybody starts to arrive.'

Jude had followed her into the kitchen and Suzie turned to him with a huge smile of relief. 'She's staying. Isn't that great?'

'Took a bit of persuading.' He glanced across to Lucy and smiled. 'But I think I've convinced her now.'

'Oh.' Suzie was clearly taken aback. 'So you're properly together again, are you?'

Lucy found she couldn't bear to look at Suzie.

'Perhaps if she'll have me.'

Suzie shook her head. 'You'd better get her upstairs.'

'Excuse me!'

'Hot water,' Suzie snapped. 'She'll want a bath.' It was as if Lucy wasn't there. 'She'll want a hot bath and a clean towel and if she doesn't hurry up she won't get either.'

Lucy looked down at her jeans, caked with mud, felt the rain in her tangled wispy hair. 'I could wash and get ready and then perhaps there's something I could do to help?' she suggested awkwardly.

'It's all done, darling,' Suzie said airily, still not looking at her. 'Don't worry about that. The caterers are here. The band's setting up . . . ' She looked out of the window. 'I can see the rain has arrived early.'

'But that doesn't matter, Mum,' Jude said reassuringly. 'We'll be inside, it'll be dark, the weather doesn't matter at all.'

'Yes, darling. I'm quite aware of that.'

She'd snapped at him, Lucy realized in surprise. But Jude, on his best behaviour now, didn't rise. Instead he walked over to Suzie and pulled the plug out of the sink. 'Leave this,' he said. 'I'll finish it off. You must have better things to do.' He smiled at her. 'It's your party, Mum, you should be painting your nails or reading the paper or something, not messing about in the kitchen.'

Suzie protested, but she allowed Jude to steer her away from the sink and then broke away from him and walked over to the door.

'Luke is at the bottom of Tindle Hill. Dad asked him to chop up a tree. Did you meet him, on your way back?' Now she was looking pointedly at Lucy.

'I saw him,' Jude answered for her. 'I was wondering where he was going. What's he doing that for?' He looked out at the rainy night.

'Because it's fallen on a fence, Jude. You know Dad, nothing can wait until morning. But I wonder if you'd go and fetch him, please. As everyone's been invited for seven-thirty I think it's very inconsiderate of both of them not to be here.'

Luke was at the bottom of Tindle Hill. Not in the house, not anywhere she might find him. And she went cold at the thought that he could have seen her and Jude coming back from their walk. She bit her lip in agitation, then looked up and saw Jude watching her, a strange bright look on his face.

'I'll go and find him now,' he said slowly, still keeping his eyes on Lucy. 'And you,' he went on, 'your bathroom awaits.'

He led her up the stairs, along to the hall to her bedroom door. 'You'll be OK?'

She nodded quickly, moving to the door,

but he stepped forward, took her gently by the shoulders and turned her round, and then his mouth was searching for hers, his arms holding her tight, and she had to step back, pushing him forcefully away from her.

'Hey!' He kept his hands on her shoulders, trying to see her face. 'Don't do that. Just tell me not to.'

'I'm sorry.'

He held her away from him, looking hurt.

'I'm sorry,' she said again.

'I'm not expecting anything of you, Lucy. Just because of what happened before . . . it doesn't mean that I'm presuming it's going to happen all over again.'

She laughed uneasily, trying to make light of it. 'You mean I don't have to dance the smoochy dances with you?'

'Yes, you *do* have to dance the smoochy dances with me.' He pushed open the bedroom door. 'Go and get ready. I'll see you later.'

★ ★ ★

Lucy drew the curtains, then pulled off all her clothes and stepped into the bath, which was wonderful and hot. After a long time she climbed out, wrapped herself in a towel, and went to the cupboard for her dress. She

338

slipped it off its hanger and laid it out on the bed, then went back into the bathroom, brushed her teeth, returned to the bedroom, found some underwear and went to the dressing-table.

She dried her hair into a head of loose curls, then pinned up the ones over her face so that she could work on her make-up, determined to look her best, to put it on carefully, with none of the slapdash she usually got away with. She looked at her face, making herself smile as she started to work on her cheeks — foundation, blusher, a dusting of bronze. She moved on to eyeliner, eyeshadow, brow highlighter, mascara, then lipstick, the exact same pink as her dress. And then she stopped and looked at herself again and saw a fearful looking ballroom dancer staring back at her. She exhaled a long wobbly breath, found her cleanser and a tissue, and wiped it all off. Then she began again, this time only lightly brushing her cheeks and her shoulders with bronzing powder, leaving off the foundation com-pletely, touching her eyelashes with mascara and adding just the briefest of gold lines to her lids. She shook out her curls, added a spray of scent, and went over to her dress, lifting it carefully over her head, reaching behind her to tug up the zip. It slipped over her body so perfectly, fell in exactly the right way as she walked, clung and stretched in just the right places, the sequins winking gently, that for the first time in a long while Lucy began to feel better. Give her a big glass of champagne and she'd survive anything.

She went back to the cupboard for her sandals and stepped into them. Then she went back to the dressing-table and looked at herself in the mirror. It was a party, that was all, it would be over, one way or another, so soon. And tomorrow she'd be back on that train, leaving them all behind.

She bent to her make-up bag and added another line of glittery gold to her upper lids, then headed to the door. She wished she had someone to walk down the stairs with. More than anything she wished she could magic Jane there beside her. She looked at her watch. Seven-thirty. Perhaps other people might already be there? Perhaps downstairs the rooms would be full of people and she could slip in unnoticed.

She trod carefully down the stairs and towards the hall. She could hear voices ahead of her, Sophia's high-pitched giggle, and she hesitantly pushed open the door and looked inside.

'It must be Lucy!' A grey-haired man who looked like a gnome leaped to his feet and rubbed his hands delightedly. 'And looking absolutely stunning, my dear.' He came over to her and took her hands in his. 'I'm James. What a pleasure it is to meet you at last. Such cold hands, come over to the fire.'

The elusive James. She gratefully allowed herself to be led into the room, catching sight of Luke and Jude sitting side by side on the sofa, Sophia standing talking to Suzie and every so often tossing back her hair, dressed in spiky high heels and a white backless dress that showed off her tan.

'Lucy, what a stunning dress,' Suzie said, breaking off her conversation with Sophia and joining her husband in front of Lucy.

'Thank you.' Lucy smiled, accepting a glass of champagne from James, thinking how his eyes twinkled as if he were constantly in the middle of a wonderful private joke. And yet he was clearly a force to be reckoned with too. Lucy could see where Luke had inherited his air of command and authority. If James wanted a tree chopping or a drain unblocking at the bottom of his field, she'd probably try to do the job for him.

Jude hurriedly pushed himself to his feet. 'Let me in. I want to see her,' he insisted, and when he'd manoeuvred his father to one side he stopped and looked at her. 'My God. But she's beautiful.'

'Don't sound so surprised.' Suzie laughed.

'I mean, you look amazing.' He came forward and whispered in her ear, 'It's the pink dress, at last I'm getting to see it.' He kissed her cheek then turned back to the others, his eye alighting on Luke. 'Doesn't she look fantastic?'

'Very nice.' He was staring back at her, unsmiling, swilling his champagne around in his glass.

And then suddenly there was a loud knocking at the door and immediately both dogs started barking noisily.

'Get it, James,' Suzie cried in relief. 'And Jude or Luke, would you shut these two dogs away? We can't have them barking every time someone arrives.'

Into the room came a tall grey-haired woman in a long velvet cape which she swung away from her shoulders to reveal a full-length scarlet dress and a spectacular diamond necklace. Behind her came two teenage girls, both in tiny dresses, both with impossibly long legs and long blonde hair. They were pink-cheeked and beautiful and giggling together, and looking at them Lucy suddenly felt terribly old.

'Bethany, Abigail.' Suzie greeted them warmly and put a hand on each of their shoulders. 'So you were allowed out for the night? Mum wasn't sure if school would let you come.'

'Oh yes.' Both girls nodded, eyes bright, and Suzie turned to Lucy to explain. 'Bethany and Abigail are at boarding-school near Oxford. Don't you worry,' she added in a stage whisper, turning back to the two of them, 'you'll find you're not the only two young ones.'

'Oh, yes, we know,' Abigail or Bethany replied enthusiastically, in a high-pitched, very posh voice. 'Sam and Josh Pemberton-Leys are coming, aren't they? And Miles Hadlow. And loads of other girls from school . . . '

And then, all at once, more guests arrived, pouring into the house in a steady stream, unwrapping themselves from velvet stoles and long fur coats, picking glasses of champagne off heavy silver trays, marvelling at the weather, the room, the fireplace, how wonderful it was to see Luke and Jude there too, and looking so happy and well.

Not that Luke looked well or happy. He looked unapproachable and dark. As Lucy sipped her drink and was introduced around the room, she was aware of him all the time, how guests would be brought up to him, or would cautiously make their own way over to him, and how they'd get a moment of his

343

attention and then seconds later would move away.

Jude, on the other hand, seemed to be the life and soul, refilling everyone's glasses, laughing and chatting, circulating and cracking jokes, but always coming back to Lucy, gamely introducing her into one conversation after another. He was back in his old role, she realized, watching him as a horse-faced young woman leaned eagerly towards him and then burst back in delighted laughter. He was back where he was supposed to be, at the centre of attention, the dashing, electrifying charmer he'd always been. And she was amazed that the transformation could have occurred so fast, that it was all so simple for him.

He caught her eye and immediately came over to her and took her hand. 'Listen, the band's begun. Come and dance?'

'Jude!' She smiled at him. 'People are still arriving. You're on duty.'

'No, I'm not. Luke can do that.'

'But they'll still be doing sound checks, tuning up. They won't want us in there yet.'

He shook his head. Determinedly he took her hand and led her out of the hall, out of the house and along the dark cloister and in through the door to the ballroom. It was dark but for the flashing lights bouncing off the walls and the huge glitter ball that was now suspended from the ceiling. Self-consciously Lucy allowed Jude to lead her into the middle of the room, and seeing them there, the band immediately fell into a song, their lead singer, a bosomy middle-aged woman in a long split-to-the-thigh silver dress, stepping forward to the microphone and giving it her all.

And dancing with Jude turned out to be fun. For all her uncertainty, confusion, doubt, she was perfectly happy to be held against the scratchy wool of his dinner jacket, feeling his arms loosely wrapped across her back, letting him catch her hands to spin her around the room or guide her slowly left and right, never catching her eye with a meaningful stare, never trying to pull her towards him too hard. He was so sweet and undemanding, knowing intuitively what she wanted, and she found that she danced on, through one song and on to the next, and then on again, losing herself in the music and the rhythm, finally letting go.

'Thanks, Jude,' she said when the third song finished.

'But they've hardly begun. Wait till you hear what else is on my mother's playlist.' He kept his hands around her waist. 'You sure you don't want to rock around the clock?'

She smiled. 'Later on, we could. But don't you think we should be getting back to everyone now? You especially should be back in the house.'

'No.' His arms tightened around her. 'I'd rather stay here with you all night.'

Other people had heard the music and were appearing in the doorway, peering in uncertainly and then, seeing Lucy and Jude in the middle of the dance floor, following their lead and coming in to join them, starting to dance. Above them on the far wall the flowers flickered in time to the beat. Lucy could see people noticing them, pointing them out to each other. And then she saw Luke entering the room with Sophia, watched how he was dragged unwillingly across the dance floor, Sophia looking more like an angel in her long white dress. How stiffly Luke stood as Sophia danced gamely beside him, his hands loosely clasped around her tiny waist.

She found herself stopping, standing still on the dance floor.

'Are you all right?' Jude asked immediately.

'I'm fine.' She nodded. 'I think I need to sit down, that's all.'

He took her hand and led her away, back to the cloister, where there was a long bench running along the wall.

'Not too cold here?'

'No. Thanks.'

346

He left her alone while he disappeared to find them a drink, returning with a bottle of champagne, wet from its ice bucket, in one hand and a couple of glasses in the other. He sat on the floor at her feet, turning his back on the guests who passed them by, pulling off the foil and beginning to work out the cork. Then James chose that very moment to appear at the other end of the cloister, and Jude smoothly changed his aim and fired the cork at him. Miraculously James caught it and lobbed it straight back at him.

'So you've abandoned the party already, you hopeless pair?' He turned to Lucy. 'Don't disappear completely, because I'm expecting a dance with you later. And I would suggest you come and eat something soon, before it all disappears.'

'Was that an order?' Lucy asked Jude when they were left alone again. The truth was that while dancing with him had been fine, sitting with him out here all alone with nothing to say was proving much more difficult.

'Are you hungry?'

She nodded. 'Yes, a little.'

'Then we should eat.'

He rose to his feet again and for the first time she caught a look of impatience in his eye. She knew that she was being awful, lousy company, her hopeless inability to think of a word to say to him only too obvious. What must he be thinking of her now? She stood up, then caught the back of the bench.

'Are you OK, Lucy?'

'Yes.'

'I feel I'm asking you this all the time.'

'I know you are. I'm sorry, Jude.' She shook her head. 'Don't ask me again. Go and find someone else to talk to if you want to.'

'Is that what you'd like me to do?'

She looked back up at him. 'Give me another couple of drinks and I'll be fine.'

'I think I should find you something to eat.'

He took her back to the hall and left her alone sitting in an armchair, looking at the fire and listening to the wind, which had got up in gusts and squalls. She could hear it howling down the chimney in the main hall, and she rose to her feet and walked to the window and looked out at the black night, rain spattering at the windowpanes. She checked her watch. It was nine o'clock. She could see her face in the reflection of the window, and she touched her cheek with her hand. Then she went back to the fire and sat down again, leaning back against the chair and watching the flames.

'Hello.'

She turned fast, the colour rising in her cheeks, and Luke came towards her, bending down and briefly kissing her cheek, producing such a flood of longing that she could hardly pull her thoughts together enough to answer. He went towards the fire, spreading his hands to its warmth.

'Never ever let my father catch you at a loose end. There's a party? Forget it! He's just sent me to check on the cows. Our cows!' He smiled uneasily. 'And don't think wearing a dress will put him off. He'll have you out in your high heels mucking out a stable if he gets half a chance.'

'So I heard.'

He moved away from the fire and sat down in the chair opposite her.

'If Jude hadn't come to Tingle Wood to bring us back we'd probably still be there now.'

She nodded.

'You know he's a good-for-nothing bastard and he doesn't deserve you.'

'Are you joking?'

'No.' He leaned back in his chair, staring at her through half-closed eyes. 'But after all the work I've put in for the pair of you, I'm happy enough, I suppose.'

How could it be so painful to hear him talk so calmly, as if he really couldn't care either way?

'I thought about interrupting when I saw

you kiss him outside the house, then decided I shouldn't.'

She flinched at the thought, feeling a guilty flush spread across her face. 'If you saw it, you'd know it was a brief insignificant little kiss.'

'No it wasn't.' He looked at her witheringly. 'Anyhow, I'm sure you'll find plenty of opportunity to pick up where you left off.'

'Luke,' she said desperately, 'I don't know what to do.'

'It's done. Don't think about me. Look forward now.'

'Is that what you want me to do?'

'Oh, Lucy,' Luke said quietly. 'Lucy Blue.' He shook his head. 'I guess I'll survive.'

She couldn't believe that he was standing up, leaving again before she'd hardly said a word. Yet with him like this, so utterly remote, she wondered what else she might have found to say.

'I wish you well,' he said quietly from the doorway. 'Having spent the last year ruining Jude's love life, I'm pleased for you, truly I am. Happy it worked out.'

And then he was gone, and moments later, Jude was back, with two plates piled high with food.

'Come with me.'

Like a puppet she allowed him to steer her

away, following him as he shouldered open a door into another room that she'd not been into before and led her to the far end, pulling aside a long blue velvet curtain that revealed a wide windowseat, covered in deep cushions, that looked out into the dark garden.

'I know I'm supposed to be hosting this damn thing, but I need you to myself for a little while now, no interruptions.' He smiled at her. 'Do you mind? We can eat and then we can be sociable afterwards.'

She shook her head and went to sit beside him, thinking how she would not be being sociable afterwards; she would be leaving the party as soon as she could, waiting in her bedroom for morning. The window was wide enough for them to sit facing each other, balancing their plates on their knees, and once they were settled he let the curtain swing again in front of them, closing them off from the rest of the house.

'Hey, Jude,' she said, giving him a half-hearted smile.

'I think you've used that one up already.'

He waited, but she just looked down at her plate of rare roast beef, tiny Yorkshire puddings, roast potatoes and dark green beans, wishing she could think of something, anything to say.

'Lucy?' She could tell from the tone of his

voice that he wasn't about to crack a joke.

She looked up at him.

'Try telling me what's changed. When we were out walking together today, it felt as if everything would turn out OK — better than OK, I thought it would turn out perfectly. And then you came down into the room this evening and you were wearing your pink dress and I thought it was some sort of sign for me. And you looked so beautiful and happy to be there with us all. And now, forgive the cliché, it's as if the light's suddenly gone out of your eyes. And try as hard as I can, I can't seem to turn it back on again, and I don't know why.'

And Lucy thought this is why I'm here, for this moment, to be here with him, sitting behind this curtain now. This is what I've been leading up to, for so long. I must not think about Sophia. I certainly must not think about Luke. This is the moment when I'm meant to reassure him, to do what I've come to do. She picked up their plates, leaned precariously down off the windowseat to place them gently on to the floor, then faced him again.

Evidently he decided it was all right to move forward, to put a finger on the line of her collarbone and slowly let it slide around the back of her neck, at the same time drawing her closer, closer, until he could touch her lips with his. Then he moved forwards on to his knees, bending over her and cradling her face with his hands.

'Why do I always have to kiss you in such bloody awkward positions?' he whispered, coming forward again.

And then the curtain was pulled wide open and Luke was standing there.

'Get away,' Jude said good-naturedly, grabbing it back and pulling it closed again. 'Silly bugger!' he said. 'Doesn't he realize a closed curtain has to mean someone is behind it?'

The curtain opened a second time.

'Luke, for God's sake leave us alone! What's the matter with you? What do you want?'

'I want you out of there. What the fuck do you think you're doing?'

'Trying to kiss Lucy,' Jude said simply.

'You should be with the rest of us, hosting this party.'

'Don't give me that crap.' Jude climbed off his seat and squared up to his brother. 'Leave us alone. Give us a chance to get to know each other again.'

'You can do that later. Right now you should be out here, both of you should. We have guests, Jude.'

'For Christ's sake, Luke! What's the matter with you?'

'I have to go,' Lucy blurted, startling them into silence.

They both stopped, looking at her in astonishment.

'Where?' said Jude.

'Anywhere away from the two of you.'

'Don't say that, Lucy.' Jude was turning back to her, reaching for her hand, pinning her to the chair and laughing at her, still misunderstanding how serious she was. 'Stay with me, please. I'll get rid of him again, watch me.'

But she was talking to Luke, not to him. 'I can't bear to watch the two of you like this,' she told him. 'And I'm making it worse now, not better. And I'm sorry I'm not turning out quite as you planned. Not for you, not for Jude. Not for Suzie, not even for bloody Sophia.'

'Lucy?' Jude was still trying to stop her but she was rising up off her seat, sidestepping the plates of food on the floor. 'I didn't realize. I didn't understand.' He was looking wildly from her to Luke. 'I'm sorry, I didn't know.' Then he was turning back to her again. 'Why are you so upset? What's wrong? Both of you — Lucy? Luke? What's wrong now? I don't understand.'

She pushed past the pair of them, still hearing Jude asking again, 'What's the big deal? I don't understand.' And then she was escaping from the room, through the door at the far end and into the main hall. She slipped along the highly polished floorboards of the drawing-room, passing guests, turning left and right, running into and out of the rooms she now knew so well. She climbed the stairs two at a time, turning on a heel and feeling a stab of pain in her ankle but stamping down on it again grimly.

'What's the matter?' a stranger asked as she passed him on the stairs, his eyes full of concern. 'Are you all right?'

'I'm fine, fine,' she muttered, then stopped and turned back to him, to where he was still standing, looking after her anxiously.

'Would you tell Jude that Lucy's going home, please?' she asked him, politely enough. 'Tell him I'll call him tomorrow and I'm sorry I couldn't tell him myself but not to worry about me, please.'

The man nodded at once, as if he understood completely and wasn't surprised at all.

In her room she ripped off her dress, stepped out of her shoes, pulled on her jeans and her shirt and jumper, found her socks and trainers and pulled them back on to her feet. Then she threw everything else into her bag — bottles and wash-things, T-shirt and pyjama bottoms — pulled the sides of her bag together and zipped it shut, then shrugged herself into her coat.

Five minutes, that was probably all it had been since she'd left them both behind the curtain. She closed her eyes. *Please God let them still be there shouting at each other.* Would that man have found Jude yet, she wondered? Would Jude guess she was planning to run away? Not just to slip up the stairs to her bedroom but to leave the house and go for good. She knew what a coward she was being, slinking away into the night, and she felt hopeless and full of shame that she wasn't saying goodbye to Suzie after all they'd said and done together that day. But at that moment it felt as if it was the only thing she could do. Flee the house, out into the night, away from the lot of them.

She slunk down the stairs, anxiously looking ahead in case anybody noticed her, half expecting to see Jude or Luke or even both of them waiting for her, but although there was a throng of people down there, neither of the brothers was among them and no one noticed her slipping round the side of the banisters and quietly walking across to the front door. And once she had turned her back on the Middletons and had her hand on the door-handle, she didn't care if anyone noticed her leaving, if anyone was wondering who she was or where she was going. She saw a torch on the floor in the corner of the porch and picked it up. She'd send it back to Suzie from London. Then she shut the door quietly behind her and walked out into the night, looking up at the thousands of stars and the bright clear moon in the midnight-blue sky and feeling a certain poignant peace descend upon her. As crushed and hopelessly confused as she felt, at least she was getting away.

She ran down the drive, her feet crunching loudly on the gravel, her bag swinging against her back as she ran, and then she turned right on to the gated road and began to walk, following the lane, past the war memorial, starting to climb the first long winding hill that led towards the station.

She was more than glad of the torch, realizing within a few strides that without it she would have had no hope of finding her way. Used to London, she couldn't believe how deeply black the night could be. She waved the torch into the hedgerows, imagining foxes and badgers staring at her silently as she passed, and felt the first ripple of unease. Then she reminded herself of what waited for her back at the house, told herself that she was glad to be there on the road, getting away, that anything was better than staying at the party, feeling so false and miserable. That however many miles she would have to walk, however long it would take her, however slim the chances were that she'd find a train going anywhere from little Lipton St Lucy station tonight, it was better to be beginning her journey home. She'd sit in the waiting-room, wrapped up in her coat. She'd sleep a little and she'd catch the first train in the morning, wherever it was going. She didn't care.

The certainty started to slip away after the first half mile but still she walked, swinging her bag on to her other shoulder, her footsteps very quiet on the tarmac road. With each step forward it got harder to imagine turning back, yet, with every stride it seemed more stupid that she was out there at all. And then with a rush she started to cry, silently, at the hopelessness of it all, the loneliness of walking on her own in the dark.

She reached the brow of the hill, lifted the torch again and could make out the lane snaking away below her, disappearing into a shadow of trees. She hefted her bag on to the other shoulder again, huddled into her coat, and walked on. Ten minutes later, at the bottom of the hill, she came to a T-junction she didn't remember having seen before, and a signpost with the names of two villages, neither of which she recognized. She stood uncertainly in the middle of the road, panic starting to rise inside her. How far had she come? She'd been walking for twenty minutes, perhaps, but the thought of choosing the wrong road, walking further and further into nowhere . . . She looked round again, feeling the night closing in all round her, even the road behind her, leading back to Lipton St Lucy, suddenly looking terrifyingly impenetrable. She looked back to the signpost, desperately trying to work out which route she should take, but she couldn't make herself go forward in either direction.

And then she shone her torch back along the lane to Lipton St Lucy for a second time and realized that she had only one choice: not to go back, slink through the front door and pretend she'd never been away, but to go back and find Luke. And immediately, from stepping out hesitantly, tentatively, she strode forward, wondering why it had taken her so long to realize that of course that was what she had to do. Why she had left at all? She thought back to the moment when he had pulled back the curtain. Why had she run away instead of confronting him? How was it that at that moment she'd become Teddy's

Lucy again, so hesitant and uncertain? And suddenly the urge to be back there, to run into the house, not up the stairs to her bedroom but to find Luke, made her start to run, her bag bumping hard against her back.

Then, for the first time since she'd left the house, she thought she heard a car. She stopped, hearing it again, definitely coming closer, accelerating around the bends and bearing down on her fast, and she leaped up off the road in fear, leaning back against the hedge and holding her bag straight out in front of her as if it might keep her safe.

Headlights swept towards her and she lifted the bag further, shielding her eyes. But instead of passing her, the car slowed as it reached her and then stopped square in the middle of the lane just in front of her, its hazard warning lights suddenly starting to blink brightly in the dark. A dark figure leaped out of the car and came towards her and she saw that it was Jude.

'What are you doing? Where were you going? You silly fool.'

'I was going to the station,' she said sheepishly, then made herself look up at him. 'Jude, I'm so sorry. I thought I couldn't bear to stay any longer, listening to the two of you always fighting, losing your temper, Luke so sad, you so angry.' She shook her head. 'I know it was a stupid, horrible thing to run out on you without explaining . . . and in a way,' she shrugged, giving him a helpless smile, 'this scary walk did me good. I'd turned around. I was coming back. I need to find Luke.'

'I came to find you.'

'Yes, thank you. I can see that. It was very nice of you. It was a long way to the station, further than I thought.'

He nodded.

'What's the matter, Jude?' She came forwards, unsettled by the stiffness in his face, the way he seemed to be holding himself so tight and still. 'Are you so furious with me?'

'Get into the car and I'll take you home.'

She came forward and gripped his arm. 'Is Luke OK?' She had a sudden thought that something terrible had happened.

'Going berserk looking for you.' He forced out a smile. 'But otherwise he's fine. Oddly, it didn't cross his mind that you might have left. But once I'd had a word with Colonel Everett — who passed on your message perfectly, thank God — I knew where to find you.'

'So what's wrong, Jude?' She still had hold of his arm. 'You sound so strange. What's happened?'

'There are two things I have to tell you.' He

looked away from her, his handsome face tight with strain. 'And I don't want to tell you either of them. But I'm going to have to before I take you home.'

'Tell me now!'

They had reached his car, and he opened the door for her then started the engine and drove them further down the lane to a lay-by. He stopped the car again, turned off the engine and turned to her in the darkness.

Lucy sat, huddled in her coat, and waited.

'Somehow being in the car with you again, looking at your face — and it's dark, I can hardly see you at all — it reminds me of before, makes me think of our journey together. How close we were. I'm thinking perhaps . . . Well, I can hope at least that you might remember I'm not all bad.'

'Just tell me what it is, please, Jude.'

He nodded. 'Luke told you about Gabriella, didn't he?' he said.

'Gabriella?' She looked at him in surprise, but he was staring blankly through the windscreen. 'Yes.'

'There was something *I* had to tell Luke about Gabriella and me, about the night I picked her up from the station.'

'No,' she gasped. 'You weren't. Please God don't tell me that.'

'No,' he said, 'we weren't.' He paused, still

not looking at her, and then went on quietly. 'But I suppose it would be fair to say that I'd have liked it if we were.' Finally he turned to her, caught the distaste on her face and immediately looked away again. 'Yes,' he said. 'I knew you'd look at me like that. But nothing ever happened between us, nothing ever would. She was too much in love with Luke.'

'So?' she asked cautiously. 'Why are you telling me this now? Why did you have to say anything to Luke?'

'Because . . . ' He took a deep breath in, exhaled slowly. 'On that afternoon, when she rang to say she'd caught an earlier train, I was the only one home.'

Lucy nodded. 'Luke told me about that.'

'But what Luke wouldn't have told you, because he didn't know himself until just now, was that as I got into the car I saw them all coming home from their walk.' He was looking at her again, defying her to look away, but she held his gaze, transfixed. 'Luke had reached the gate. I could have called to him, I could have let him know, could have let him go to the station instead of me, but I didn't do it. *I* wanted to go. I wanted to go to the station and pick her up. I wanted to get her on her own.'

Wordlessly Lucy dropped her head into her hands.

'So tell me what you're thinking,' Jude went on. 'Tell me what a sad, fucked-up bastard I am, to try to nick my own brother's girlfriend.'

She shook her head miserably.

'And then we had the smash. And afterwards, I could never tell any of them, could I? How I shouldn't have been there at all.'

Lucy looked up at him. 'And now you find you can't be around Luke any more?'

'I suppose. At times I've kidded myself that it was no big deal — not compared with what happened afterwards — and that I hadn't been planning to *do* anything. I tell myself I just wanted the fun of flirting with her for a few minutes, that not calling out to Luke was a little misjudgement but not a major crime.' He paused. 'But I know that's not true.'

She looked at him, sickened by what he'd thought he was capable of and yet, at the same time, wanting to reach out to him, to tell him that it was all right, that he'd suffered enough, that everyone at times had thoughts they shouldn't have, behaved as they shouldn't behave. The tragedy was that Jude, because of the accident, had been forced to live in that moment for ever, to have that bad thought, be that shameful person, over and over again.

She touched his arm. 'How do you know that's not true? Perhaps a little misjudgement is all it was?'

'I know because I'd have done the same thing all over again with you.' He said it so quickly that she had to listen again to his words in her mind to take in what he had said, and then she felt the shock punch her. 'Because you were just like Gabriella, suddenly you became a challenge. You are the second part of my confession tonight.'

'How am I?'

'He's in love with you, Lucy, completely in love.'

'What?' She felt herself swoop and dive at his words.

'I saw he liked you straight away, but then, of course, I realized it was more than that, much more.' He breathed in deeply and then held his breath and closed his eyes. 'And instead of backing off, thinking how wonderful that he could feel such things again, for somebody else, it made me want you for myself.' His eyes flashed open again and he turned to her. 'Not that I hadn't always thought you were wonderful, fantastic. But it had always been about that one day, to me. Even when I saw you again, and then . . . ' He laughed bitterly. 'I realized that Luke had his eye on you too.'

'You said something to him in Tindle Wood, didn't you? When you went to find him, what did you say?'

Jude turned back to her, staring at her in the dim light inside the car. 'I thanked him for finding you for me. I told him how happy we both were. How we couldn't believe we'd found each other again.'

'You are a bastard,' she said.

'Yes, over and over again.'

'But you're also here, telling me this . . . about Luke.' She started to laugh, tears in her eyes. 'And for that I could almost love you! Oh Christ, Jude, to be honest, all I can think of is him there, at home now, looking for me. Will you take me back? Are you sure it's true? You're not making it up?'

He shook his head. 'Tonight, when he pulled back the curtain and I saw his face, I can't believe you didn't see it too. And I felt sick at myself. I knew what I was doing to him. But it wasn't until you ran away that all the energy, all that determination to hang on to you, to make it work, just stopped. I stopped. And I realized I didn't want to be that person any more. That in a way I was being given another chance and that this time, instead of running away, I could put it right. Luke brought you here for me, thinking he was doing the right thing. And in a way he was, and now I can bring you home to him.'

He nodded, started the car again and drove them cautiously out into the lane. And Lucy suddenly, in her mind, saw the red-headed girl in the tube station, smiling at her, remembering the girl's absolute conviction that Lucy would be with the man who'd drawn the poster, how certain she was that Lucy would find him. 'When you find him, you'll know I was right.' And she was, she was.

Jude took her hand. 'You've come here and you've turned me round, sorted us out. And I owe you everything for that. I'm glad you forced me to tell Luke the truth.'

'Just out of interest, how was Luke when you told him all this?'

'He didn't hit me, if that's what you're wondering. But he didn't exactly hug me tight and tell me not to worry either.' He smiled. 'I don't expect him to. Perhaps he won't ever feel like doing that. But right now, that's OK. I can bring you back to him. Perhaps that will make a difference to him in the end.'

'It will,' she said. 'Of course it will.' She saw the pain in his eyes despite the smile of bravado. She thought of the long journey they'd made together, begun in Inverness airport only two weeks ago, about how far they had come since then.

'Find him, Lucy,' he said, turning briefly to her once more. 'Walk back into that party and find him now, that's all you need to do.'

And then they were in the drive, pulling up alongside the other cars, and Jude took her hand and helped her out of the car, keeping his arm close round her as they ran towards the front door and in through the hall, under the surprised stares of Suzie and Sophia, who was sitting on the edge of the sofa in front of the fire, hand in hand with a beautiful man. Lucy was aware that everyone stopped talking when she came in, their drinks frozen in mid-air as they took in her face, her jeans, her muddy trainers, but Jude's arm was protectively around her shoulders and in any case she really didn't care.

Suzie seemed to understand everything in an instant. She caught Lucy's eye, nodding her through the open door to the hallway beyond. And without a word, Lucy left them all behind her. There was another crowd of people in the next room but she didn't see any of them, only Luke.

As she stood in the doorway he turned, and for a long moment he didn't move, just looked at her with such love and hopeless longing that she wondered how she'd ever doubted it before. And then Jude came up behind her and nudged her forward, and the crowd around Luke seemed to step back from him to let her in. And she walked towards him, and it was as if he finally understood and a great exultant smile broke across his face and he opened his arms and pulled her towards him, crushing her against him as if he would never let her go.

'I've been looking for you,' he told her, his face so close to hers. 'In the barn, round the garden, down the gated road, everywhere I could think you might be. And then Jude said he had an idea — that he thought he knew where to find you.'

'I was coming back to you but Jude found me and he brought me home.'

She looked up at him, tight in the circle of his arms, and he reached down and kissed her softly on her mouth.

'Yes?' he asked in a whisper. 'Does that feel right?'

'It does,' she whispered back, hardly able to speak because it had felt so utterly, completely perfect.

He stroked her hair. 'Lucy Blue, I found you.' He looked down at her, tenderly stroked her face. 'Perhaps there'll have to be another poster?'

'No, Luke,' she told him, smiling back at him, coming forwards to kiss him again. 'This time, I found you.'

Other titles published by
The House of Ulverscroft:

CALLING ON LILY

Louise Harwood

What do you do if your best friend is about to marry the wrong girl? Buy the matching bathrobes and keep your mouth shut? Or kidnap the groom on his stag night and hold him in a remote cottage in the Welsh borders until the wedding day has safely passed? Hal's friends know what they want to do, but they haven't reckoned on being overheard by Lily — who has already witnessed the devastation of her sister's wedding day, and is going to do anything she can to save this one — and Kirsty, Lily's friend, initially more interested in pulling the groom, but swift to take up the challenge.

LOVING HIM

Kate O'Riordan

Connie and Matt Wilson, once childhood
sweethearts, have worked hard to achieve
their dreams — their lovely London home,
their three beloved sons and a stable
marriage. When they go to Rome for a
romantic weekend, they enjoy exploring,
eating, drinking and making love. But a
random encounter sets off a chain of
events that turns Connie's existence from
predictable but blissful, domesticity to
dangerous obsession, when Matt
announces that he is not coming back with
her and she returns to London — and
their three boys — alone.

FOR MATRIMONIAL PURPOSES

Kavita Daswani

'Who needs you to be happy? I want to see you married this year.' This is the view of Anju's mother, in the time-honoured tradition of all mothers, but particularly that of the fond Indian parent. Anju now works in New York, living the sophisticated American lifestyle — almost. But when she returns home to her parents in Bombay — usually for another family wedding — she finds herself reverting to the traditional daughter role. At each visit another prospective suitor is brought forward. But what sort of man does the very modern Anju want? How important are her family, her country, her traditions?

EAT, DRINK AND BE MARRIED

Eve Makis

Anna's head reels with plans to escape life behind the counter of the family chip shop on a run-down Nottingham council estate. Her mother, Tina, wants nothing but the best for Anna. She thinks that Anna should forget going to college, learn to cook and find herself a suitable husband. Mother and daughter are at loggerheads and neither will give way. Anna's grandmother, Yiayia Annoulla, is her ally, telling her stories about the family's turbulent past in Cyprus. Anna longs for the freedom enjoyed by her brother, Andy, but it is only when family fortunes begin to sour that she starts to take control of her own destiny . . .